CAUTION DEATH AT WORK

A DCI WARLOW CRIME THRILLER

RHYS DYLAN

WYRMWOOD
BOOKS

COPYRIGHT

ISBN 978-1-915185-03-7
eBook ISBN 978-1-915185-02-0

Published by Wyrmwood Books.
An imprint of Wyrmwood Media.

EXCLUSIVE OFFER

Please look out for the link near the end of the book for your chance to sign up to the no-spam guaranteed VIP Reader's Club and receive a FREE DCI Warlow novella as well as news of upcoming releases.

Or you can go direct to my website: https://rhysdylan.com and sign up now.
Remember, you can unsubscribe at any time and I promise won't send you any spam. Ever.

OTHER BOOKS by RHYS DYLAN

The Engine House

Ice Cold malice

CHAPTER ONE

'OH MY GOD, Dad, I swear we're going around in circles. I saw that sign to Peniel ten minutes ago.' From the back seat, Amelia Rewston extended her arm over her father's shoulder and pointed through the windscreen at the rusting post opposite.

They'd pulled up at a junction and, much as he hated to admit it, Chris Rewston thought she was probably right. The post leant precariously to the left and a smear of bird droppings that all but wiped out the 'P' of Peniel helped contribute both to its unique appearance and uselessness as a sign.

Best to confess, Christopher. He gritted his teeth. 'It's the damned young farmers, I tell you. I swear they move the signs for fun.'

'Use the satnav, Dad.' In the back seat next to his sister, twelve-year-old Benjamin muttered the suggestion without looking up from his Nintendo Switch.

'Can't. No signal up here.'

'You're telling me.' Amelia sat back, arms folded in a sulk, phone face down in her lap. 'Why did we have to come back through this stupid forest, anyway?'

In the passenger seat, Rachel Rewston half turned to contemplate her fourteen-going-on-twenty-year-old daughter. 'It's not a stupid forest. It's Brechfa Forest. And every time we visit your Uncle Peter in New Quay, we've promised ourselves that we'd make this run on the way home so you could see it.'

'The trees all look the same,' Amelia muttered.

'It's getting dark, too, Mam,' Ben remarked.

'It wasn't an hour ago. But you wouldn't notice with your nose buried in that thing.' Rachel's comment was a groove in a stuck record.

Ben looked up, frowning. 'It's not a thing, it's Mario Kart.'

'This forest is a national treasure, you two,' Chris said. 'Amazing walking and biking trails. It's ancient. Part of our heritage.'

Amelia let out a long-suffering moan and squeezed her folded arms a little tighter. 'Not the H word again.'

'We're not that far from home now.' Rachel tried appeasement. Her specialist subject as a mother of two. 'We just have to hit the main road.'

'You said that twenty minutes ago.' Amelia sent her a poisonous glare.

'I reckon if we turn left here, we should be okay,' Chris mused.

'I'm hungry,' Ben muttered without looking up.

'We all are, *cariad*. Once we get a signal, I'll ring for a pizza. It'll be there by the time we get home. How about that?' Rachel gave him a bright smile.

'Bribery will not work.' Amelia huffed air out through her nostrils.

'Yes, it will.' Ben looked up with a perky smile, earning a withering glance from his sister.

The road curved sharply on Chris's right into a blind bend. He eased off the brakes but slammed them back on with a jerk just as lights lit up the tops of the trimmed hedgerow. Seconds later, a red hatchback hurtled around the corner and zoomed past at high revs.

'Wow.' Ben sat up. 'What was that?'

'A death-trap, that's what.' His mother looked across at her husband with alarm.

'They used to hold rallies up here,' Chris explained. 'Some people still think it's a circuit.'

'Can we just go home, please?' Amelia's sigh was deep and prolonged.

Chris turned off onto a lane as narrow and as unlit as all the others they'd navigated for the good part of thirty minutes. Grass had found a foothold and grew down the middle of the tarmac. The way was wide enough for one vehicle only. Ah well, the best laid plans. He had to admit he was hungry, too. His brother and sister-in-law had only offered them twee sandwiches and crisps as a snack despite inviting them over for a meal.

Bloody cheapskates. Chris's stomach rumbled. The sandwiches had been hours ago, and pizza suddenly sounded wonderful. Especially accompanied by a cold beer. Buoyed by the thought, he pressed on. The hedges were high on both sides, and when they petered out as they climbed and the fields gave way once more to forest, the trees encroached to the very edge of the road. They were what, ten miles from the county town of Carmarthen and major roads? Yet it seemed so remote, with no lights from buildings anywhere around them.

'It's spooky here,' Amelia said, echoing his thoughts.

'Isn't it great to know you can drive a dozen miles from home and find something like this?'

'Yeah, great.' Amelia rolled her eyes. 'Real *Eden Lake* territory.'

'Have you seen that?' Ben whispered, eyes wide.

Amelia shot her mother a glance. Probably best not to

admit it, though she doubted her mum would know anything about horror films.

'Maybe,' Amelia whispered back.

'They say it's sick,' he hissed.

'Shut up, Ben.'

'They say some people actually threw up in the cine—'

He got no chance to finish. Though the road had flattened out ahead of them, well-lit by the SUV's twin beams, Chris held his speed at only twenty, praying that there'd be no more boy racers around. But what he hadn't bargained for was what stumbled out from the trees and staggered into the road thirty yards ahead, making him slam on the brakes for a second time in almost as many minutes.

Amelia screamed.

The car slid to a smooth stop and, for one moment, the only sound was the engine's idling hum.

'Dad, what is that?' Amelia broke the silence.

In the headlights, blinking into the lights, dressed in cycling shorts and a stained fleece that once may have been light blue, crouched a man. Mud caked his legs and smudged his wild, bewildered looking face.

'Stay here.' Chris opened the door.

'Where are you going?' Amelia protested, half a tone short of hysterical.

'That man looks hurt, love.' Rachel turned in her seat to address her daughter.

'He looks like a zombie,' Ben yelped in a voice that made him sound five years younger than he was.

'Shut up.' Amelia rounded on him and slapped him gently on the thigh.

'Just sit tight,' Chris ordered.

'Dad,' Amelia wailed, but by then Chris had both feet on the lane.

He reached into the door's side pocket and took out

some gloves. 'Busman's holiday, it looks like.' He smiled weakly at Rachel.

'It's okay, Amelia.' Rachel squeezed Chris's hand. 'Your dad knows what he's doing.'

Chris walked toward the man who'd stood up on shaky legs, swaying with a hand up over his face to ward off the glare of the headlights.

'Hello? Are you okay?' Chris shouted.

The man staggered forward and fell to his knees with a grunt. Chris broke into a trot. Behind, from inside the car, Amelia let out a little squeal of fright.

As he got nearer, Chris held a hand out and introduced himself quickly. 'Hi, my name's Chris. I'm a paramedic and I can see you're hurt.'

A pale face, streaked with blood from a matted wound on his scalp, looked up.

'Help,' he croaked.

Chris knelt and put a hand on the man's shoulder. 'What's your name?'

'Rob.'

'Okay, Rob. Have you been in an accident?'

A shivering Rob shook his head.

'So what—'

'I ran... I... got away.'

'From what?'

Rob's head dropped between his shoulders, and he let out a sob. 'I couldn't do anything. I couldn't help... It was dark... I...' Slowly, he turned his head to glare white-eyed over his shoulder into the dense blackness of the trees behind him. 'We need to get help.'

'Sure. But we need to get somewhere where there's a signal. It's useless here. I know because we've been trying. We'll get an ambulance. As soon as...'

Rob sent Chris a desperate look and shook his head. 'Too late for an ambulance. We need the police. It's Andy.

He's still in there.' He threw a rueful glance over his shoulder into the darkness of the forest.

Chris followed his gaze. 'Andy? Is he lost?'

Rob heaved in a ragged breath. 'Not lost. I think… I think he's dead.'

CHAPTER TWO

EVAN WARLOW WATCHED the woman hurry towards him on a lane two miles out from the hamlet of Nevern in North Pembrokeshire. He gave a slight tug on the lead with his right hand and muttered, 'Steady.'

The woman was young, female, earbuds in. The white kind that didn't use wires. She strode with purpose, arms swinging, legs striding, kitted out in tight-fitting leggings and weatherproof jacket. Essentials for West Wales walking. Twenty yards apart, she and Warlow made eye contact. He gave her a polite smile. He got a nervous, toothless, half-smile of acknowledgement in return, before the woman's eyes slid down to the shiny-black bundle of energy padding at his side. The walker's smile broadened into a grin. Good teeth, wide mouth, cheeks flushed from the great outdoors.

Sometimes people stopped, knelt, and beckoned to the bundle. Occasionally, they'd ask permission to touch. The odd one might ask for a name. Warlow always obliged because though whip smart and, at two and a half, still a little boisterous, Cadi wouldn't answer for herself. Even the most intelligent of Labs didn't talk.

But this walker didn't tarry. She was clearly on a fitness mission, even if seeing Cadi caught her attention. Shame. If the girl stopped, she'd receive a furry, tactile welcome to remember. And Warlow was keen to see if his attempt at training the dog not to jump up at strangers was paying off. Proofing is what it was all about.

But there were no other people around and the nearest house was a good seventy yards away. A young woman alone in such a situation needed to be wary. He approved, though she need not have worried.

Warlow was no predator.

In fact, he was the exact opposite. The walker's brief interaction with man and dog would be the safest few minutes she'd have out in the world that day, week, month, year even. But he didn't carry a sign announcing himself as a Detective Chief Inspector, and so the woman was not to know. All she saw was a man somewhere on the other side of fifty, a little below average height with salt and pepper hair cut short above a high forehead, swathed in waterproofs that masked his wiry frame, walking a cute black dog.

Ten yards after passing, the walker broke into a trot. The sudden change of pace drew Cadi's attention, her chase instinct triggered. But Warlow called her on and the walker was forgotten. A hundred yards further up the winding road, man and dog veered off onto a lane whose stoned surface gave way to tarmac fifty yards in, at a point marked by a closed five-bar gate in the hedgerow guarding a two-acre field. In summer, the field contained cattle. Today it was empty but reeked to high heaven from the recently sprayed liquid cow dung lying thickly upon it. The cattle were all holed up in a shed somewhere, dreaming of spring and making more manure for the farmer to distribute.

The rousing chorus from 'The Circle of Life' – the last

word of the title substituted with 'Shite' – surged into Warlow's head. It would be funny if there was anyone around to hear him sing it.

There wasn't. Except for the dog. And she took no notice.

At his feet, a raised concrete ramp acting as both a conduit for diverting surface water into a ditch and as an incidental Sleeping Policeman marked where the tar began and ended. Someone had once begun a petition to replace signs announcing "Sleeping Policeman Ramp" with "Sleeping Police Officer Ramp" in a moment of woke madness. It failed and Warlow had been surprised at how delighted he'd been on hearing that.

Not that any traffic calming was needed here since the only people who came down this lane were Warlow, the taciturn farmer called Emyr who shared the access with him, and a postal worker pathologically committed to wearing shorts in all weathers. He'd waved to that very postman in his red van as he'd turned the corner prior to passing the female walker a few minutes before.

Still, funny term, Sleeping Policeman. He smiled at the irony of it, shelved the thought, and addressed the dog.

'Let's see what old posty's left us, eh, Cadi?'

Inside, with Cadi watered and fed with a chew treat, Warlow picked up his mail from the doormat. A handful of bills and circular invites to change service providers from banks and electricity providers, and something about local elections. They all went into his favourite filing spot without passing go. The bin was going to need emptying soon.

He recognised one envelope because his name and address had been typed. It had franked postage, too, with a return address of a hospital in Swansea. He tore it open and took out a letter, read it, and then stuck it on the fridge with a magnet in the shape of a Kangaroo – a present from his eldest son who lived in Australia. The letter was a reminder for a hospital appointment in two months' time.

Appreciated but hardly necessary. Warlow was unlikely to forget. The three types of medication in his bathroom cabinet was reminder enough.

One more envelope remained. This one had been readdressed from his old house, the one in Whitland he'd moved out of when he and his wife split up several years ago.

Several? Christ, was it that long ago? He'd sent the new owners his new address when he moved into the Nevern cottage because Police HQ in Carmarthen were getting fed up of him using them as a post office box for stray letters.

But the brown envelope he stared at now was no stray letter. He recognised the crossed-out handwriting of the person who'd written the original address. Knew exactly who it belonged to.

Karen Geoghan.

Wife of Derek Geoghan, currently serving twenty years for manslaughter.

'Chief cheerleader of the Evan Warlow fan club,' as the crusty Detective Chief Superintendent, who oversaw the case where Warlow secured Geoghan's conviction, had announced with a hefty dollop of sarcasm.

Cheerleaders sang your praises. But that's not what Karen Geoghan did. Far from it. Old Karen screamed out Warlow's name in a banshee wail like a curse. Yet, he had to give it to her, she was consistent. Easter, Christmas, Geoghan's birthday, her birthday, and Warlow's birthday, he'd get a card. As a reminder of her thinking of him. He already knew what would be in it. The same thing as always. Some hair, other stains he dared not consider the origin of. Sometimes bits of dead animal. And, inevitable, some wise words.

I hope you and your family die soon.

Or,

I've cursed you and yours. You will suffer a slow and painful death.

Or,

One night you will look around and I will be standing there.

Karen wasn't going to get a job at Hallmark any time soon. Worryingly of late, some words had appeared in a language he didn't recognise. He'd sent a photo to his younger son, Tom, who was into sci-fi and fantasy. He'd texted back that he'd thought it was Runish, as opposed to what Warlow had suggested: bullish and shittish. It looked like old Karen was delving into the arcane. It came as no surprise to Warlow to learn that she'd become a witch. Hell, if she turned up on a broomstick, he'd hardly turn a hair.

It would have to be a big and strong broomstick, though.

But a witch, fine, Warlow was all for that. Maybe someone would get around to burning the nasty piece of human waste or dunking her in a lake tied to a stool.

Beneath the not too kind words on the card, there'd be the greeting:

For what you did to Derek.

Warlow always thought this a bit rich considering what Derek and come to think of it, Karen Geoghan, had done to other people. Cheated, lied, stolen and, ultimately, killed. They specialised in the vulnerable. Befriending them, defrauding them and, in one final act of real cruelty, getting someone to change their will before snuffing them out with a pillow.

Real charmers the Geoghans. As they kept proving to him regularly.

Still, old Derek wasn't likely to be out for some while. And so Karen kept sending reminders. Bless her.

Warlow slid on some gloves and used a knife to slit open the envelope. Better safe than sorry.

It was a simple card, depicting a Hangman's noose. Black against a red background.

Inside, in Karen's handwriting.

Happy birthday to my Darling Derek.

Death and suffering to the pig who put him inside. This card is laced with Ebola. Enjoy.

(For what you did to Derek.)

THERE WERE ochre stains on the surface and on the inside. He momentarily considered sniffing one, but shook his head immediately as common sense kicked in. Why even bother? He suspected that this was blood, but whose, or what's, was anyone's guess. A toad's maybe? Or perhaps a newt's?

Hubble bubble. The words popped into his head and immediately annoyed him. Common Macbeth misconception. He'd put himself out of his misery by looking it up online. The actual quote with the three witches communicating their intent was of course, *Double, double, toil and trouble: Fire burn and cauldron bubble. Cool it with the baboon's blood, then the charm is firm and good.*

He doubted Karen Geoghan had sourced baboon's blood. But Christ, he wouldn't put it past her.

He put the envelope and card in the bin for burning later, making sure it was out of the dog's reach.

Cadi tilted her head with interest until Warlow discarded his gloves and riffled the fur between her ears. 'Not nice. Takes all sorts, eh, *cariad*?'

The dog wagged her tail.

In Warlow's long and successful career of putting lawbreaking scum away, Karen Geoghan was not the only criminal who despised the ex – now back in the saddle –

DCI. That kind of hero worship went with the territory. He was careful what pubs he visited and always checked who was behind the bar in case his pint might get an extra bit of spittle in the froth, or worse, a widdle top up. He'd once spotted a recidivist shoplifter working at the chip fryer in the kitchen of a takeaway in Saundersfoot. They'd exchanged glances, and the venomous look she gave him made him cancel his order and take his hunger elsewhere.

No telling what she might have deep fried for him and passed off as a rissole.

But Karen Geoghan was probably the most persistent of all his haters. She'd served four years for theft, but it was Derek that took the fall for the manslaughter of James Kinton, a gentle soul in his early twenties with a learning disability who lost both elderly parents over a period of four months before falling into the clutches of the Geoghans.

If it had been up to Warlow, good old Derek would serve life, not twenty years, because everyone knew that meant fourteen with good behaviour, twelve of which had passed already. Thinking of the case still made his skin crawl. They'd found James after a tip off from an animal feed delivery driver. Found him chained up in a shed with a dog bowl full of water and nowhere but a bucket in the corner of the cold, damp, six-by-eight prison for him to use for his ablutions. While the Geoghans, like a pair of plump, insidious cuckoos, took over the detached property. Not only that, but they let James's beloved hens starve.

The Geoghans deserved everything they got.

His mobile's ringtone jerked Warlow out of his dark musings. He looked at the number and knew who it was right away.

'Sion, what can I do for you?'

Detective Superintendent Sion (The Buccaneer) Buchannan ran Dyfed-Powys Force's Pembrokeshire BCU, but had other responsibilities within CID, which, after toying with a few other acronyms, most of the detectives within Dyfed-Powys had defaulted to being known as. One of those responsibilities was as mentor to detectives training for Senior Investigating Officer status. A national qualification which both he and Evan Warlow held. Currently, they were helping Detective Inspector Jess Allanby get enough experience to take the SIO course. So Warlow knew what this call might be about. He wasn't wrong.

'Nasty one up in Brechfa Forest. One dead, another injured.'

Warlow pressed the button to put the call on speaker while he refilled Cadi's water bowl. 'When?'

'Last night. Didn't see the sense of bothering you then. Let Jess do the legwork.'

'She's up there now?'

'She is.'

Warlow turned off the tap and slid the dog's bowl onto the floor before straightening up and arching a stiff lower back. 'In the forest, you say?'

'Take wellies,' Buchannan said and Warlow didn't like the little chuckle that accompanied it. Still, he was yet to hear of a murder scene in the royal suite at the Ritz. 'I'll get someone to text you directions. If you get lost, light a fire and send up smoke signals.'

'Out in the wilds, is it?'

'Let's just say you won't find a takeaway coffee there.'

Warlow chuckled. 'Okay. Let the troops know I'm on my way.'

CHAPTER THREE

THE CRIME SCENE, like most Warlow had been too, had a surreal air to it. White tents sat incongruously in a clearing in the trees. People in white paper suits leant over numbered flags plonked in the moss-covered ground, swabbing, or photographing or measuring. Tape markers led the way in and out from the path to a forestry road that Warlow had navigated for a quarter of a mile to get to the spot. He took a moment to take in the surroundings. He'd been briefed by DS Catrin Richards on the way up, listening to her on the speaker in the Jeep. But he needed to breathe this in.

Absorb it.

The technical term for where the tents stood would be a glade. A spot where the soil was too rocky and thin to support tree growth, but where grass might survive. But the word didn't sit right in Warlow's ears. It was too… twee. Reminiscent of poetry or summer walks. He searched for another, better, more descriptive word or two.

Killing field came to mind. He stuck with that.

All around the dark trees stood sentinel against a background of grey and sodden sky. It wasn't raining at the moment. But it would, and the sky pressed down in warning. As isolated and, dare he say it, Godforsaken a spot as he could remember for a murder.

But then, was there ever a good place?

A long career had made him no stranger to death. Accidents, suicides, murders all featured. And Warlow had the sort of mind doomed to remember not only the bodies, but the dejected atmosphere of their surroundings. The eerie quiet of a hanging wood. The abandoned dustiness of a forgotten pensioner's trinket filled room. The crashing churn of waves on a shoreline slick with blood beneath a cliff face.

He walked to the edge of where the tape restricted access and stood, observing. Besides the tents and the white clad Crime Scene Techs, there were the little flags in the ground. Some around black churned up earth, or flanking tracks leading off towards an obvious path heading back uphill towards the trees.

'Lovely day for a walk in the woods, DCI Warlow?' The voice, off to his left, he recognised immediately. Alison Povey was a seasoned crime scene manager that Warlow had worked with before. Having been out of the loop for a couple of years, he was pleased to see a face he recognised, even if that face was two-thirds hidden by an elasticated paper hood. Under that, there'd be a short haircut and no jewellery, possibly a smidgen of make-up. All part of her no-nonsense approach to a job she enjoyed and was enthusiastic about. She pulled down her mask to talk to him.

'Alison.' Warlow grinned. 'Another idyllic setting, I see.'

She puffed out a visible exhalation into the cold air. It plumed forward a good four feet before evaporating. 'Can't fault it. The great outdoors.' She opened her arms wide.

'What have we got?'

'A shitload.' Povey's suit rustled as she turned and pointed to the nearest Tyvek tent. 'Body was found on top of a one-man pop-up. There's a second pop-up under the other SOC tent.'

She had a camera in her hand. An expensive digital SLR. One of several used at the scene to record every little detail. Povey turned it so that the back screen was visible to Warlow and pressed some buttons. These were night shots, but well-lit from arc lights. The victim was face down, dressed in a fleece and cycling shorts, both stained heavily with dark blood. She scrolled through a carousel of different viewpoints and close-ups. Both prone and after the body had been turned. The face showed a young man of around thirty, eyes and mouth open in an undignified moribund expression, cheeks smudged with what looked like black mud. But which could just as easily have been blood.

Warlow nodded when he'd seen enough.

'There's a survivor and so we have a lot to work with.' Alison stepped to her left to a marker in the soil. 'Motor-bike tracks. The survivor says someone came in on a bike, buzzed around them, ran over their bikes, and then the tents.'

She motioned towards two mud-spattered bicycles lying on their sides in a tangled heap with thick tyres coated with mud. Both were expensive looking, sporting thick back-wheel spindles heavy with a mound of gears. The wheels looked buckled and bent beyond repair.

'So, the story is that the victims emerge from their tents and are attacked by the rider. Multiple stab wounds to the deceased. Blood spatter confirms that. The second man got away and alerted you lot.'

'Where do the tyre tracks lead?'

Povey pointed to a gap in the trees. 'That's a cycle track. Motorbikes are not meant to use it, but in this instance, someone did.'

Warlow nodded. 'Victim's name?'

'Andrew Geary.'

Warlow took out his notebook from the pocket of his lined weatherproof jacket and wrote as Povey spoke. 'Survivor?'

'Rob Hopley.'

'Has the HOP been?'

'Yeah. Body's gone to Cardiff too.'

'Who was it?'

'Tiernon.' Povey spoke the name with exaggerated cheerfulness.

Warlow smiled thinly. 'Ah well, that's where the dream team ends.'

Povey grinned. The oval frame of the paper hood pinched the flesh of her cheeks and made her look like a slightly mad chipmunk. 'He was on good form. As miserable as ever. He'd already been out to a floater in a reservoir in Margam. Wasn't exactly whistling the chorus to "*Happy*" when he got here.'

'It's a Home Office Pathologist's lot. He'll get over it.' Warlow glanced around. 'When's he doing the autopsy?'

'This afternoon, he said.'

'I can hardly wait.' Warlow's gaze drifted across the trees, the track, and the Tyvek tents before settling back on Povey. 'So far what you've seen tallies with the witness statement?'

She nodded slowly. 'There was a motorbike, definitely.'

'Just one?'

'Yep.'

'What about footprints?'

Povey pushed an extended, booted foot into the ground for Warlow's benefit. 'It's grass and moss. Spongy stuff that's useless. The tyres churned up some soil, but unless the killer stepped in that there won't be much. We'll take casts of the tyre track, obviously. We'll keep looking for footprints, too.'

'Murder weapon?'

Povey shook her head. 'Nothing yet.'

'Alright. I'll leave you to it. How's the little one?' From somewhere he'd dredged up a memory of Povey and her partner having a baby sometime in the recent past.

The CSI's eyes lit up. 'He's three, so not so little anymore. Meena's got him into the *meithrin* in Ammanford. Proper little know-it-all now he is.' She'd opted for the Welsh word for nursery. Common parlance in this predominantly Welsh-speaking area.

Warlow grinned. 'Great. That's what happens. They grow up.'

'I'd show you photos, but probably not appropriate.' She shrugged and wrinkled her nose.

Warlow shivered inside his coat. 'No. Probably not.'

Povey nodded, pragmatic as ever as she stepped away. 'Good to see you, Evan. I'll get these photos over to you as soon as so you can catch this bugger. Boys are already calling him Evel Knievel.'

CHAPTER FOUR

EXPERIENCE HAD TAUGHT Warlow that driving around the parking lot in the Heath Hospital for half an hour trying to find a spot did nothing for the blood pressure. Instead, he parked down a side street off King George V Drive at the top end of Heath Park and walked into the sprawling complex of the University Hospital of Wales in Cardiff. The mortuary wasn't that well signposted, although the Forensic Path Unit was one of the busiest in the country. Still, he found it quickly enough. He'd been here many times. Too many times.

A technician let him in, showed him into a changing room, and asked if he needed any help with the kit. Warlow shook his head. Scrubs first, then white coveralls with an apron, mask, and gloves. The whole PPE shebang.

In full fancy dress, Warlow hesitated outside the door for a moment. He hadn't done one of these for a couple of years and he reminded himself that they were never as bad as you thought they were going to be, so long as you started from a baseline of absolute awfulness. The first half dozen were the worst. After that, you hardened yourself and settled with knowing your job was going to be to nail the bastard that caused you to attend in the first place. Some he remembered better than others, even if their names sometimes didn't stick.

Some he could never forget for many reasons. Age, level of violence, or simply the petty and tawdry circumstances that sometimes led to violent crime.

He stuffed a Polo mint into his mouth before pulling up his mask and pushed through the swing doors into a white-tiled room. Three people clustered around a gurney looked up. He nodded at the two shorter figures. The taller of the two with dark hair was DI Jess Allanby. The other, paler, slightly freckled, DS Catrin Richards.

The third figure stood rake thin with a beaked nose, dressed in the same fancy dress as Warlow but in a different colour – green – as befitted his top banana status. Dr Colm Tiernon was a senior clinical lecturer and the Home Office Pathologist who'd caught their case. Under the mask, only Tiernon's eyes were visible, but they were enough to demonstrate the man's imperious distaste for the DCI.

'Nice of you to come, Mr Warlow.' Tiernon's Irish brogue lent his accent a soft edge.

'Just can't keep away. Something about this place keeps dragging me back. Been dying to revisit.'

'I find that in extremely poor taste,' Tiernon said, regarding Warlow with undisguised distaste. 'And we started fifteen minutes ago.'

'Traffic is a bugger.'

'I will not start again.' Tiernon peered down his nose at the DCI.

Warlow smiled under his mask. Tiernon was a caustic narcissist with a degree in condescension. He enjoyed the rigmarole. Enjoyed being top dog. And he was pretty good at it, though there were better. Warlow let him have his affectations because he was an excellent pathologist. But he'd play to the audience, especially if he could find someone new to act up to. Then the schoolyard bully in him took over. Warlow had seen it happen to young DC's and the odd DS. And the older lags let it happen. Co-conspirators, enjoying seeing the younger officers squirm. But Warlow wasn't an indulgent sort of person. Probably why Tiernon's eyes narrowed in disappointment at seeing him. Either that or the guy's piles were throbbing.

'Wouldn't dream of it. My colleagues can brief me later,' Warlow said, delighted to see the little frown of irritation on Tiernon's brow deepen on realising the policeman refused to joust.

Andrew Geary lay naked on the metal gurney. He had nothing to be self-conscious of in death and, looking at him, his reasonable physique probably meant he did not need to be afraid of showing it off in life, either.

With any luck, all Tiernon discussed in the first fifteen minutes were blood screening, stomach contents, and underlying health problems. Warlow's guess would have been a clean-ish slate from that perspective. From the look and circumstances of the crime scene, Geary had been a serious cyclist and a bit of a fitness nut.

The chest and neck showed multiple dark slits around an inch long. Lots of them on either side of the breastbone. The two in the neck were on the left side. They looked almost innocuous like this, washed clean and with no blood oozing. But that belied their deadly nature. What looked like nicks on the surface went deeper, through muscle and sometimes bone. Slicing and dicing the vital internal structures.

Both Catrin and Jess had notebooks and pens in their hands. Warlow glanced down at the pages. Jess's had a few neat sentences. Barely a square centimetre of white remained on Catrin's.

'Right, we'll continue.' Tiernon turned to the body.

'We counted twenty-two stab wounds to thorax and neck. Most of them are deep, between five and seven inches.' Tiernon leant into one slit four inches down from the middle of the clavicle on the left side. 'Here you can see an oblong impression of the knife's hilt or guard. It means that the attacker used a lot of force.'

Catrin peered at the place where Tiernon pointed. The pathologist reeled her in. 'Come on, Sergeant, take a closer look. He won't bite.'

Warily, Richards leant in close to the corpse. To a point where the smell of dead meat would be at its darkest, strongest, and most cloying.

Warlow never got used to it. Sometimes when he'd walk Cadi in the woods, she'd catch a whiff of something and head right for it. A dead bird, the odd badger, once a bloody great deer. Warlow would follow and eventually his nose would pick it up, and he'd know instantly the cause when it reached him. A stench that caught in the back of your throat and sometimes wouldn't let go until whatever you'd eaten that morning came up to meet it.

It hung about this room like a miasma. It would be disgusting from where Catrin was. Warlow sucked on the Polo mint a little harder and wished he'd been able to give one to the sergeant earlier.

But the DCI knew this show and tell had little to do with eliciting details that would help in the investigation. Tiernon singled the DS out as the weakest in the herd. Catrin was no wimp, but that didn't matter. This was a power trip. The pathologist flexing his professional and intellectual muscle to amuse himself. And once upon a time, Warlow might have let it slide. Let the sardonic git get his kicks.

But this wasn't once upon a time. This was here and now, and things were not as they used to be. Warlow had picked up the reins after an eighteen-month self-induced lay-off wrapped up as a supposed retirement. But the force, namely Superintendent Sion Buchannan, asked him to return after a successful partnership where he'd consulted on a nasty case with Jess Allanby and they'd blown wide open a drug and human trafficking racket. And so here he was doing the same thing as he'd done for the last fifteen years as a DCI and five before that as a DI.

Well, not exactly the same thing. Some people, given the opportunity to reflect on a long career, might have mellowed in the interim. Warlow, had not. Reflection, in his case, had hardened an intolerance of unacceptable behaviour into something cold and clinical. An intolerance already calloused by years of experiencing just how disappointing humanity could be.

With two sons of around about the same age as Catrin Richards, Warlow had a paternal soft spot for the sergeant. Tiernon, no doubt, was grinning under his mask. Enjoying the big joke. But what Warlow witnessed here did not make him smile. Too many times he'd been in situations like this, aware of the fact that speaking out loud in the moment could bring regrets later. Treading on eggshells fed by the knowledge that he might have to work with Tiernon again.

But that ship had long sailed. Tiernon's little jape was nothing more than unpleasant bullshit. Time to call the man's bluff.

'Yes, Catrin. Get your nose right up to that corpse,' said Warlow.

Richards, leaning forward, turned her face towards her superior with surprise and disappointment in her eyes. But Warlow wasn't finished. He flicked his gaze from the sergeant to the pathologist. 'Still got that place in Newport, Pembs, Dr Tiernon?'

Tiernon narrowed his eyes.

Warlow's grin, were it visible under the mask, displayed a lot of teeth but very little warmth. 'Because if you do, maybe DS Richards could return the educational favour. You come down what, every other weekend? We'll get her to track you on ANPR and blue light you to Haverford-west nick. An inside track to our side of the job. Show you the cell our least favourite junkie has redecorated with his own intestinal doings. He can be very creative can Play-Doh. We'll let you get your nose right up close, just like this.'

Warlow switched his gaze back to Catrin still leaning forwards. 'You up for that, Catrin?'

The DS straightened, nodding. 'Yes, I… yes, sir.'

Tiernon made a noise like a tyre losing air. 'You wouldn't—'

'Try me,' Warlow said, still with his hidden shark's grin, not letting the pathologist finish.

'I was only—'

'Arseing around,' Warlow interrupted a second time. 'While we would like to get on with the serious job of catching the bastard who did this.'

Tiernon's mask moved as if he was about to say something. But he thought better of it and moved down the corpse towards the forearms. When he spoke next, it was more formal. More business-like. More… professional.

'Multiple lacerations here. Defensive wounds. From these, you might conclude that it had been a frenzied attack.'

'The knife?' Warlow asked.

'Long, serrated, an inch wide with an oblong guard.'

'Which blow killed him?' Jess asked.

'This one, the topmost neck wound nicked the carotid.' Tiernon pointed to the spot.

'So, lots of force. Male, you'd say?' Warlow inquired.

Tiernon nodded. 'And right-handed.'

'He was lying on his front when they found him,' Warlow said. 'Was he stabbed in the back, too?'

'He was. Another dozen times. I'll forward the photos. Whoever did this wanted to make certain, that's for sure.'

'Time of death?' Jess asked.

Tiernon paused to think. 'Can't say from the body, but given that they found the survivor at eleven thirty, I'd say between seven and eleven that night.'

There would be more, of course. Blood tests that showed no STDs or worse. No sign of any sexual attack. No semen in any orifice.

'He bled out from the neck wound?' Warlow asked.

'Yes.'

'So there'd be a lot of blood?'

'A fountain.'

'It's likely the killer would be bloodstained?'

'I'd say that was inevitable.'

Warlow exchanged knowing looks with the female detectives.

Tiernon had a tendency to see these post-mortems as a teaching exercise where he could listen to his own voice droning on into an explanation of the time it might take to bleed out from a neck wound. Warlow tuned out and wondered if Povey had any luck with blood spatter patterns on the mossy ground. He tried to remember if it had rained hard that night or not. Another variable to dial in to the mix.

Tiernon would forward a formal report, but so far there was little or no doubt as to Andrew Geary's cause of death: exsanguination from a stab wound. Warlow would take that as a reasonable starting point.

As he left the autopsy suite, a couple of technicians who'd been standing at the side gave Warlow the thumbs up as he passed, quickly dropping their hands as Tiernon turned. Obviously, they knew the kind of class A prat they were working with. Clear, too, from their response that they'd enjoyed seeing the git brought down a peg or two.

CHAPTER FIVE

JESS AND CATRIN SHARED A RIDE. Warlow followed them west down the M4 after arranging a stop in Costa in Cross Hands. They sat at a corner table. Warlow bought the coffees and added a couple of fruit flapjacks to a plate in the middle. The women split one, Warlow ate the other.

Jess sipped her flat white and grimaced. 'Why do they always make the thing too hot?'

'Basic error. Nothing worse than burnt milk.' Warlow nodded.

'Why I stick to tea.' Catrin gave them both an irritatingly holier than thou smile.

'Plan?' asked Warlow.

This was how they played the game. Jess Allanby had been a DI for nigh on a year. She needed cases under her belt in order to get qualified as a Senior Investigating Officer. Sion (the Buccaneer) Buchannan had hit on the idea of putting the two of them together – with Jess as Warlow's deputy SIO – after the Engine House case a few months before. The Buccaneer had run that case but, like all good managers, he'd taken a step back and put Warlow in the driving seat. Jess had not objected. Warlow's question about a plan was all to do with mentoring.

'I'd want to talk to the paramedic that found the survivor first-hand. Get his impression of things,' Jess said.

'Agreed.'

'Also, get the autopsy briefing entered into HOLMES and interview the victim's relatives.'

'I'd do the same.' Warlow's flat white sloshed around in the cup. Too much milk and not enough froth, in his opinion. He could make a better stab at it than this dishwater.

'Um, I've more or less typed up everything,' Catrin said.

Warlow raised an eyebrow.

'Knowing this was what you'd want,' Jess explained, 'I drove while Catrin typed on her laptop. It'll be a cut-and-paste job for the entry.'

'Slick.' Warlow was impressed. 'Is the paramedic available?'

Catrin checked her phone. 'I texted him. He's come back to me to say he's at work delivering a patient to Glangwili. He'll be in the ambulance station in Carmarthen next to the hospital within the next hour.'

'Okay. We can work with that. Catrin, you come with me. Jess can go back to the office.'

'Sounds like a plan,' Jess said.

And yes, it was a plan, but far from an ideal one. They were shorthanded and having an experienced investigator like Jess stuck running the office was almost criminal. Warlow toyed with saying exactly that, but never got the chance because Catrin stood up abruptly.

'Five minutes?' she said, before heading to the loo.

Jess watched her leave over the rim of her cup. 'She thinks you're wonderful. Must be nice to be hero worshipped.'

'Amazing what a flapjack will do,' Warlow said, with his customary tendency to bat anything complimentary away.

'Don't be coy. Tiernon is scared stiff of you, too.'

Warlow rotated his hand in a so-so movement. 'He's a good pathologist. Trouble is, he spends too much time with the dead and it's rubbing off. Has been for years. The cadavers may not have any feelings but other people, the inconveniently walking around ones, do.'

'I enjoyed it.' Jess grinned.

'Catrin's a good kid. She didn't deserve a mortuary piss-take.'

'Even so. Tiernon—'

'Won't send me a Christmas card. Boo-hoo. I can live with that. When it comes to him, leave all the bad cop stuff to me. You're going to work with him more than I am. But there are four HOPs. That's three to one in your favour. So Tiernon gets the hump. What's the worst that can happen? I've already retired once, remember? This is all extra time for me.'

Jess smiled. 'Nice position to be in.'

Warlow sipped his coffee thoughtfully and let whatever he was thinking curve his mouth into a lopsided smile. 'Notice how his face changed when I mentioned the blue lights?'

'Ooh, he wasn't happy,' Jess said.

'Everyone's got something to hide, Jess.'

'Even you?'

'You do not want to know.'

Jess sent him an eyebrows raised look. Luckily, Catrin's return spared Warlow any further interrogation.

Someone's phone chirped. Jess picked up. 'Text from Molly. Photo of her and Cadi practising her frisbee catching.' She held the phone up and Warlow saw his dog with a frisbee in her mouth, looking as pleased as punch, inches from a pretty girl's grinning face in a distorted selfie. The text read, *Tell Cadi's daddy she is the best frisbee catcher ever.* Followed by a smiley face with hearts for eyes.

Warlow had dropped the dog off with Jess's sixteen-year-old daughter that morning, knowing he'd be out most of the day. He'd toyed with putting Cadi in a kennel, guessing that a case like this would suck most of the time out of the next few days. But on hearing that, Jess had suggested Molly, who'd jumped at the chance. Since the schools were on a break, it seemed the obvious answer.

'They're getting on okay, then?' Warlow asked.

'House on fire doesn't even come close. She's always wanted a dog.'

'I had noticed since she keeps telling me in your presence whenever she gets the chance.' Warlow stood up, cheered by the message. 'Right, I'll drink the rest of this in the car. Or, more likely, hurl it out of the window. Let's get going.'

———

THE CARMARTHEN AMBULANCE station was a low brick building accessed off Abergwili road near a flyover above the A40, with Glangwili District General Hospital looming behind it. Chris Rewston was in uniform, and they chatted in a tiny office with a window looking out to the parking bay where three yellow and green ambulances sat.

Catrin had already made the introductions and had spoken to Rewston on the phone.

'Run us through what happened, if you would, Chris,' Warlow said. 'You don't mind if DS Richards records this. For our records.'

Rewston gave the police officers the two seats in the office and positioned himself on the edge of a desk. He nodded and began speaking. 'We were on the way back from the Cardigan coast visiting my brother in New Quay.

I'd decided to take them back through Brechfa Forest. It's a pleasant run, but I'd got a little too enthusiastic and hung about in the viewpoints for too long. I know it was dark, but you can see the lights in the distance and on a cloudless night the stars are incredible. And yes, I took a few wrong turns. The phone signal is patchy up there and the satnav sent us in circles. The signage is not helpful either to say the least.'

'You said you saw a red car travelling at speed a few minutes before you came across Mr Hopley?' Catrin asked.

'Yeah. We were at a junction. Did you get the map I sent? I tried to retrace where we ended up.'

Catrin nodded. 'We did. Very useful, thanks.'

'We'd pulled up at this junction, about to take a left to get back to a better road when a red Peugeot came hurtling round the corner. Must have been doing forty, which doesn't sound a lot, but on those roads…' Rewston shook his head.

'Did you get a plate number?' Warlow asked.

'No. Too fast and too dark. All I remember is that it had a spoiler and some kind of yellow sticker across the back windscreen. It hurtled past us in a flash. I took the left and we'd gone maybe fifty yards when Hopley appeared on the road right in front of us. Scared the life out of the kids.'

'Do you remember where he came from?'

'Out of the trees. He sort of stumbled down onto the road. I mean he looked in a bad way. He was bleeding, had a head wound, clothes matted with dirt and, what I later found out, blood.'

'So you stopped the car?' More a statement than a question from Warlow.

'I did. I wasn't sure what best to do for a minute. I had the family with me and… he looked a sight. Ben, my youngest, thought he was a zombie.' Rewston chuckled. 'I tell you, these video games—'

'But you got out of the car?'

'I did. Training I suppose. When I got to him, he collapsed on to his knees. I told him to stay put and we'd get some help. And he said something about it being too late for an ambulance and that we'd need the police. He mentioned an Andy. That he was still in there. And then he said he thought he was dead.'

'What happened after that?' Catrin asked.

Rewston shrugged. 'I decided I'd stay with him, and I sent Rachel, that's my wife, with the kids to find a signal so we could call it in. Luckily, it only took them ten minutes to get to the Carmarthen Road. She called it in, and the police came and… you know the rest.'

'Did Hopley say anything else to you while you wait-ed?' Warlow pressed the paramedic for details.

'He went quiet at first, as shocked people do. Shivering a lot. I'd fetched a towel from the car to wrap him in before they left.' Rewston grimaced. 'You're going to tell me I shouldn't have because I may have contaminated evidence, right?'

Warlow shook his head. 'You acted in good faith. No one can object to that.'

'He kept saying that he couldn't help Andy and that he'd run away. That he shouldn't have run away. He was crying a bit. He said he'd hidden in the trees until the attacker left, then he went back to find Andy. As soon as he saw he was dead, he went to fetch help. He had a shoulder injury but not bleeding too badly. I kept him moving for warmth and stayed with him to engage him, half listening for that lunatic in the red car in case it came back.'

'And you saw no one else? Heard nothing else?' Catrin asked.

'Nothing.' Rewston shook his head.

Warlow sat back. 'We'll probably ask you to come in and give a formal statement when you can, Mr Rewston. Mrs Rewston too if possible.'

'Be happy to.'

'How are the kids? Must have been an ordeal for them?' Warlow asked.

'They never want to go back again, that's for certain. They've now renamed it *Coedwig y Bwystfil*.'

From the way he said the words, Warlow guessed that, unlike him, Rewston wasn't a natural Welsh speaker, though his wife and children might well be. Education in the county was mandated to be bilingual, slipping and sliding between English and Welsh at the drop of a '*het*'. The DCI did not need a translator for *Coedwig y Bwystfil*. Monster Woods seemed appropriate enough after what they'd witnessed.

'They should, though. Go back I mean. You all should. In summer, on a warm bright day.' Warlow knew the forest from walking with Cadi and, when they were younger, biking with his boys.

'I'll try my best.' Rewston hesitated before adding. 'Any idea who might have done this?'

'Not yet.' Warlow stood up and shook Rewston's hand. 'But we will find out.'

Back in the car, Warlow watched as Catrin wrote furiously in her notebook, unable to hide the brief glint of amusement in his eye. When she caught it, she stopped writing. 'I find it's better if I write things down right away. Leaving it only muddles my thoughts.'

'Don't let me stop you.'

'No, I've finished.' She folded the pocketbook and put it away in a backpack.

Warlow doubted she had finished, but self-consciousness was a beast. 'And what are they, those thoughts?'

Catrin took a deep breath and let her eyes fix on some

passing fields as she composed a reply. 'Rewston seems like a reliable witness. We'll run a check on him to see if there is any link to the deceased. But since the rest of the family were in the car at the time they came across Hopley, my feeling is we can accept what he says. He couldn't have known Hopley and Geary were in that section of woods.'

'Agreed. Actions?'

'Find the red car. Double check satnav signals out near where Hopley was found, just to verify.'

This was his second big case with this team, and the DS continued to impress him. Diminutive in stature, she might have been, but thorough and big in the detail department.

Warlow slowed down to a crawl behind a tractor pulling a trailer. No point being aggrieved about that. This was the countryside and farm vehicles were a fact of life. The farmer would turn off eventually. Meantime, he concentrated on trying not to drive through the biggest of the clumps of dung the tractor kept shedding onto the road from its tyres and the trailer itself.

'Oh my God,' Catrin said, wrinkling her nose. 'That smell is disgusting.'

Warlow pointed to the glove box. 'Fancy a Polo mint?'

CHAPTER SIX

THEY'D SET up the Incident Room and it was taking the shape of all the others that Warlow had been in: desks, laptops, monitors, and, at the front, a white board plus something more beige that was useful for sticking thing to, like Post-it notes and photographs. They referred to the beige as "the Gallery". And the white board – with stuck on instructions, actions, and contact details of various experts/sources/witnesses – as the "Job Centre". When he and DS Richards entered, there wasn't a great deal on either board but that would soon change.

Stickler Sergeant Catrin Richards would make sure of that.

You needed a stickler in a murder enquiry.

There was a room at the back for the SIO, separate from the crowd, with its own desktop computer and phone. By and large Warlow didn't use it, unless he wanted to get his head down for an hour when things got really manic. But he preferred being in here with the rest of the team most of the time.

Catrin went straight to her desk and fired up the computer.

Jess stood at the beige board sticking the autopsy photos up underneath what the crime scene bods had already sent over.

'Ah, you're back,' she said over her shoulder. 'We've got the kettle on. Rhys? Must be your turn.'

A lanky DC called Rhys Harries looked up from his desk. 'Is it me or is it always my turn?'

'For now, yes,' said Jess. 'Tea, or any hot beverage of your choice accessible from a tin in the kitchenette, is an essential weapon in our fight against crime.'

'I've learnt that already, ma'am.'

'Good, lad.' Jess beamed at Rhys who stood up and headed for the kitchenette.

The back of the room had a few Uniforms and civilians already setting up.

'So not just the four of us then?' Warlow remarked.

'Indexers and secretarial help already. Some more bodies tomorrow. As for the primary investigation team, we're it for now. I'm hoping we'll get someone else, but…' Jess let the sentence hang. There was never a slack time in an investigation like this. Just as Povey, whose job of preserving the scene until everything was photographed or measured or swabbed or plaster cast, faced a constant battle against the Welsh weather, the clock was ticking for collecting evidence from witnesses. Warlow felt the dull anxiety gnawing at him.

Resources were always limited. Warlow's colleagues were all busy with projects and operations. And worst of all was the fact that they'd recently lost a seasoned sergeant. Collateral damage from the drug and trafficking case that had brought Warlow out of retirement. Mel Lewis, fallen from grace, had been a friend as well as a colleague. His absence still left a bitter taste in Warlow's mouth.

'Doesn't have to be a sergeant. A DC would do.

Someone to help Rhys with the donkey work. I'll have a word with the Buccaneer,' Warlow said.

He retreated to the SIO room and fussed around with some online paperwork until Rhys returned with the tea. He joined the team for refreshments, took a mouthful, and smacked his lips. 'You are getting very good at this, detective constable.'

'Thank you, sir.' Rhys offered a grudging smile.

'If only the rest of your work was as thorough in the making.'

The DC blinked, crestfallen. 'If it's about the car, sir. I'm on it.'

Warlow narrowed his eyes and sent Rhys a sideways glance. 'It wasn't about the car, but since you mention it, what about the car?'

Jess, still facing the board, chuckled softly.

Rhys, looking nonplussed, said, 'Uh… I'm waiting on a call from Uniforms. They said they'd ring me back an hour ago, but they haven't. I was going to give them ten more minutes and then—'

'You lost me at Uniforms,' Warlow said before he could finish.

'It'll all become clear at the debrief.' Jess's big eyes were smiling above the rim of her mug.

But Rhys hadn't finished. 'I promise I'll try to pull my weight with this case, sir. And not get stabbed again, sir.'

They all looked at him as they might a puppy who'd lost a toy. Even Catrin stopped typing to peer up over her monitor.

Warlow sighed and put down his mug, then steepled his hands over his abdomen. 'Right, DC Harries, write this down.'

Rhys scrambled for a pen.

'First, if we didn't think you were pulling your weight you would not still be on this team.'

Rhys got to the last word, frowned, stopped writing, and looked up, blinking.

'Second, regarding the stab vest, never apologise to me for some miserable scrote trying to kill you while on duty. If it happens again, make sure you write his name in blood before you snuff it so we can nail the bastard.'

Rhys nodded and kept writing. The noise of a poorly restrained guffaw breaking free to take on a life of its own and resemble the snort of a pig emerged from Catrin, half-hidden behind a tissue.

'Third, we've booked you in to the RAW detection course.'

'RAW?' Rhys asked.

'Yes, RAW. Recognising A Wind-up. As in when the DCI takes a slurp of tea that you made and says if only the rest of your work was as thorough in the making. Got it?'

Rhys kept blinking.

'He means keep up the outstanding work, Rhys.' Richards dabbed her eyes as she got up from her seat to add something to the Job Centre. 'It's irony.'

'Oh,' Rhys reddened.

Warlow held up the tea and winked at the DC. 'I can see this is going to be a slow and painful apprenticeship for both of us. But well worth it for the tea.'

'I think we're ready,' Jess said.

Warlow stood, put the tea down, and picked up a pen before facing the boards and the crime scene photos of the deceased.

Time to get to work.

———

'OKAY,' Warlow began. 'Andrew Geary. Aged thirty, from Woolwich, stabbed to death in a clearing in Brechfa Forest.' He used a pen to point at the image of the young man posted on the Gallery. Geary's photo was a candid shot, half a smile raising one eyebrow. He had a full head of swept-back hair not yet flecked with grey and the inevitable five-day stubble that was de rigueur for that age these days. Both Warlow's sons flirted with facial hair, whereas the DCI preferred a daily wet shave borne out of a regimen of early rising and getting set for the day. Not shaving just seemed lazy.

Geary's image oozed confidence. Whoever had taken the shot had blurred the background and drawn the eye to the man's slightly sardonic expression. Warlow would have enjoyed delving behind that outward projection. Alas, no one was ever going to do that now.

He scanned across to a map with a red circle drawn in the middle of an enormous expanse of green. 'Reported dead in fact by his friend, Rob Hopley, who was found wandering dazed and confused, in the dark on a lane in the forest, approximately four miles from the village of Brechfa.'

'That must have been a shock for whoever found him, sir.' Rhys squinted at the map.

'It was. Lucky for Hopley, said finder was a paramedic who kept his head and called us.'

Warlow stepped across to the autopsy images Tiernon had sent through. 'Twenty-two stab wounds, front and back, the ones in the neck doing the fatal damage. Crime scene confirms that the attack took place where Geary and Hopley had set up camp for the night.'

'I didn't think you could camp in Brechfa,' Catrin remarked.

Warlow nodded. 'You can't. Not officially. So we'll need to find out why they were. You can see from the images that both men were cyclists.'

'Where was their car, sir?' Rhys asked.

This time, Jess replied. 'Though Geary's address is in

London, he has local connections. His parents have a small holding here.' Her turn to point at the map. 'It's on the... Ridaroo road.'

'It's Rhydyrhiw ma'am,' Catrin explained. 'Pronounced Reed uh rew, as in crew.'

Jess sent her a grateful look. 'I swear these names will be the death of me.' Having been in the Dyfed-Powys Force for less than a year, DI Allanby's Mancunian accent did what it could with the tongue-twisting Welsh place names. 'It's been a holiday home for the family for twenty-five years and now Geary's parents live there full-time. Andrew Geary and Hopley used this as a base and cycled across to the forest.'

'No one's interviewed them properly yet I take it? Geary's parents?' Warlow asked.

Head shakes all round.

'Okay. They're on my list, too. Siblings?'

'None.'

Warlow turned to Rhys. 'We need background checks on the Gearys, both dead and living.'

Rhys jotted things down. He was going to be busy.

'What about the witness, uh, Rob Hopley?' Warlow pointed towards a headshot of a fair-haired man with a darker beard. The incongruous, smiling pose looked like it might have been taken for an employer. When he commented on it, Catrin said, 'I got it from his LinkedIn profile, sir.'

'Nice smile,' Catrin remarked.

'I doubt he's smiling much now.' Warlow observed grimly. 'Still in hospital, I take it?'

'Glangwili.' Catrin read from her notebook. They were still getting used to the formal change of name. For years, the old place had been known as West Wales General. 'Under observation. Some deep lacerations to upper arm and shoulder, defensive wounds on the forearms. Oh, and a nasty head wound, but otherwise nothing life changing.'

Warlow turned back to the crime scene photos. 'Hopley says they were disturbed while they slept. The attacker came in on a motorbike. I've seen tracks at the scene, so we need to chase that up, see what forensics can come up with.' He stared at the Gallery. 'What else?'

Rhys cleared his throat. 'About the car, sir?'

'Car?' Warlow frowned.

Jess put him out of his misery. 'Rewston, the man who found Hopley, reported seeing a hatchback shortly before. Red thing with a spoiler driven by a wannabe Louis Hamilton.'

'Yes, I know. What about it?'

Jess nodded towards the DC. 'Rhys here has a theory about that.'

Warlow perched on the edge of a desk and put on his best attentively listening face.

Rhys swivelled in his chair to face the DCI. 'It's a thing kids do. Even I used to. Once you're old enough to drive and get a car, we'd cruise up to Keepers with a couple of cans. You'd park there, have a laugh, and drive home. Or even race each other home.'

'Keepers?'

'It's a big car park. There's a forestry educational unit there where they do play days for kids and outdoors skill courses. That sort of thing.'

'So drinking and driving is something you've done in your criminal past?' Jess folded her arms.

Rhys's neck bloomed a bright red. 'As a passenger, ma'am. A few illicit c-ciders, that's all,' he stammered.

'It's a wonder you're not on death row.' Catrin tutted.

'The reason I'm saying all this is that sometimes you'd get older kids there with better cars spoiling for a race. I've talked to Traffic…' He sent Catrin a glance. She returned it with an 'and-your-point-is?' expression. Warlow remembered that Catrin's partner was a Traffic officer.

'I asked if they remember seeing any red Peugeots that night,' Rhys continued. 'No answer yet. We're already scanning CCTV. But I thought it might be worth a trip up to the car park, sir. Sometimes you'll find discarded cans around the bins there. Might be lucky with some prints.'

'Sounds good,' Warlow said. 'Local knowledge, Rhys. Can't beat it. I'll leave that with you then.'

The DC beamed, looking pleased.

Warlow turned back to the Gallery. 'Right, we've all got enough to do. But first things first, I need to talk to Geary's parents.'

'Sir, I think his fiancée is going to be there too,' said Catrin.

'Hmm,' grunted Warlow. 'In which case, Sergeant, you're with me.' He threw Jess a glance. 'I don't enjoy seeing you stuck in the office like this, Jess.'

She waved him away. 'It's fine. Someone needs to do the paperwork.'

Running the office in a major investigation was a job all in itself. Something they'd all done in their time. But it wouldn't make best use of Jess's skillset.

'It's not fine. You'd be more use out and about. I'll see what I can do.' He turned to Catrin. 'You have an address for the Gearys?'

'We do, sir. I've also warned them it's likely we'll be visiting them today.'

Warlow smiled. He toyed with saying 'you'll make someone a wonderful wife someday,' but put a lid on it instantly. The force was still a male dominated workplace. And whereas he might still say such a thing to a male colleague in jest and in certain situations, he wouldn't dare say it to a female colleague. Even if, in his heart, he thought it actually might be true. Catrin Richards was organised, thoughtful, and attractive. Positive attributes in any partnership. Not for him, obviously. He was old enough to be her dad. But such quips and even such thoughts were, these days, like dancing in clodhoppers in a minefield, blindfolded. Best to say nothing contentious. Easier to stick to swearing and praise masquerading as insults.

Those he was good at.

'You're driving,' he said, as he slid on his coat. 'I need to phone Superintendent Buchannan and then look up Brechfa Forest on the bloody inter web.'

CHAPTER SEVEN

THE A40 from Carmarthen took them east along the Towy Valley with the river on their right snaking its way to the estuary at Llansteffan. They'd taken a job car. A BMW3 series. Not built for pursuit. But good enough to get them from A to B.

While Catrin drove, Warlow picked up his phone and dialled Buchannan's number.

'Evan, how's it going there?'

'We're just getting in to it.'

'Good. The press will get wind of it by the end of the day. They'll suddenly find an untapped interest in forestry, no doubt.'

Warlow said nothing. A necessary evil was how he viewed the hyenas, as he liked to call the press. 'We're thin on the ground, Sion. Jess is stuck in the office. It would be good to have her in the thick of it.'

'I've asked. Carmarthen say they cannot spare anyone.'

'Surely—'

'But I have someone spare in Ceredigion. A DS who's been tied up with Operation Alice.'

Operation Alice was a multi-force child abuse investigation that had been running for at least two years hoovering up personnel and resources.

'It's Gil Jones. Know him?' Buchannan added.

'I don't.'

'He's a good lad. Dedicated, but wants a change from being knee deep in the trenches. And he deserves that. He's been around the block more than once, so knows the score. He'll be with you tomorrow.'

'That's great,' Warlow said, genuinely relieved. 'So what's the catch?'

'None. It's just the way things have fallen. Ops coming to an end and tailing off, you know the drill. Gil will be an asset. Where are you now?'

'On the way to visit the victim's family.'

A slight hesitation on the line told Warlow that the Buccaneer had something else to say. 'And how are things? In general, I mean.'

Warlow glanced over at Catrin. The radio was off, but he didn't think she could hear the other side of this conversation.

'Things, in general, are good. Thanks for asking.' His reply emerged as a stilted warning.

'Someone in the car with you?'

'Yes.'

'Right. I won't say anything else then. But I'm here, Evan. Any time.'

Warlow killed the call but kept his eyes front. As euphemistic conversations went, that had been a good one. He appreciated Buchannan's discretion. He was the one man aware of why Warlow had taken early retirement. Why he'd been reluctant to return. Why he still had doubts over how well he could function in the role.

'Everything alright, sir?' Catrin looked over, sensing the DCI's preoccupation.

'Fine,' Warlow said, with as much finality as he could

muster. It seemed to work. He opened up a browser on his phone and googled Brechfa Forest. Found the natural resources Wales site and read out the relevant bits for Richards.

'Here we are. Used to be called Glyn Cothi Forest because of the Cothi river. The navy chopped down all the oak for ships and now it's six and a half thousand hectares of conifer and bike trails.'

'What's a hectare?'

'Hold on.' Warlow punched in another question. 'Ten thousand square metres.'

'That's a lot of pine needles.'

'It is.'

It took fifteen minutes to get to the A40 turn off and another twenty winding north to find the Gearys' cottage – Journey's End – down a two-hundred-yard driveway in a V-shaped clearing in the forest. The stoned track gave way to mud just where they turned off into hard standing. Warlow looked through the windscreen at the stone building with the unusual sight of a tree in the middle of a turning circle in the yard. The branches stood dark against the sky. No leaves this early in March, despite the mild weather. Several lichen-covered stone outbuildings had been converted into garages and rooms. Next door was a paddock, but there was no sign of horses.

The place was well kept, the stone matching the green-coloured window frames and doors painted in a shade reminiscent of National Trust buildings. It looked a very des res although it was a little too remote even for Warlow's tastes.

Second homes dotted the countryside from Carmarthen to St David's. This far west, where the language and culture still lived, residency remained a bone of contention. Further north, the local authority in Gwynedd had already implemented a one hundred per cent council tax premium on unoccupied second homes. Market forces often left communities defenceless and the old chestnut of privilege riding rough-shod over local needs reared up periodically. The Assembly ducked its head on talk of a licensing system for conversion of properties and, ironically, local council motions often failed. Abstentions were common because the fox was in the henhouse when it came to councillors declaring an interest. Disapproval of interlopers existed, but not enough to murder someone in a desolate forest, surely.

They parked and crossed the gravel to a front door.

Warlow knocked. Firm, no-nonsense, making sure the occupants knew it was serious business. Not that they'd have much in the way of footfall or passing trade out here. At the second knock, the door opened. A man stood in the hallway dressed in twill trousers, a checked shirt, and a turtle-neck sweater. He looked firm and upright, though there were deep lines on his stony face. Warlow would have bet a tenner he'd been in the military.

'Afternoon, Mr Geary.' Warlow had his warrant card out. 'DCI Evan Warlow and this is DS Catrin Richards. We're sorry to bother you at what must be a difficult time. But there are things you might help us with. Things we need to understand about what's taken place.'

Ralph Geary looked out over the DCI's shoulder with a pained expression, blinking into the evening light as if he was expecting, or hoping, someone else might be there. 'Come in.' He spoke in a gruff, clipped, no-nonsense way.

Ralph led the officers in to sit on chairs at a table in an uncluttered living room. Warlow glanced about and let his eyes settle on a sideboard covered in framed photos. Andrew Geary from child to man took up most of the space. In school uniforms, on bikes, sailing, skiing. Images of a privileged upbringing. One showed a younger Ralph Geary posing rigidly in uniform, arm in arm with a pretty woman in a bridal gown. That same woman, thirty-five years on, was sitting on a sofa. Geary introduced her as Celia. She stood up and offered both Warlow and Catrin tea. A few minutes later she served it in little cups that clinked when Warlow picked his up.

'Sorry to have to do this now.' Warlow declined the offer of a biscuit when Celia proffered a plate. 'But we need to establish Andrew's movements as soon as possible.'

At the mention of his name, Celia Geary squeezed her eyes shut and ran one hand over the other in her lap in a writhing movement. As if she was washing them without water. Ralph Geary put his own hand over them, but it didn't stop them moving.

'In your own time,' Warlow said and nodded at Catrin who took out her notebook.

Ralph took a breath and exhaled sharply. 'Andrew came down the day before yesterday. Drove down from London. It's his stag weekend.'

'I didn't know that.' Warlow shifted in his seat.

Ralph nodded. 'They were bound for the coast. An adventure weekend. Andrew and half a dozen others. That's all off now, of course.' He stopped there, as if realising the callousness of what he'd said. 'Rob, that's Rob Hopley. He was to be Andrew's best man. He was staying with us. The boys... they go back a long way. From school. Rob used to come here in the summers and he and Andrew used to go off on their own. *Famous Five* sort of stuff.'

'Is that what they were doing in the forest?' Catrin asked.

Celia Geary spoke up to answer. Her accent mirrored her husband's. 'They wanted to relive what they'd shared as boys one last time. Go off and do a bike ride. Camp out like they used to do when they were children. Just one last innocent adventure...' Her expression hardened. Warlow guessed it was the word 'last' uttered in innocence but loaded with a different meaning from what was intended.

'So they left here on their bikes?' Catrin asked.

'Yes. They got the bug here,' Ralph explained. 'Riding through the bike trails in the forest. Used to go off all day, come back filthy. It's an ideal place for that.'

'You have a lovely property here,' Warlow said.

'Picked it up for a song when it was just a crumbling barn. Did it up bit by bit. Now we're down here most of the time. Pop up to the Finchley flat when we visit…' Ralph caught himself, swallowed loudly. 'Visited Andrew.'

Next to him, Celia Geary choked back a sob.

Warlow clinked his toy teacup onto its saucer. 'Did anyone else know they were back?'

Ralph frowned. 'Only the other boys on the stag weekend.'

'We'll need their names and contact details,' Catrin said.

Ralph's frown deepened, but he nodded vaguely.

'Did you hear from either Andrew or Rob once they'd left here?' Warlow kept his gaze on Ralph. Celia didn't appear to be in a fit state to answer.

'No. That's a standing joke out here. Mobile phone reception can be patchy.'

'Did they tell you where they were going?'

Celia shook her head. 'To the forest. That's all they ever said when we asked them. Even as kids.'

Warlow took the second and last swallow from his cup and told himself not to let it clatter when he put it down again. He studied the couple on the couch over the rim. They sat up, leaning forward on a sofa with a backrest that angled back. To sit back was to lounge. And neither of them felt like lounging, he felt sure.

Instead, they took an awkward position that he'd seen people adopt dozens of times over the years. An uncomfortable physical manifestation of their psychological state. A fight between desperately wanting to be somewhere else where they could be alone with their grief and a need to be of use. Everyone in this room knew damned well that whatever they did or said, none of it would bring Andrew Geary back from the mortuary gurney in Cardiff. Their discomfort was a kind of torture. Like grief, something to be endured, hoping perhaps it might ease the suffering.

Warlow touched his cup to its saucer with barely a chink. 'This can't be easy for you both and some of these questions I ask might seem a little bit off. But I need to ask them. Can either of you think of anyone who might have wanted to do Andrew any harm?'

Ralph shook his head. 'Andrew lived in London. He came back here for the odd weekend. Christmas, birthdays, that sort of thing. But his life was in London.'

'And you have no enemies here? No disputes with anyone local? Sheep getting out into someone else's garden, land disputes?'

Celia Geary shook her head. But then stopped and frowned to herself. As if something in her memory had surfaced. Warlow saw it, waited for her to speak. When she didn't, he said. 'Say whatever you think. No matter how trivial.'

She sent her husband a glance. Warlow's antennae twitched. He felt sure that glance had a question in it. But Ralph was already shaking his head. Dismissing the suggestion. 'There's nothing. We live a quiet life here. Celia is in a choir. I fish. I keep a few hobby sheep. Everyone around us is kind. It's taken some time, but they have accepted us into this community. English interlopers though we are.' The ghost of a smile touched Ralph's mouth for a second.

'Nothing has ever happened that might make you nervous about being here?' Warlow persisted.

'No,' Ralph said.

Warlow turned his eyes on Celia, but her gaze had fallen back to her constantly moving hands. He was about to ask her the same question when a door at the far end of the room opened. A young woman stood there, tall but diminished and hunched in her grief. Fair in colouring, eyes red from crying, dressed in jeans and roll-neck sweater with the sleeves hanging over her hands. She had striped socks with no shoes and wore an imploring look on her face.

'I'm sorry, I… I couldn't bear not knowing if you'd found out…'

Ralph Geary stood up. So did Warlow. 'Oh, Fran,' Ralph said. 'Come in, darling. This is Detective Chief Inspector Warlow and Sergeant Richards from CID. They're here to ask some questions about Andrew.'

The girl responded with a series of rapid nods.

'Mr Warlow, this is Francesca Dee, Andrew's fiancée.'

'Miss Dee, I'm very sorry for your loss.' Warlow stepped forward.

Fran squeezed her eyes shut. A fresh tear cascaded down her cheek, but there was no accompanying noise.

Geary took her elbow. 'Come and sit down. Let me get you some tea.'

'How about we two go into the kitchen,' Warlow said. 'I'll make the tea. We can chat there while Sergeant Richards takes some names and addresses from Mr and Mrs Geary.'

'Will you manage?' Mrs Geary looked horrified.

Warlow sent her the briefest of smiles. 'We're trained to make tea under all situations and circumstances, Mrs Geary. Essentially par for the course. Do not worry.'

CHAPTER EIGHT

JESS AND RHYS pulled in to the Keepers' car park in the Brechfa Forest. It was getting late. Another half hour of daylight at the most on this drab day, she reckoned. The DI made an executive decision at half past four and left the Incident Room in the hands of a couple of secretaries and a CID sergeant with strict instructions that anything from forensics was to be put through to her. Rhys had been like a lost dog all afternoon, following her around, itching to get out and explore his boy racer theories.

In the end, she'd relented. They were in her VW Golf parked twenty yards from a dark barn-like structure which, Rhys assured her, was the 'forestry school.' The road wound up from Nantgaredig and Rhys had made her drive another half a kilometre to a different car park, a smaller one, that the drivers sometimes used. But they'd found no debris or empty cans lying around, so they'd backtracked to Keepers.

Only two other vehicles sat in the muddy car park and there was acres of room, but Rhys had pointed to a spot which was closest to an overflowing bin.

'Should I look?' Rhys asked, as they both sat in the car.

'I'm following your lead, Rhys. How far are we from where Andrew Geary was found?'

Rhys paused with his hand on the door handle. 'Couple of miles as the crow flies. But from here, I think we'd need to go deeper in before we could access it.'

'You have gloves?'

'Yes. Ma'am.' He reached into his pocket and pulled out a pair of blue nitriles.

Jess opened her door.

'You coming too?' Rhys asked.

'The chance to examine a rarely emptied refuse bin? Wouldn't miss it for the world. Go on, I'm right behind you.'

Rhys got out and walked across to a stained and rusted barrel. Jess went to the boot and donned a pair of ankle-length galoshes that she slipped on, tucking in the bottoms of her trousers before walking across to observe the DC, but keeping a good ten yards back.

'Mainly dog poo bags,' Rhys said with distaste.

'Bring one of those back for Mr Warlow. He'd be delighted, I'm sure.'

'Really?' Rhys looked up.

Jess rolled her eyes.

The DC grinned. 'Good one, ma'am. They're only on the top anyway. There must have been a few walkers since… wait, underneath, yes, cans of Strongbow.' He reached in and pulled out an empty.

'I thought you said people threw stuff on the floor?'

Rhys looked around at her, eyes bright from his find. 'They do, but the other people who come here, the walkers, they're a different breed. Environmentally aware. They'll pick up any trash and put it in.' From a pocket of his anorak he pulled out an evidence bag. Jess took photos. There were three cans in total.

When he'd finished, Jess strode past him towards the

building and the wide descending track. She stopped at a noticeboard to study a map of the trails.

Rhys joined her, cans clanking in the bag. 'We going for a walk, ma'am?'

'Mmm. Just a couple of hundred yards.' Jess looked around at the massive trees. 'I want to get a feel for the place.'

The track was wide enough for vehicles for the first quarter of a mile. Then a sign, a blue rectangle with a white footprint, pointed off to the left down a steep stoned path. After thirty steps, they were in a different world. The road above them disappeared and a broad woodland track flanked by tall conifers wound its way down into a little valley. Within five minutes, a hush descended. Above them, the trees hissed and moaned in the wind. Below them, the gurgle of a stream burbled up. The trees were not dense, and between the trunks, Jess looked right and left across the slopes.

'Is this a looped walk?' she asked.

'About a mile and a half there and back.'

The curving path made a half circle to a point where she could look down to the valley floor and a wooden bridge leading to an ascent on the other side. She looked up and stopped. Through the trees, across the valley, a lighter patch of land came into view. A green field and grey buildings.

'Is that a property?'

Rhys followed her gaze. 'It is. There aren't many up here, but one or two are dotted within the forest itself.'

Jess manoeuvred herself between the branches of a tree to get a better view. 'It looks remote. What was it, a keeper's cottage?'

'This forest has always been here. One of the few that wasn't cut down during the Bronze Age. Different trees, but the same location. People have tried to manage it over the years.'

Jess sent Rhys an appraising glance. 'How come you know all about this stuff.'

'I have a few cousins in the Towy Valley. Sometimes we'd drive up here.'

'Your criminal youth.'

'Not that bad, ma—'

'Chill, Rhys. I'm pulling your leg.' She turned back to look across at the cottage. 'Can't be easy access to these places.'

'No.'

The DI shivered.

'You cold, ma'am?'

'No. But it's getting dark and I've had a long day with the promise of longer ones to come.' What she didn't add was the creeping sense of unease she had that they weren't alone in this place. Jess wasn't squeamish and, with a sixteen-year-old daughter who considered the outdoors her playground, she was no stranger to long hikes, beach walks, and treks to seek surf of adequate height, speed, and volume. But an uncomfortable sense of being watched had come over her the minute they'd started the descent. Entirely possible that a dog walker might come the other way, of course. But still…

'No point going on. I only wanted a taster. I'll have to come back on another day and explore with Molly.'

'Bring a picnic. There's a lot to explore.' Rhys grinned.

From somewhere, the whining buzz of an engine broke the silence. It wasn't near but waxed and waned making it almost impossible to say where exactly it might be.

Jess held up a finger and narrowed her eyes. 'Chainsaw?'

Rhys shook his head. 'Dirt bike, ma'am. It's how most people get around out here.'

'Sounds like a mad bee.'

The two officers turned and retraced their steps back to the car park.

Jess got into the car and started up. 'I'll drop you off at HQ. Get those cans to forensics. See if they can get prints. Then we'll see what your theory throws up.'

———

FRAN DEE LOOKED like a broken doll as she stood in the kitchen. Warlow opened cupboard doors and grabbed a couple of decent sized mugs instead of the china cups, threw in some tea bags he found in a usefully labelled tin, and waited for the kettle to boil. While it did, he kept the conversation light.

'You came down from London today?'

She shook her head. 'I was meant to be at a girlfriend's for the weekend. I was on the way there when Ralph called. I turned the car around and drove straight here.' Her expression crumpled, more tears threatening at any moment.

'You live together in, Wandsworth, is it?'

'Woolwich.'

Warlow nodded. 'I was based in Southwark for a while. Back in the day. Before they completed the Shard. That's how old I am.'

Hardly scintillating conversation. But bland was what he was aiming for. He knew this would be one way. She was in no state to initiate any chat.

The kettle boiled, he poured in boiling water, then opened the fridge.

'Milk?'

Fran nodded.

Warlow took out the milk and put it on the countertop,

un-poured. 'I'm not an add milk to the cup with the tea bag in man. We'll let it steep for a few minutes.'

Fran looked at the mugs and said nothing.

'You feel up to answering some questions?' he asked.

She was hunched forward, arms folded across her chest. Warlow noted the manicured nails painted a dark purple colour. She'd done her best to deal with the smudged mascara but was fighting a losing battle there. Her reply, when it came, ignored his question. 'Can you tell me what happened?'

'The straight answer is no I can't because I don't know yet. But that's why I'm here. To find out what I can so that it'll help me. It's the way these things work. We begin by building up as full a picture as we can.'

Fran swayed a little and for a moment Warlow wondered if she was going to pass out. He reached out a hand and said, 'Why don't you sit down?'

Fran shambled forward and pulled out a chair from under a small breakfast table that, Warlow assumed, the Gearys used when they had no visitors.

He pulled out the only other chair and sat. Fran Dee was twenty-nine. He already had that information. He knew she was bright, an actuary in the City. He knew she was from Surrey. But the woman that these labels applied to – capable, hardworking, confident – wasn't the one sitting next to him at this table. She'd long gone and, in her place, sat a frightened, miserable girl trying to cope with a loss that was all the more unacceptable for its sudden and brutal nature.

Warlow spoke softly. 'We're going to have a chat and I suspect you might think that some of my questions will sound stupid and irrelevant. But it's a part of the process. You okay with that?'

She looked up at him and, though her distraught

expression didn't change, he acknowledged understanding in her eyes.

The DCI stood, fished out the teabags, and added milk. He put the mug in front of Fran and saw her clutch it with both hands through the long sleeves. As if its warmth, more than anything else, gave succour. Warlow spooned in one sugar and offered the bowl to Fran. She shook her head. Warlow sipped. It was hot and sweet. Not bad at all.

He looked around the kitchen. Blue tiles, an Aga, slate on the floor, wooden kitchen cupboards that looked expensive. A clock on the wall said half four. Fran Dee's fiancé had been dead for less than a day. Time to get a move on then.

'Sorry that we have to meet under such horrible circumstances, Miss Dee,' he began.

'Can you tell me how? No one will tell me how.'

'I can. As far as we can tell, Andrew and Rob were attacked last night in a glade in the woods. They'd camped there. It looks like someone came in and a knife was used.'

Fran brought a hand up to cover her mouth. Her breath started to heave in and out.

'A lot of people are working on finding out what exactly happened.' Warlow leant in. 'I'm here with you but there are investigators at the scene.'

Fran's bottom lip was wobbling. The only word she managed to say was, 'Who…?' it came out high and thin.

'We don't know. But we will. I can promise you that.'

She looked at him, eyes wide, lip trembling until her hand covered her mouth again.

Warlow put his mug down. 'I'm not going to pretend to say I know what this feels like for you. But we are going to do everything we can to find out what happened. A lot of people are going to help me. And that will include you.'

'How can I…?'

'What we have now is a jigsaw. We have big chunks of

it already completed. But there are other pieces we need help with. Did Andrew contact you yesterday?'

Fran nodded. 'In the morning. He texted. Said he and Rob were off on an adventure.' She sniffed.

'Nothing after that?'

'No. Not until Ralph called.' She squeezed her eyes shut and pulled a tissue from her sleeve to dab at some fresh tears.

'You know Mr Hopley, I presume?'

Fran nodded. 'Andy and Rob… they wanted to have a day or two together before the others came down.'

'Did Andy see much of Rob?'

'Not as much as he used to. Rob was in Cardiff, we were in London. Busy jobs, you know.'

'Of course. Did Andy ever say anything to you about anyone wanting to do him harm?'

Fran sucked in a wracking sob. 'No. Andy… I know he could be a bit brash sometimes. He couldn't sit still. That's why Rob organised a stag full of mad things. Canoeing, coasteering, archery. Everything was a competition. Rob knows Andy well.'

Warlow waited for her to qualify the tense, but she didn't. Neither did he press the point.

'But underneath all that Andy is…was… really sweet…' Fran shook her head.

'No problems at work? He wasn't in any trouble financially?'

'No. He was doing really well.'

'What was his job?'

'He worked for Janders. M and A.'

'M and A?'

'Mergers and acquisitions. They're a merchant bank.'

'Right,' Warlow said, making a mental note.

Fran sipped her tea. It seemed to help. 'We were planning on getting married in May. Over the bank holiday.

We'd booked Bingley Hall in Gloucestershire. He was paying for all that. We weren't going to ask our parents for anything.'

Warlow nodded.

'They went out on a bike ride like they'd done a hundred times before,' Fran said with a defiant tone. 'There's no reason for anyone to... to attack Andy in the middle of nowhere. How can there be?'

'That's what I'm going to find out, Fran. It's little enough under the circumstances, but I will promise you that.' Little enough succour in his words, he knew. But he also wanted her to realise he meant every one of them. 'We're going to take his laptop. I don't suppose you have any idea of his password, do you?'

'I do. We had no secrets. Gearyyme336.'

'That's great. We'll want to look through it. Just in case.'

'Of what?'

'I don't know. Probably nothing, But we won't know unless we look.'

Warlow reached into a pocket and fished out a business card. 'This is me. You can ring me day or night if you think of anything that might help. Doesn't matter how trivial. Ring me.'

Fran took it and it disappeared under the sleeve of her jumper.

Outside, a car pulled up. Warlow stood and through the window saw a marked police car arrive and a woman in uniform get out. He turned back to Fran.

'The person arriving now is a specially trained officer. She's very good at helping in these situations. You can talk to her, too. About anything.'

Fran nodded.

The doorbell rang. Warlow heard Ralph Geary answer

it. Low murmurs in the hall followed before Geary opened the kitchen door. 'Your colleagues, DCI Warlow.'

'Family liaison?' Warlow asked the uniformed officer.

'PC Mellings, sir,' said the uniform. Young, attractive, confident.

'This is Fran Dee, Andy's fiancée.'

Mellings' mouth compressed in a sympathetic smile. 'I'm so sorry to meet you under these circumstances, Miss Dee. I've already introduced myself to Mr and Mrs Geary.'

Warlow gulped his tea. It was still hot but he'd developed an asbestos mouth. He turned again to Fran. 'Officer Mellings will be staying with you. She'll keep you informed of any progress we make. Perhaps you could fetch Andy's laptop?'

He nodded to the uniform. She followed Fran into the body of the house. All part of the little song and dance he'd performed far too many times. He went into the hallway, beckoned to DS Richards and, once Fran had provided the laptop, said his goodbyes to the Gearys.

A minute later they were driving away from a house that suddenly looked small and cramped, as if it was being squashed under the weight of an irredeemable grief.

CHAPTER NINE

WARLOW AND RICHARDS called in to the crime scene on the way back. When he'd suggested it, the sergeant jumped at the chance.

'I'd like to see it, sir.'

She'd go far this one, he thought.

As it turned out, the Crime Scene Techs were packing up the van when they got to the parking area on the forestry road. But, as expected, Alison Povey was still on site. As usual, the last to leave.

She stood outside the cordon for once, and the paper hood of her suit had been swept back to reveal her short dark hair.

'Anything new?' Warlow asked, dispensing with the niceties.

'We've got a match on the tyre impressions. That report should be with you tonight or tomorrow.' She walked parallel to a narrow strip of tape, pointing to the space between. 'The motorbike came in and out this way.' Warlow followed Povey's pointing finger and another bike track leading off into the woods.

'Does it go anywhere?'

'Joins up with another forestry road running west to east. Not much help there, I'm afraid.'

Warlow nodded.

'But we also think we know which way Hopley got out. It was dark, a bit of moon but not much. There's another bike trail leading south-east. I've walked it and it brings you out more or less on the lane where the paramedic found him.'

'It would make sense if he stuck to a path,' Catrin said.

'How's he getting on?' Povey asked.

Catrin answered. 'I spoke to the hospital this afternoon. He's still under head injury observation. None of his wounds are life threatening, though. We should be able to speak to him tomorrow.'

Warlow looked around at his surroundings. 'There's no way anyone would have stumbled on this spot. Someone knew they were here.'

'Think they were followed?' Povey asked.

'Maybe. Or someone knew they'd end up here.'

The investigator tilted her head. 'What's going on in that devious mind of yours, Evan?'

'Nothing that hasn't already gone on in yours.'

'If only I could believe that.' Povey grinned.

———

HE GOT BACK to the Incident Room a few minutes before seven. Warlow bit back disappointment on seeing not much difference in terms of additions to the Gallery. Both Jess and Rhys had gone home. But an unfamiliar figure stood gazing at the Job Centre, studying the actions and to-do list. He was bigger than Warlow by half a head, heavier, and wider, too, by some measure. He wore a short-sleeved shirt and had both hands on his hips. A stance which showed up all the hair on his brawny forearms.

'Help you?' asked Warlow.

The man turned with a surprisingly light movement. A broad, clean-shaven open face with arched eyebrows and a receding hairline contemplated Warlow before breaking into an engaging grin.

'DCI Warlow is it?'

There was something familiar about him that Warlow couldn't quite pinpoint. The lanyard around his neck arched forward over a bit of belly which, Warlow surmised, didn't bother this man too much.

'DS Gil Jones.' The man started forward, hand outstretched, and added a greeting in his native language. *'Shwmae?'*

'Iawn diolch,' Warlow replied. Then it clicked. He hadn't physically met Jones but, now with the man standing in front of him, he remembered where he'd seen the photos on the Dyfed-Powys intranet site. The DS had been commended on more than one occasion for his work.

Warlow shook a big meaty hand and defaulted back to English as was the norm in a work setting. A couple of civilian admins were tapping away at desktops in the room, not that they needed to hear any exchange. It was merely force of habit.

'Gil, good to see you. The Buccaneer said you'd be joining us. But I was expecting you tomorrow.'

Gil nodded. 'Wanted a head start, sir. My daughter lives near Llandeilo. We're staying there tonight, get an early start in the morning. Thought I'd call in and take a look.'

'Not much to see yet.' Warlow added a forlorn exhalation.

'Nasty though.'

Warlow nodded. 'I've just come from the scene and before that the relatives. Here's the deceased's laptop. You any good with that stuff?'

Gil raised one eyebrow theatrically. 'Not really.'

'Me neither,' Warlow conceded. 'We'll get Rhys Harries or Catrin Richards to look at it first thing before sending it to the cyber nerds. They seem to know their way around tech.'

Gil glanced at the laptop Warlow placed on the desk. 'Tidy. I'll check it in, no problem.'

'The Buccaneer said that you'd been working on Alice?'

A downturned smile reshaped Gil's mouth momentarily as he nodded.

'That can't have been much fun.' Warlow tilted his head in sympathy.

'No, it wasn't. Still, we put some sick buggers away.'

'You have kids?'

Gil looked a few years older than Warlow so it was a fair guess. 'Grown up daughters. Three grandchildren. My wife's come with me to Llandeilo. We're toying with moving down to be close to the kids.' The DS's open face smiled.

'That's good to hear. Great to have you here, Gil. The change will do you good.'

Gil half turned back to the Gallery. 'Looking forward to it.' He contemplated the post-mortem snaps before adding, 'Says something about the job when photos of a man stabbed to death are a relief from the sort of thing I've been looking at for the last six months.'

Warlow let out an understanding snort but said nothing. Child abuse ops like Alice inevitably spilled over into related crimes such as child pornography. Often the officers involved needed counselling. Sometimes they only needed a reaffirmation of normality. Some reassurance that the world wasn't always a cesspit. Spending some time with your grandchildren seemed as good an antidote as any.

Warlow jangled his keys. 'Right. I'll see you first thing. I'm off to pick up the dog from the sitter.'

———

JESS AND MOLLY ALLANBY rented a house in Cold Blow in Pembrokeshire. Warlow knocked on the door and the younger Allanby opened it. At sixteen, she was a slightly smaller version of her mother. Same dark hair, big grey eyes, and good skin. The main difference showed in the lack, or rather the dismissal as unnecessary, of social skills. But he'd already sussed that out. Molly's parents had just separated, she and Jess had upped sticks forcing her to navigate the choppy waters of a new school in a different country. Still Britain, but West Wales wasn't Manchester. Most of her sarcasm emerged as pure defence mechanism. And because he understood that, Warlow took no offence. Molly needed to show the world how tough she was. And Warlow suspected that men, especially those old enough to be her father, were open season. It was almost entertaining to see the number of ways Molly could find fault.

'You are so late,' she said, arms folded.

'I know. Sorry about—'

'I told Cadi you'd be back ages ago. She was beginning to think I was lying to her.'

With that, a black bundle of energy burst out from behind Molly, pushed past and writhed and wriggled against Warlow's legs.

'Hello, Cadi, *cariad. Wyt ti wedi bod yn ferch dda? I ti wedi cael amser da?*'

'She has been a good girl, and yes, she's had the best time.' Molly accurately interpreted and answered the rhetorical questions from Warlow's customary greeting of the dog in Welsh. 'We've had a huge walk and played find the slipper like a hundred times. She is getting really, really good at that. I mean dead brilliant.'

Molly, like her mother, retained her Mancunian accent, extending her vowels, glottalizing her t's and dropping more h's than not. Neither of them had been in West Wales long enough for it to change. But Warlow had the feeling Molly wouldn't let it change since it fed into her abrasive teenage vibe.

Behind her, Jess Allanby appeared in off-duty jeans and sweatshirt, complete with fluffy slippers on her feet.

'Hi. I see that Molly's not bothered inviting you in.'

'He never comes in,' Molly protested with a fixed grin. 'Unless it's for a free meal.'

Warlow shook his head. 'That's harsh and factually inaccurate. But I still won't. I've troubled your daughter enough for one day.'

Molly bristled. 'Cadi is no trouble. I don't even see the point of you taking her home. You'll be back in like, ten hours.'

'I need a Cadi fix, too, you know,' Warlow said.

'Molly's right though, if you want to leave her here overnight, you're more than welcome,' Jess offered and Warlow had the feeling that the coming nights might be late ones judging by how the case was shaping up. They always were in a murder investigation. And Jess was not one to run home when work demanded even if it meant leaving Molly alone. Warlow sensed the subtext. It would do no harm for a sixteen-year-old girl to have some canine company.

Warlow nodded. 'I might take you up on that. I'll bring a spare bed over just in case.'

'No need,' said Molly. 'She can sleep with me.'

Jess sent Warlow a long-suffering glance. 'If you have a spare dog bed, that would be great.'

Molly rolled her eyes. 'Waste of time.' She knelt and

hugged the dog. 'See you tomorrow, Cads.' With that, she turned on her heel and ran upstairs. The dog watched her go, tail wagging.

'Our help has arrived by the way,' Warlow said.

'Help?'

'A DS. Gil Jones. Lots of experience. He was in the office when I left. I think he'll be good for us.'

'How did it go with the Gearys?' Jess adopted a wary tone.

Warlow blew out his cheeks. 'As expected. Devastated.'

Jess nodded. Some things never changed

CHAPTER TEN

WARLOW GOT up at six the next day. It was a good forty-minute drive from his cottage in Nevern to the Incident Room in Carmarthen. And even though he'd dropped off Cadi – complete with bed – at seven, he'd been surprised to note that Jess had already left. By the time he arrived, they were all waiting for him. He sensed the atmosphere as soon as he walked in. A little buzz. Some definite positivity. Whether the imposing presence of the new DS or the inevitable excitement of the chase had lit the fuse, it didn't matter.

But he sensed it.

'I see introductions have already been made,' Warlow said, shedding his coat.

'All done,' Jess sent Gil a flashing smile before holding out a mug of tea to Warlow.

The DCI took it, sipped, and nodded. The tea was good and hot. Someone must have spotted him arrive in the car park. This was teamwork. His kind anyway. 'Right, I'd like to officially welcome DS Gil Jones. I don't need to tell the rest of you how experienced Gil is. And how much of an asset him joining us will be. For now, he'll be running the office, which will free up DI Allanby. Catrin, you do the honours. Let's see where we are as of now.'

Catrin stood in front of the Gallery, chin raised, up for it.

'The tyre tracks found at the scene are Yamahas. Common on motocross bikes. I'm checking registration for owners in the area.'

'Good. What about the laptop?'

Rhys turned from his desk. 'I have it open, sir. I'm going through what I can now.'

'What about Geary's phone?'

'Haven't been able to open that yet.' Rhys wrinkled his nose. 'It's new, so it opens either with a digital password or facial recognition, not a thumbprint. I left a message with the FLO to ask Fran Dee if she knows what it is. If it stays unlocked for forty-eight hours, it reverts to passcode.'

'She said nothing to me about a phone passcode.' Warlow paused for thought. 'What if you unlock it with facial recognition within forty-eight hours?'

Warlow looked at Jess and Gil. They both smiled. Rhys merely looked confused. 'How would that work, sir?'

'Ever seen *Shaun of the Dead*, DC Harries?' asked Gil.

Rhys grinned. '*Shaun of the Dead* is one of my all-time favourite films.'

'Well, this is your chance to be in your very own fan flick.' Gil delivered this all smiles.

Rhys opened his mouth, but nothing emerged as he struggled to follow the DS's train of thought.

Everyone turned to look at the Gallery. It took Rhys a long ten seconds to catch on. 'You don't mean... not the mortuary?'

Gil sucked in air through his teeth. 'Geary's face is intact. I'll give the technicians a bell. You'll be up and back from Cardiff by lunchtime.'

'Really?' Rhys said. Or rather, warbled.

Gil dropped his voice. 'Pop the blanket back and ask him to say cheese. If he sits up you have our permission to leg it, okay?'

Everyone grinned. Everyone except Rhys whose eyes were rapidly blinking orbs. 'So, I have to hold the phone over a dead man's face?'

Catrin waited ten more seconds before putting him out of his misery. 'No, you do not. That never works. The phone allows facial recognition attempts only half a dozen times before reverting to passcode. At least half a dozen people will have looked at that phone since they found it. You're safe.'

'So I don't need to go to Cardiff?' Rhys demanded clarification.

'No. But chase up the fiancée for that PIN,' Catrin said. 'And you could give the mortuary a ring and ask if anything has come through that they haven't put on HOLMES yet.'

Rhys wrote everything down, glancing up accusingly at Warlow and Gil who exchanged amused and very-pleased-with-themselves glances.

'We're awaiting forensics on the cans found at the Keepers' car park. Rhys came up trumps there,' Jess added.

Warlow raised a mug at the DC, who still looked a little shell-shocked after his narrow escape from interacting with the deceased victim. 'Okay,' Warlow said. 'That leaves Hopley. He's top of my list today.'

'Nothing from the hospital yet, sir.' Catrin said.

'Doesn't matter.' Warlow walked to the boards. 'We can't wait any longer. And we need to chase up the other stag do attendees. I doubt formal interviews are needed, but a quick chat to establish where they were and what their thoughts are will do.'

'I'll get on with that,' Gil said.

'Good.' Warlow checked his watch. 'Looks like we've all got our jobs to do. By the time I come back, I want some answers posted up under all these questions.' He nodded at the Job Centre. 'So that leaves you and me out and about, DI Allanby.'

'My car or yours?' Jess asked.

———

AT THE HOSPITAL, Warlow spoke briefly to the Sister in charge of the surgical ward who told them Rob Hopley was doing well. The knife wound to the left shoulder had gone into bone, and the lacerations were worse on the left forearm, too. But they were expecting him to make a full recovery. His neurological observations remained normal.

She went in before them and had a quick word. From outside, Warlow saw Hopley nod. He had bandages on both of his arms and the left one in a sling. His head had been bandaged, too, but he was sitting up, reading something on his phone when the nurse interrupted him. She walked back out and nodded at the two officers.

Warlow had his warrant card out as he walked in. Probably no need, but sometimes best to play by the rules. Or at least establish some. Jess did the same. Introductions over, Warlow got on with the interview.

'Sister tells us you're feeling better,' Warlow said.

'I'm fine. Better than Andy anyway.' Hopley's voice sounded ragged.

The DCI continued. 'There's never going to be a good time for us to do this, but we're grateful for you agreeing to talk to us.'

'I've had the press on the phone already.' Hopley glanced at his phone and put it face down on the bed. 'How the hell did they get my number?'

Warlow's face clouded. The buggers were like wild dogs in a case like this.

Jess answered. 'They're resourceful. My advice would be to say nothing. We have a press officer. You can refer them to us. We'll be holding a press conference soon anyway.'

Hopley nodded.

There were flowers and two cards on the little table next to Rob. The cards had been propped open. Warlow read the names Ralph and Celia in one, Fran in the other.

'Are you up to answering a few questions about the attack?' Warlow asked.

'Of course. Anything I can do to help.'

'Mind if I tape this?' Jess waved her phone. 'Saves us writing things down.'

Rob shrugged.

Jess pressed some buttons and placed the phone on the side table with the app running.

'In your own words then, Mr Hopley,' Warlow said.

Rob frowned. 'I know it sounds weird, but I've been lying here, knowing you were coming and trying to think what I should say. I mean, it was dark. It happened so fast, I—'

Warlow cut him off. 'Start at the beginning. Why did you go to the glade?'

Rob puffed out red cheeks. He reached for some water and winced. Warlow helped him and waited while the injured man took a swallow. He noted the rusty coloured hair and freckled features and the prominent nose. A flushed face added unflatteringly to the palette.

Rob finished the water and glanced at Jess's phone before beginning. 'Andy wanted to go into the woods. Like we used to do. The last time we did that, we were eighteen or nineteen. The glade has always been there. We'd stay overnight and get up just before dawn. There's a run,

Ram's run. We get up there for the dawn. You can watch the sun come up over the Black Mountains from the top. It's spectacular. Andy wanted to do it one last time.'

'That was the plan, then?' Jess asked. 'Get up early for the dawn?'

Rob nodded. 'We camped. It got dark early, so we lit a fire, had some bangers and a beer or two. We'd been out most of the day and we were knackered, so we crashed at half nine. We'd heard a bike—'

'A bike?'

Rob nodded. 'Yeah, a motorbike. You hear them all the time in the woods. People aren't supposed to do motocross in there, but they do. Way in the distance. Once, it got louder, but I thought nothing... I mean it was dark and my guess was that it could have been someone heading home. I was half asleep when it suddenly got very loud and I saw a light coming towards us through the trees. I got out of my pop-up in time to see Andy out of his tent and the bike... the bike went for him. It hit the tent and knocked him over.'

'Did you see a face?'

'The rider was dressed in dark clothing. He had a headlight on over a helmet. He ran Andy down and then ran me down. I jumped out of the way and fell. When I got up, the bloke was off his bike. I couldn't see clearly, but it looked like he was hitting Andy who'd fallen to his knees. Not punching, more like striking at him. I yelled and ran forward, and then the bloke turned on me. I felt something sharp, and I fell again, rolled over. He hit my shoulder and he stumbled. But by then I'd scrambled away.' Rob shut his eyes, head down. 'I should have gone back, I should have gone to help.'

'It was an armed man, Rob,' Jess said. 'You couldn't have helped.'

'What about the bike? Had you seen any sign of it before the attack?' Warlow pressed.

'As I say, we'd heard it. Or something like it. But you do up there. Sometimes, there are people working in the forest. A chain saw can sound a lot like a bike.'

'And what about cars?'

'No. Nothing in the forest. Nothing… oh, hang on. There was one thing. We were cutting across from one trail to another. It meant us being on the road for half a mile. We were two abreast and some idiot in a car came right up behind us, sounding his horn because he wanted to pass.' Rob shook his head. 'We were on a bend. It wasn't safe to overtake, anyway. The road straightened out after that and he passed us at a ridiculous speed. The engine sounded souped up. We pulled in for a drinks stop, but then we heard the car further down. He turned around and came back past us again on the other side of the road, leering at us. We heard him stop further up and then come back again two minutes later. At speed. Some people think they own the road, don't they?'

'Did you see the car again?' Jess asked.

Rob reached for the plastic cup and took another sip of water. The beaker trembled in his grasp. 'Like I say, we could hear him so we veered off the road into the woods onto a trail. He must have pulled up at the spot where we'd been resting. The driver shouted a few obscenities, but we'd long gone. It happens. Some motorists hate cyclists.'

'What do you remember about the car?' Jess asked

'It was red, I remember that. If I had to swear to a make, I'd say a Peugeot. One of those hot hatches with a custom paint job.'

'You left-handed, Rob?' Warlow jabbed a finger towards Hopley's bandages.

'No. Why?'

'Your left arm's taken the brunt of the injuries. South-paws usually hold their left arms up as guards.'

'It was pure reflex.' Rob said. 'I wasn't thinking. There are cuts on my other arm too.'

'So, you didn't have a weapon in your right hand? A stick or a branch? If you did, we can look for it, check it for fibres. Maybe some DNA if you got lucky.'

'No. I was… I was too scared.' Rob's head fell forward, and he sighed. 'Sorry. It all happened so fast. I think I was pretty lucky to get away with just these injuries.'

'You were,' Warlow said.

Rob looked back up at the DCI with a haunted expression. He clutched at the bedclothes with his right hand, bunching up the material in his fist. 'He was my best friend.' His eyes lifted to the ceiling, face crumpling as if a new pain was surging through him at the memory. 'So I ran and hid until it stopped. The attacker got back on his bike. He didn't go. Not right away. But I was in the trees. He had no way of finding me. He sat there and I waited like a total coward for about ten minutes until he'd gone away. But he came back again. I think he was trying to trap me. I don't know how long I hid for, but he went eventually and I found my way back to Andy. I'd dropped my phone. But there was light from the fire. Enough light to see…'

This time he looked straight at Warlow, tears swimming in his eyes. 'I was his best man. I sorted out what was meant to be the best weekend of his life. And look what happened.'

Warlow stepped forward and leant in. 'Our forensic people found your phone. They'll get it back to you once they've finished DNA analysis and the like. We'll find out what happened, Rob. Evidence has a habit of turning up. We'll find out, I promise you.'

CHAPTER ELEVEN

It was a ten-minute journey from the hospital back to HQ.

The road through the town was slow and choked with traffic. Jess could have taken the bypass on the other side of the river, but it was much of a muchness. Warlow didn't mind. He was happy to sit and let his mind absorb what he'd just heard as they wormed their way past terraced houses, takeaways, and the old Priory hospital now converted to swish flats.

On the surface, Carmarthen appeared a sleepy little county town. Tourists come here because of the glorious countryside and wow-factor natural beauty: the beaches south and west and the mountains to the north. And because it was safe. Warlow suppressed a laugh. Simple mistake to make, that. What poisoned the idyll were the two-legged buggers that ran around on all that lovely land. Not the majority. Oh no. The majority, he was well aware, were all right. Carmarthenshire remained rural. Most of the inhabitants still clung on to a belief in community. Naive perhaps, but most were salt of the earth. People he had a fondness for – not that he'd ever tell anyone that.

But other things existed in the earth besides salt.

Things with blind eyes and dark hearts that lay around waiting to pounce on the unwary. He'd met a few on these very streets. He suspected that the forest in Brechfa might have had its fair share, too.

'So, what did you think?' Jess asked. They'd come to a stop at the traffic lights on Jail Hill. Warlow had said little of anything since they'd left Hopley, preferring to stare out of the window at the flat water of the river snaking its way west to the Bristol Channel. The DI's question drew him back into the here and now. He answered with a question of his own.

'When are they going to let Hopley go?'

'Today. I had a word with the Sister. He's going to stay with the Gearys.'

Warlow nodded. 'Good. We'll give him today to recover. He'll need to give a formal statement.'

'He knows that. But you still haven't answered my question.' Jess looked across, determined not to let Warlow evade her question.

'What do I think?' Warlow pursed his lips. 'It's a bloody odd story is what I think. I mean, attacked in the middle of nowhere like that at night? Whoever rode in on that bike must have known his way around. I almost got lost both times I've walked into the crime scene.'

Jess shook her head. 'Not the sort of place I'd want to be alone in at night.'

'What he says seems to fit. But we need to get Tiernon to look at the photos of his injuries, too. Confirm it's the same weapon.'

Jess frowned.

Warlow persisted. 'Only dotting the i's. He's our only witness, so we need to squeeze as much detail out as possible.'

'But you think someone knew they were there?'

Warlow shrugged. 'Or knew they were going to be there.'

'So they were followed you reckon?' Jess asked.

'Hopley didn't mention hearing a following motorcycle. It's more likely someone knew where they were going and waited for them nearby.'

The lights changed. Jess eased off the brakes, and the car rolled downhill towards the Carmarthen bridge. They lapsed into silence until Warlow added what they were both wondering. 'But what's so special about that glade?'

———

'How was he?' Gil asked, as Warlow and Jess walked back into the Incident Room.

'About how you'd expect. Cut up about it. In more ways than one,' Warlow replied.

That earned him a raised eyebrow look from Catrin who had Geary's laptop open in front of her.

Warlow dismissed her censure by asking, 'How goes it with the laptop, Sergeant Richards?'

'I'm getting there slowly, sir,' Catrin replied. 'There are a couple of encrypted folders, but I've accessed his emails and there's nothing helpful here.'

'Probably porn,' Rhys said from his own desk without looking up. 'In the encrypted file, I mean.'

'DC Harries,' Jess said with mock offence. 'How would you know that?'

For once Rhys didn't turn crimson. 'Seen it in a couple of cases now, ma'am.'

'Do you have an encrypted file on your laptop?' Catrin asked.

'I do not.'

She dropped her eyes and muttered, just loud enough

to be heard. 'That's because you use a VPN and an incognito browser for your gratification.'

Rhys swivelled in his chair and this time did flush a dusky red. 'How do you—'

'*Arglwydd mawr.*' Gil let slip the curse. 'Are they even speaking English?'

Catrin put him out of his misery. 'VPN means virtual private network. It's a way of masking your IP address when you're online. And incognito browsers are a less effective way of hiding your browsing history. All the big ones have the option now: Google, Firefox, Safari.'

'Oh, right. Glad that's cleared up then,' said Gil, clearly none the wiser.

'All I know is that this emphasis on privacy and the tech that goes with it makes it a damn sight harder for us to do our jobs,' said Jess.

'Too bloody true,' Warlow chimed in.

Rhys's phone rang and he was spared further scrutiny. He muttered yes five times in between long tranches of whatever the other party was saying, scribbling furiously in his notebook before putting down the phone and tapping his desktop keyboard like a man possessed. Since he seemed not ready to share anything, Catrin continued. 'I've looked at Geary's browsing history. Nothing exciting.'

'So he wasn't using this PVN stuff?' Gil asked.

'VPN,' Catrin corrected him, with a look that suggested he'd deliberately changed the order of the acronym for comic effect. 'No. Why bother if you don't share your laptop with anyone? Umm, from what I can see most recently he was planning a trip to the Far East. Researching flights to Thailand, hotels, that sort of thing. And digging further back still, it looks like it's not the first time he's been there.'

'We got something back this morning from the post-mortem, too,' Gil told them. 'I've emailed you all details, but the gist of it is that the toxicology screen showed up alcohol and a bit of wacky baccy. Nothing else.'

Warlow shrugged. 'Two blokes under the stars having a few beers and smoking a joint. Neither here nor there.'

'Oh, and Alison Povey phoned to say that they haven't found Geary's drinks bottle.'

'Why is that significant?' Warlow asked.

'That she didn't say,' Gil said.

'Something tells me I better find out.' He looked at the room. Jess was busy writing up their initial interview with Hopley. Something he was grateful for. Catrin was peering at the laptop, Rhys engrossed in his screen. 'Think I'll give her a buzz.'

He retreated to the empty SIO room, found Povey's mobile number, and pressed the call button. Povey's voice responded after three rings.

'Evan, what can I do you for?'

'The drinks bottle. Significance?'

'We've had a good look. A really good look. We've had Uniforms doing fingertip searches until their manicured nails bled. No sign of it.'

Warlow gave her space.

'Only Hopley's was there. From what I know of these downhill cyclists, they go lycra'd to the eyeballs all prepared. And Geary's kit is top of the range stuff. His bike was a four thousand quid job. A *Santa Camino* Trail bike. His tent half a grand's worth. Hopley's not the same standard. But Geary had the works. I find it strange he wouldn't have had a basic drinks bottle.'

'Hardly a smoking gun,' Warlow muttered. 'But thanks for letting me know.'

'How are you getting on?'

'More or less done. We'll have the killer behind bars within the hour.' Warlow sighed. 'In other words, we're floundering. Hopley can't remember much. Too dark to see. The motorbike is our priority, obviously. But I will ask him about the drinks bottle. Thanks, Alison.'

He filed away the information for future use and wandered out of the office. It was mid-morning. Time for a tea break, surely. But as he entered the room, he sensed the change. Everyone clustered around the Gallery. Something at last. Warlow felt a little thrill of anticipation as he strode forward.

'What have we got?'

'Aaron Key.' Rhys's look of triumph lit up the room. 'That was the lab on the phone. The prints on the cans threw up a name. I've just pulled him up.'

Warlow stared at the photo. A standard custody shot of a still-pimply twenty-something with his face composed into what he thought of as a hard stare. What came across was the petulant defiance of an irritating little scrote.

Rhys gave them the relevant. Key was known to the local constabulary as a petty criminal and a not so petty pain in the arse. Theft and burglary, with a special interest in expensive car parts.

'He's also the registered owner of a red Peugeot 208 GTI. A boy racer's wet dream.'

'Hmm,' said Warlow. It came out as a loaded growl. The kind a wolf made when it sensed prey.

'How did it go with Povey?' Gil asked.

Warlow didn't take his eyes off the photograph of Key when he answered. 'Our crime scene terrier isn't happy that we can't find a drinks bottle. Got a bee in her bonnet.'

Catrin turned to stare at Warlow with an expression he was coming to appreciate as one that usually preceded something significant from the sergeant. He realised it was pavlovian, but he loved seeing that look on her face.

'What?' he asked narrowing his eyes.

'The drinks bottle,' she said and walked around to the desk. 'We haven't opened Geary's phone yet, but he was an Apple guy through and through: MacBook, watch, iPhone. So photos taken on his phone are uploaded via the cloud to his photo app which is shared software.'

Gil stared at her with a pained expression. 'Do you speak Mandarin as well?'

Catrin swivelled the laptop around and, leaning forward, tapped keys. A minute later, an image appeared. Two men in cycling kit, helmets on, standing on a viewpoint with a backdrop of densely wooded hills and sweeping views out towards a distant horizon. They were both astride their bikes. On the left, Andrew Geary, wearing black and blue to match a sky-blue bike, one hand out of shot, presumably holding a selfie stick. On his left, Warlow recognised Rob Hopley, all smiles, one hand on the handlebar of a red and black bike.

Both men had their hands up in a toast. Hopley held a green plastic bottle. Geary, too, had a gloved hand around a bottle. Blue to match the bike, and, as Catrin enlarged the photo without Warlow even asking her to, fragments of words appeared around the gloved hand.

Warlow peered at the image and read 'Sant' and 'Cam'.

'Taken on the morning before the attack,' Catrin explained.

'So we know he had a drinks bottle. It's possible the killer might have taken it as a trophy. Good old Povey.' Warlow turned from the photograph. 'I presume we have an address for Key?'

'It's in Burry Port, sir.'

'Right!' Warlow slapped the desk in triumph. 'Get on to Traffic. Get them to drive by and see if the car's at the address. If it is, he's unlikely to be far. Looks like he kisses the bloody thing goodnight before he goes to bed. If it's there, Jess and I are off to the seaside.'

'But…' Rhys looked as if he was about to protest. The lost-toy puppy look had returned with a vengeance.

Warlow exchanged a look with Jess, who said, 'We could do with some back-up,' and managed to deliver it with a completely straight face.

'I've never been back-up before,' Rhys said, beaming.

Warlow shook his head. 'Fine. But only because you found the prints. And don't forget your stab vest.'

CHAPTER TWELVE

RALPH GEARY STOOD in the corridor just outside Mared Ward at Glangwili Hospital, waiting for Rob Hopley to appear. He'd brought clothes in, and a smiling staff-nurse told him to wait while they finalised the discharge.

He knew the hospital. He'd visited a few people from the fishing club here when they'd fallen ill, but he'd never been a patient here himself, thank the Lord. He had private insurance and either went down the road to the local BMI or up to Cardiff to the Spire. It always struck him how tawdry the place was. Beginning life in the Second World War, it was in need of, at the very least, a facelift if not a bulldozer. There'd been talk of a new hospital for years. Almost as long as he and the family had been coming down…

The thoughts trickling out of his head froze when his consciousness locked on to the word.

Family.

There were no seats in the corridor. Only bare walls. And it was to one of these he half stumbled to for support as realisation once again crashed down on him. He'd made himself keep busy since the police turned up at their door.

Finding things to do. Paperwork, cancelling insurances, talking to banks.

But he couldn't shake off the dread of remembering that two o'clock in the morning knock. He'd come awake with a start, wondering if he'd been dreaming. But the second knock confirmed it. An insistent knock. Harsh and loud in the complete quiet of the forest. Impossible to ignore. A harbinger of something awful.

He'd looked out of the bedroom window and seen the police car and known that something bad had happened. Why else would the police turn up in the small hours like that?

He'd thought accident. He'd thought maybe the boys had got drunk and made nuisances of themselves. They'd done that before.

A tiny part of him hoped it was a mistake. Because mistakes happened.

Andrew bought Celia a new iPhone last Christmas, the kind that had that one extra step to switch off the power. A final screen with an emergency SOS option for desperate measures. Only Celia had a tendency to hold the buttons for too long. If you did that, then the automated SOS signal kicked in after five seconds.

In the middle of January, just before midnight, two police officers had turned up to say that they'd received an emergency call from Celia's phone at half past eleven. They were polite, apologetic even. It happened all the time, they explained. But because Celia's phone had then switched off, they had no option but to follow it up to check on the number and the person who owned the phone.

Ralph had been bewildered. He'd woken Celia, and the young officer, satisfied that it had been an error, explained the scenario. He'd asked them to be careful when they switched off their phones from now on. They'd even laughed about it later when they'd told Andrew via a WhatsApp call.

And so Ralph half hoped this was déjà vu. That Celia had been a little cack-handed. But because the boys were out in the forest, he couldn't help but fear the worst.

An accident perhaps?

You sometimes heard cars on the quiet forest roads, especially in summer. He'd complained to the police more than once about it.

Or perhaps Rob had come off his bike and done some damage. He refused to believe it might be Andrew because his skill level was so high. But they came down those hill trails so damned fast on the bikes. All part of the adrenaline rush, he knew. But only a hidden root or stone away from going over the handlebars at speed, too.

But it wasn't an accident or an SOS error message the police turned up at 2am to report. It was something else. He hadn't expected the looks on the two uniformed officers' faces. A look he'd worn himself when he'd turned up at widows' doors in the days when he'd been in the army. The commanding officer's bane.

The corridor wall was cold underneath Ralph's hand.

Family.

The trigger word. Because there was no family now. It would be only him and Celia.

His legs buckled. He'd never fainted in his life, but his eyes darted around, looking for a seat somewhere because leaning against the wall was drawing stares.

No wedding for Andrew and Fran. No dinners for the four of them around a London restaurant table. No prospect of grandchildren. A prospect Celia had been so looking forward to in her own quiet way.

A man in scrubs walked past him. 'You alright?'

Ralph pulled himself together. Straightened up and

dredged up a smile. 'Yes, thanks,' he muttered. 'Fed up of waiting, that's all.'

'You look a little pale.'

'Had some bad news.'

Up the corridor, a bandaged Rob finally emerged with a nurse carrying his cycling clothes in a plastic bag. Rob was limping, pale, and weak.

Ralph waited. Though Celia and Fran had been in to visit, this was the first time the two men had met since Andrew was killed. Ralph desperately tried to hold it together. Rob's lower lip wobbled.

'I'm sorry, Ralph. I'm so sorry. I couldn't stop—'

Ralph shook his head. 'Say nothing, Rob. It's not your fault. Come on, let's get you home.'

———

WARLOW, Jess, and Rhys sat in the DI's Golf on Elkmar Terrace in Burry Port, staring out at the pillar-box-red Peugeot. It had a red spoiler and black alloys. The windows were tinted and the car sat low on the ground. Warlow hoped there were dice hanging from the rear-view mirror. All it needed to make this a boy racer's wet dream.

Key had parked on hard standing behind a corner property. The kind of place that had once been a big house, but which now had three separate back entrances: one offset, the other two next to one another.

'Separate flats,' Warlow observed.

'I've never been to Burry Port before.' Jess undid her seat belt.

'It's an interesting place. Started life as a harbour for coal exporting,' Warlow said. 'Now there's a marina and pubs and caravan parks and no coal.'

'My father blames Thatcher.' Rhys's voice emerged from the back of the car where he'd been shoe-horned in and sat with his long legs on one side and his body in the other of the two seats.

'There is that,' Warlow agreed. 'But it was a rough and dirty job. Take one look at someone with pneumoconiosis and you'll understand why.'

They'd waved off the marked car that had babysat the property for them while they'd driven over and now sat, observing the layout.

'So, what's the plan?' Rhys asked. He'd been antsy all the way over. Warlow had half expected him to say, 'Are we there yet?' at any moment.

'We, that is DI Allanby and I, knock on his door and ask, politely, if he'll answer some questions while you hang about at the back in case he takes off in his bat-mobile.'

Silence bloomed. After several seconds, Rhys spoke. 'The bat-mobile is black, sir.'

Jess shook her head. 'I swear you and my daughter must have taken the same courses in irrelevant pedantry. FYI, DC Harries, the bat-mobile is a made-up vehicle which exists in comics.'

Rhys allowed a few seconds to pass before adding, 'And films, ma'am.'

'See what I mean?' Jess appealed to Warlow.

'You insisted on him coming,' Warlow muttered, grabbing the door handle.

The address must once have been quite a grand house. It had views overlooking the railway line, but beyond that the harbour lighthouse and the sea. But the "For Rent" sign in a ground floor window spoke of a less glamorous existence now.

Key's flat had a single door access from a side road. Three steps to the pavement. Warlow stood back as Jess knocked. A dog barked somewhere inside. A small noise advertising a small dog. Nothing for Warlow to worry about.

Jess knocked again. The door opened on a chain lock and Key stood there, as pimply as his photos, hair mussed, wearing a rumpled T-shirt and boxers, blinking into the late morning light.

'Aaron Key? DI Allanby, Dyfed-Powys CID.'

'Yeah?' Key kept his mouth open once he'd finished speaking. Warlow suspected he slept and breathed that way, too.

'This is DCI Warlow,' Jess jabbed a thumb over one shoulder. 'Sorry to disturb you, but we wondered if we could talk to you. We're investigating an unlawful death.'

Key woke up a bit. At least his half-mast eyelids lifted a couple of millimetres. Using the words unlawful death seemed to do the trick most times.

'I dunno what you're talking about.' He spoke with the unswerving gaze of the hardened liar.

'Look, we're not here to arrest you. All we want to do is ask some questions to help us understand a few things in what is a very serious investigation. Can we come in?'

Key sent Warlow a suspicious glance. 'I don't have to let you in.'

'No, you do not,' Jess said. 'We thought it would be more private. Away from prying eyes.'

'There's always cops around here. No one gives a stuff.'

'Okay,' Jess said. 'It's to do with your car.'

At the mention of the Peugeot, Key seemed to fully wake up. In that his sour mouth pursed into a pout. 'What about it?'

'It was seen near to the crime scene a couple of days ago.'

'Where?'

'Brechfa Forest.'

'Never been there.' The answer came back on autopilot.

'Funny that, because we found your fingerprints on

some cans of cider deposited in a refuse bin in Keepers' car park, which is in Brechfa Forest.'

Key blinked and his eyes flicked from Jess to Warlow and back, weighing up his options and suffering a sudden resurgence of memory. 'Oh, yeah. I remember now. I been there once,' he muttered. 'A while ago though.'

Warlow watched the dance. He had to admire the little git. He was good as reticent scrotes went. Deny and then backtrack from the denial with something vaguely plausible or half remembered. One step forward, two back. Keep your distance. Listen for the beat. After all, they – plod – could have no idea when those cans might have been deposited.

'Some cyclists identified your car that day.' Not strictly true, but Jess persisted in an even measured tone to get him thinking.

'Nah. No fucking way.' Key scratched his leg and repositioned one of his testicles to the opposite side of his underpants in an almost seamless movement.

Warlow's phone dinged. He glanced at it. A message from Rhys followed by a photograph. A very interesting photograph at that. He stepped forward and took out a pocketbook, flicked open the cover, and addressed Key. 'So, let me get this straight. In case there's been a mistake. You were not in the forest two days ago and you do not remember seeing any cyclists.'

'No.'

In his other hand, Warlow had his phone up to show the snap of the Peugeot Rhys had just sent. A close-up of the interior taken through the side window. 'Nice car, by the way. Custom upholstery is it?'

'Italian leather,' Key said. The lips around his open mouth were cracked and dry. Inside, the teeth were the stuff of orthodontic nightmares.

Warlow nodded. 'And is that a drinks bottle I see in the cup holder?'

'Yeah.'

'Can you tell me what's written on it?'

'Never bothered looking.'

'Let me help you. It's Santa Camino. Expensive as drinks bottles go. Matches the bike of a man who was attacked in the forest.'

Warlow watched the boy blink again. Rapid ones this time as he realised his options had exponentially diminished. In Key's book, he probably thought he was being cunning. But Warlow had studied that same book from cover to cover and knew every page, paragraph, and sentence. Whereas Key had gone for the abridged illustrated version and only ever looked at the pictures, so long as they had no speech bubbles.

The way his open mouth moved when he thought put a tin hat on it.

'Yeah, well now I remember. I got that off a bloke in the pub.'

'What bloke?' Jess asked.

'What pub?' Warlow followed up.

Key screwed his face up in an attempt to appear thoughtful. 'Can't remember the pub. But… oh hang on, I got his number on my phone.'

Key left the door on the chain lock as he disappeared into a dark interior. Warlow glanced right and left to make sure there was no traffic and started backtracking. He took ten reverse steps into the middle of the road with a view over a low wall to where the Peugeot sat. He was just in time to see Key burst from a door that opened on to the hard standing area and the blip of the car alarm being disarmed. In time, too, to see Rhys Harries extend his leg and send Key sprawling so that his shoulder thumped the boot of the Peugeot with a sickening crunch, followed by a yowl of pain.

Warlow and Jess walked around to find Key still on his knees at the back of the car, massaging his upper arm.

'Oh dear,' said Jess. 'Did you fall?'

'I think I broke my fucking shoulder,' moaned Key. He looked up at the looming DC Harries. 'This is police brutality this is.'

'Worse than that. You've dented the boot.' Warlow ran a hand over the paintwork.

Key's head flicked up with a look of abject terror.

'My mistake,' said Warlow. 'It's just a scuff. Bit like what you've done to your shoulder, I expect.' He turned to Rhys who was grinning. 'Right, DC Harries. Kindly arrest this man for theft of a water bottle.'

CHAPTER THIRTEEN

WARLOW LET Jess and Gil run the interview while he watched from the cheap seats in the observation room. Key refused the offer of a solicitor, which spoke either of his blinding arrogance or of his conviction he'd done nothing wrong. Jess was yet to say anything. She simply sat and stared at Key with her grey eyes. She'd got that stare down to a fine art.

It was a wonder, thought Warlow, *that the little shit hadn't turned to stone already*.

Gil, meanwhile, was Mr Reasonable personified.

'Okay, Mr Key. Let's just make sure I've got this right,' Gil said. 'You found the drinks bottle on the side of the road.'

'Yeah. I did. What's the big fuckin' deal? It's a poxy drinks bottle.' The end of each sentence finished with a open-mouthed challenge, followed by a sniff and the odd sinus clearing snort. He remained in constant twitching motion: a leg, an arm, neck, hand. Warlow guessed he was missing his mid-morning fix already, whatever that might be.

'And this road was in the forest?' Gil asked.

'Yeah. I just said that, didn't I?'

'The same forest in Brechfa that you swore blind to DI Allanby you hadn't visited for weeks?'

'I was confused, like. You got me out of bed. I go lots of places in the car all the time. I can't remember everywhere I go, can I?' He flicked his chin up twice, then rubbed his eyes with his thumbs, his leg vibrating on the ball of his foot, up and down like a maniac drummer.

'Have you seen his car, Chief Inspector?' Gil, with all the time in the world, turned to Jess, eyebrows raised to emphasise the question.

'Lovely colour,' said Jess, her smile fixed, her eyes not leaving Key's face. 'What colour would you say it was, Mr Key?'

'It's red, innit.' Key blurted out the answer. 'You can hardly miss it.'

'Come on, you can do better than that. How about blood-red?' Gil proposed.

'Why would you call it that?' Key looked immediately annoyed.

'Why indeed?' Jess let the sentence hang. 'Or did they come up with something cringeworthy like a *vin rouge*?'

Gil turned a grinning face to her. 'Oh, very good, ma'am. Very good.'

Key frowned, his grasp of French about as deep as his grasp of how much trouble he was in. 'Look,' he put both hands down on the tabletop. 'I found the drinks bottle on the side of the road. That's not a crime. End fucking of.'

Gil nodded and made a big show of marking a large X in his notebook. 'I'm not a big fan of profanity, Aaron. You do realise that these days, people helping the police with their enquiries get a score. Bit like *TripAdvisor*. I'm having to mark you down badly for swearing, just so you know. Now, you say you found the drinks bottle on the side of the road.

A road, in the forest you lied about being in, is that correct?

'Yes, for fu…That is correct.'

'Trouble is, there is something else,' Gil said. 'A pretty big something else.'

'Like what, for fu-fanny's sake?' Key folded his arms and shook his head.

Gil sat forward. 'Like the fact that the man whose bottle you have in your possession was attacked and stabbed to death in that same forest. Not long after you and your blood-red car tried to run him and his friend off the road.'

For the first time since entering the room, Key's mouth shut as he swallowed drily, sending his Adam's apple bobbing. He rolled his tongue between his bottom teeth and his gum as he weighed up his choices, desperately trying to put together the two linking facts that Gil had presented to him. He was blinking fast now, looking from the big sergeant to the grey-eyed DI with the laser fu-fannying stare, both of whom returned his gaze with steely interest. Of all the limited emotions in his range, anger was the one Key settled for when the thinking stopped. 'Hang on. You said I was here because of the stupid bottle. No one said anything about a killing.'

'We're saying it now, sunshine,' Gil said. 'We know that bottle belonged to the victim. We know you were on the forest roads because you tried to run him down. Put those two together and you get thirty years with no parole.'

'What?' Key's incredulity emerged as a high-pitched laugh. But there was no sign of amusement in his face. Panic crept in to replace the twitchy belligerence. 'Whoa, whoa, whoa. Time fu… time out. Okay, I buzzed them. I buzzed them, alright? Bloody prats on their bikes. They buggered off into the woods and one of them dropped his bottle. I nabbed it, okay? I did. Finders fu… finders keepers, man. I didn't take it. He dropped the bastard thing.'

'I don't believe you,' Jess said. 'I reckon you followed them. Saw where they were camping, got a bike from somewhere and went for them.'

'Bike. What bike? I don't have a bike. What's a fu… a shitting bike got to do—' He stopped, and it was almost painful to see the cogs of his brain working, floundering towards a chink in the dark curtain that was rapidly descending on his world. 'You mean a motorbike?'

'You know we mean a motorbike.'

'Coz I saw one. Later. When I was on my way back.' Key sat forward eagerly. 'I'd been up the Keepers, met with a few mates, had a little drink. On my way back this big yellow bike crosses over from one side of the forest to the other right in front of me.'

'A yellow motorbike?'

'Yeah, one of those off-road things. Scrambler type. Sound like a fu-forking wasp on acid, they do.' Key's eyes were wide now. His demeanour one of a man keen if not desperate to help.

'Do you remember where?' Gil asked.

'No, man. I was going downhill and, like, ten seconds earlier and I'd have ploughed into the twat. But it was definitely in the forest.'

Gil sat forward. 'So you're telling me that if we send a forensic team over to your flat we won't find a knife or your clothes soaked in blood.'

'On my mother's fu… on my mother's life.'

'Charming,' Gil said with a shake of his head.

Key arched forward. 'I swear I didn't do nothing. Just found that bastard drinks bottle. I swear.'

'If we take you back to the forest, do you think you'll remember where you saw the bike?' Jess asked.

'I don't know, do I?'

Jess raised an eyebrow.

Key winced. 'Okay, okay. I could try. I'm willing to fucking try, man.' He was nodding fast, looking from one officer to the other. 'Any chance I could have a fag? I'm desperate for a fag.'

Gil sucked in air through his teeth. 'Health and safety. No smoking on the premises.'

Key looked as if he might cry. 'That's mental cruelty that is.'

'Okay, Aaron. You help us in the woods and we'll see what we can do about that cigarette.' Jess pushed her chair back and so did Gil. But Key stayed seated.

'Well come on, sunshine.' Gil urged.

The mouth opened, the blinking resumed; the bouncing leg took on a life of its own. 'The forest… it's big… you're not going to bury me until I confess, or something creepy like that, are you? I can't stand small spaces. I'm cloisterphobic as fu-fork.'

Behind the one-way window of the observation room, Warlow shook his head. Both Jess and Gil looked his way, knowing he could see them. They couldn't see him, but they didn't really need to in order to share the moment.

Gil shook his head. 'Nah, you'll be fine. You do need to work on that habit of saying what you're thinking out loud, though. And I'd stay away from monasteries if I were you.'

Key stood and walked around the desk. As they got to the door, Gil turned to Jess and in a stagey whisper, asked, 'Is the shovel in your car or mine?'

CHAPTER FOURTEEN

WARLOW SENT Key out with a couple of Uniforms in a car to map out where he'd supposedly seen the motorbike. And though everyone knew what a snivelling little arsehole he was, an arsehole whose default response was to lie and lie again, Warlow felt certain that on this occasion he was an arsehole telling the truth. In case the fear of being tied up in a murder case wasn't incentive enough, Warlow's promise that unless he cooperated and that his information was of use, they'd impound and dismantle his beloved Peugeot in the search for clues. That made him sit up and beg.

It had begun to drizzle. Jess recalled Warlow telling her, when she'd complained about the weather, how he believed there might be a supernatural plumber up there somewhere whose job it was, daily, to decide on just when to start the drizzle, such was its inevitability in this land of song and... drizzle. Jess had her hood up as she and Rhys walked down the forest road. The DC was in front of her, head down studying the banking. They'd parked up at Keepers and walked down along the route Key had taken in pursuit of Hopley and Geary, aiming for where he'd supposedly seen the motorcycle, looking for the strands of blue and white police tape the Uniforms had tied onto markers to indicate the likely sites.

The first appeared half a mile from their starting point and Rhys immediately dismissed it once he'd inspected the entry and exit points to the woods on either side of the road.

'No tyre tracks, ma'am,' he'd said, kneeling to peer at the ground. 'There's a vague path, maybe used by animals, but no tyres.'

Jess let him have his head. This was his baby. He'd been the one to suggest taking prints from the cans and he had the air of a First Nation's tracker about him as he gazed into the trees, looking for… she wasn't sure what he was looking for.

It wasn't cold, but the drizzle made for an unpleasant stroll as it caressed her cheeks, driven in by gusts of wind. They rounded a bend, making sure that they were on the right side of the road to face oncoming traffic, and Rhys pointed towards another fluttering bit of tape fifty yards further on.

They were on a B road and traffic was very light. On both sides the trees formed a dense wall of dark green. Added to the dullness of the day, this stretch oozed an oppressive aura and a sense of foreboding. Once again, the thought that someone might be in those trees watching them crept into Jess's head. It was not like her to feel any kind of anxiety, but these woods were so dense and so impenetrable that it was almost impossible not to feel a little claustrophobic.

At least it wasn't *cloisterphobic*.

'Pretty dark and dismal here,' Rhys said, sensing her unease. 'Doesn't get much sun.'

'You could say that again.'

They walked on until Rhys asked, 'Molly okay is she ma'am?'

Jess smiled. Knew when to lighten the moment did Rhys. 'She's fine. Busy looking after DCI Warlow's Labrador while he's out catching killers. Only we're out catching the killers and he's nice and warm in the office.'

'I heard he had a dog.'

'Cadi.' Jess smiled. 'She's a charmer.'

'DCI Warlow ought to bring her to work, ma'am. We could use a dog out here.'

Jess huffed out air. 'Cadi's more likely to lick someone to death than hunt them down. She's a sweetie.'

They hugged the bank as a car came around the corner. Rhys raised a hand in acknowledgement to the driver who glared back at him. 'Molly doing exams this year?' he asked over his shoulder.

'She's lower sixth, so yes, we have the pleasure of all that this summer.'

They set off again, one ear open for traffic. 'She got anything in mind?' Rhys called back over his shoulder.

'I think she's more science oriented. Though surfing and canoeing come a close second. One reason we moved here. I swear that girl is going to grow gills.'

'Gillyweed does the job, ma'am,' Rhys said.

'Ah, a Harry Potter fan. You continue to surprise me, Rhys.'

'Is Molly a Gryffindor?'

Jess grinned. 'Of course she is. She read the whole lot herself and then she watched the films. She said she was glad she did it that way around.'

'The only way, ma'am.'

They got to the marker and Rhys stood inspecting the path that led off at right angles for ten yards before curving left. 'This one is well used,' Rhys said. Once again, he got down on his haunches and studied the damp earth. A muddy trail led into the woods. 'It's wide enough for a bike.'

'What is that?' Jess pointed up to the branches of a nearby fir tree. Someone had hung some sticks from a branch, it dangled unmoving in the still air, held up and together by rough string. 'A dreamcatcher, is it?'

Rhys chuckled. 'No, not a dreamcatcher. More a beast catcher.'

Jess sent him a sceptical look.

'It's an old legend thing. Some people claim that there's a beast in this forest. Some say it's a missing link, others a kind of mad woodsman that likes to dress up in a Wookie suit who sneaks up on you when you're alone. Cobblers, of course. The type of thing kids say to scare each other. We used to come up here and hunt for the Beast.' Rhys sent his eyes skywards and tried to shake the memory from his head.

'So who put that there?'

Rhys shrugged. 'Who knows? You see them now and again. Kids I expect. You also get mad buggers wandering around here at night trying to find the Beast. It's a thing. People pretending they're on *Most Haunted*, only in the forest. There's even a Facebook group.'

'What's the significance of hanging it there?' She pointed to the figure.

'Means a sighting. So I suppose it's a warning. Or it means that some nerd has put it up there to make people stop and ask what it means. Like you just did, ma'am. *The Blair Witch Project* has a lot to answer for if you ask me.' Rhys arched his back.

'Is it relevant? To what we're doing here?'

'In what way, ma'am?'

Jess narrowed her eyes. 'I'm not suggesting we investigate an urban legend. But it would give us a reason for people being in this place at night.'

Rhys considered it. 'Beast stories come and go. I haven't heard much about it for a while. Then you'll get a splurge on the internet. Someone claiming to have seen something. Funnily enough, that's usually in the summer when being out here doesn't freeze your a... when it isn't too cold, ma'am.'

Jess walked forward until she stood under the dangling creation. 'Let's see how long it takes before the crazies come out of the walls once this story breaks,' she muttered. 'Right, take some pictures. We'll add it to the mix. And make sure you send me some. Molly loves a good Beast legend.'

Rhys used his phone to snap the totems. 'Not exactly the Dark Mark, but spooky enough.'

They crossed over and inspected the opposite side. Another trail, this one descending and disappeared into the trees. Rhys got down on his haunches once again.

'Anything?' Jess asked.

'Definitely cycle tracks here, ma'am.'

She joined him. 'Bicycle or motorbike?'

Rhys compressed his lips and shook his head. 'Not sure, ma'am. The fat tyres the cyclists use are pretty wide.'

Jess stood looking down into the trees. They seemed to go on forever. It was then that the noise came. The high-pitched buzz of an engine somewhere off to their left.

'A bike?' asked Jess.

'Should we go in?' Rhys turned towards the path.

'We've got nowhere else to go, have we?'

Careful to stay off the muddy centre of the path, Jess followed Rhys in, listening to the buzz of the engine waxing and waning. The way was narrow, and she couldn't imagine riding along it on a bike at speed. But then from what she remembered of the videos of mountain bikers she'd seen, they loved nothing more than getting mud-sprayed and branch-whipped. If so, this was a made in heaven trail.

A sudden knocking brought her up short. Half a dozen rapid staccato taps from somewhere to their right.

'What's that?' she asked.

'Woodpecker, ma'am. All over the place here they are.'

The noise came again. 'Shame we can't interview it,' said Jess. 'Great view from on top of a tree.'

They walked on another thirty yards until the whine of an engine came to them again. Louder this time.

'This side,' said Rhys. He picked up the pace, pushing on, his shoes getting muddier by the minute.

The engine buzz seemed to come from all directions. Jess was on the point of calling a halt since the trail had become steep and slick when it abruptly straightened and they emerged at a junction. As well as the trail, a gravel track wide enough for forestry vehicles ran up to a ridge to their left. The sudden increase in light made her blink. There'd been some recent activity here judging by the height of the logs stacked neatly to one side and the lopsided precarious warning sign, "Do Not Climb The Stack".

Rhys stood looking around and then down at a series of deeper tyre marks and gouges in the mud where bikes turned and the trail disappeared once more into denser forest.

The engine buzz dipped away to an idle.

'Wonder where this road leads?' Jess muttered.

Rhys walked along the wider track to a point where it curved. The ground on his right fell away at a steep slope. He turned back to face his senior officer.

'Not much point going any further. But this is more pr—'

The sudden roar of an engine took them both by surprise. The bike appeared over the lip of the track, engine whining as the rider hit the throttle and sped forwards. Rhys had time only to turn before it was on him. He shifted sideways as the rider threw out an arm. Caught off balance, Rhys pivoted on one leg before stumbling wildly towards the edge of the track.

Jess had time to step back towards the protection of the logs as the bike shot past her. It roared towards the trail they'd come along and disappeared in a fog of blue smoke.

She stared after it, trying to fix the image. It was filthy and spattered in mud. The overall impression she got was of an orangey brown blob. But there was no registration plate. And the rider was a helmeted squat figure in a dark coat, equally mud-spattered. Nowhere near enough information for tracing. She whipped her head back towards where Rhys had gone over the edge, running forward, calling his name.

'Rhys! Rhys!'

They'd culled the trees on that side. Culled them and stacked them for collection. It was surprising how steep the bare incline was.

'Rhys!' Jess yelled again.

A hand emerged above the edge of the track. Waving, reassuring. Out of breath, Jess reached the edge and looked down. DC Harries sat with legs splayed out, his suit filthy, his face mud-smeared, looking sheepish but intact.

'You're alright?'

'No,' Rhys said in petulant misery. 'I'm not. Look at my suit. My mother is going to kill me.'

CHAPTER FIFTEEN

DESPITE NOT TRULY BELIEVING THAT Aaron Key had anything much to do with Andrew Geary's murder, Warlow thought it a good idea to be thorough. They got a warrant and sent a team over to Burry Port to go through Key's flat.

He let Catrin supervise and when they were halfway through Warlow called her.

'Anything?'

'He's converted a bedroom into a workshop, sir. When I say workshop, I mean a place with lots of bits of car innards on oily newspaper over ninety per cent of every flat surface. You'd think he could have used a shed.' The lack of unbridled enthusiasm in her voice made Warlow grin.

'Mucky pup then?'

'Petrol head, I think is the term a friend of mine uses.'

'Would that be the friend who works in Traffic?'

A tiny pause followed. But DS Catrin Richards was not one to be wrong-footed by her boss. 'It would. He enjoys fiddling with cars, too, but he's clean about it. Unlike Key who didn't read the memo. Too busy studying for charm school.'

This time Warlow couldn't help but let go a little chuckle.

'But the good news is it's unlikely he would have laundered any clothing worn the night of the stabbing, sir, because he has not laundered clothing since Noah's Ark set sail, as my grandmother would say.' Catrin sighed. 'With that in mind, we've had a good look and there's no sign of any blood staining on any of his clothes, shoes, or his collection of baseball hats. I especially like the one that says, "I'm sexist and I know it" but with the *k* missing off the 'know'. You couldn't make it up, sir.'

'Jesus.' Warlow ran a hand across the back of his neck.

'We did find a very interesting collection of car parts and rims.' Catrin's voice brightened. 'Some of them still in their nice unopened packaging. All of them expensive.'

'Why does that not surprise me,' Warlow replied.

'Unfortunately, nothing that helps with the Geary case though, sir. '

Warlow let go a disappointed sigh. 'Okay. Let someone else finish up there and you come back. I'd like you to finish going over Geary's laptop. I've got Gil chasing up background checks on Hopley and Dee. No point you hanging on there now.'

He killed the call. While he was mulling over the lack of evidence from the search, Gil put his head around the door and held out a steaming cup of tea.

'You okay, sir?'

'Fine. Got an itch, that's all. One I can't scratch because I don't yet know where it is.'

'Not lice, I hope?'

Warlow sent him a look.

'I remember one poor bugger in primary school. She was always having to go to the nit nurse. She was a leper at break times. Didn't help that she had a constant cold and a snot bubble in the left nostril.' His defocused eyes drifted up to the corner of the room. 'Always the left nostril. I never understood that. She'd come towards you and we'd all run away screaming. Like *Dawn of the Dead* for eight-year-olds.' Gil took a sip of tea, musing. 'Nesta Williams. Nitty Nesta was her nickname.'

'Of course it was.' Warlow shook his head. 'And I don't have lice. This is more a conviction we're missing something obvious.'

'It'll come out in the wash. Usually does.' Gil perched on the edge of the desk. 'The Buccaneer told me you're a Lazarus. Back from the dead.'

Warlow arched his back. The chair creaked beneath him. 'Yes. I pulled the plug once. I could be standing on the rocks at Little Haven fishing for mackerel now and look where I am.'

'Fishing for sharks instead.' Gil sipped his tea. 'I could have gone, too. Talked with the missus about it. She said if I was at home all day she'd go bloody mad.' He sighed. 'But if I'd have stayed with Operation Alice I probably would have.'

'How was that?'

Gil kept his eyes on the mug. It had "*I see guilty people*" written on the side in a spooky font. 'As bad as you think it could be with two spoonfuls of worse.'

Warlow thought about some of the cases he'd read about. Supposed foster carers who were nothing but preda-tors. Neglect and abuse of children, some of them babies as young as a month old. Parent addicts who ignored their kids, others with no parenting skills other than their ability to sign a form asking for council accommodation.

'They should give you a medal.'

Gil shook his head. 'Cup of tea will do fine.' He swirled the cup, brows bunched as he recalled something he probably wished he had not. It looked to Warlow as if Gil's thoughts were swirling with the liquid and he was suddenly sorry he'd asked about Op Alice.

The conversation had bumped the sergeant off the good-natured furrow he ploughed. But Warlow could forgive him that because he admired the man's fortitude. He was never sure how many of his contemporaries ended up needing some kind of emotional or mental support. PTSD was much bandied about these days, but Warlow knew they were the crosses they had to bear for haunted men like him and Gil. It didn't surprise him one bit to know that it might get too much for some. But Gil was still here, as was he. That meant they were either fools or worse, still believed in what they were doing.

When Gil looked up, he saw the DCI's expression and smiled. In an instant, the amiable Gil was back. 'What about you then, sir? What brought you back to the fold?'

'Good question. There's more than one answer, but the one I come back to is the fact that this job is like one of those hooks with a barb on the end. Once it's in you, it's a bugger to get loose.'

The nod that Gil gave in response was one Warlow liked to call knowing. He realised he'd blanked Gil's questions. But the sergeant didn't press for more. If he did wonder at a deeper reason, a darker reason, he had the sense not to pry.

'What do you think of Key? Likely candidate?' Warlow asked.

'Christ no. He's nothing but a gobby opportunist. Once he's in that car he thinks he's that bloke from *Grand Thief Auto.*'

Warlow knew it wasn't what the game was called, but he let it go. He'd got the gist.

'Take him out of his hot hatch and he's a scrawny little *cachgu*,' Gil added.

It was a Welsh word. No exact translation, but little shit would do as close enough. Gil was a man after his own heart. Warlow sat straighter in the chair. 'I'm with you there. Think he really did see someone on a bike though?'

Gil narrowed his eyes. 'We'll find out. I told him that if he was messing us about, we were going to banjax his Dinky toy for having tinted windows that exceeded the 75 per cent transparency requirement and fancy registration plates that looked more like Japanese than English. I think he lost a little trickle of pee when I told him that.'

Warlow snorted. Gil pushed off the desk and made for the door, but remembered the reason he'd come through it in the first place. 'Almost forgot. Ralph Geary rang. Says that Andrew's fiancée has come up with a couple of possibles for the passcode on Geary's phone. She's not a hundred per cent, but it's something.'

'Good. We'll get Rhys on to that straight away.'

Gil made a face and sucked in air. 'Have to wait a bit. He's out with Jess.'

'The forest?'

Gil nodded. 'Rhys wanted to check out Key's likely spots for where he saw the bike. He would have gone on his own but Jess said something about two cool heads being better than one hot one.'

'Keen, those two.' Warlow said.

'As mustard,' said Gil, grinning. 'Like good coppers should be.'

CHAPTER SIXTEEN

Rob sat on the edge of the bed, looking out at the forest through the window of the room the Gearys had given him. They had lots to choose from having converted two outbuildings into guest accommodation. It would have been a lovely set up for an Airbnb. But the Gearys weren't interested in that. These rooms were for entertaining friends. Either of their own or Andy's.

Andy. A little avalanche of ice cascaded in Rob's gut.

He badly needed a shower. But with his arms and head bandaged it was going to be impossible. Unless he taped everything up and covered them in plastic bags then it might be doable. He had to at least try because he still had forest mud all over his legs and blood over his arms and chest.

His own as well as Andy's.

His eyes fell on a framed photo on the wall. The Gearys had hung up several, but this one drew Rob's attention. Not a candid snap but a professional portrait. And not just any portrait. This was the family Geary all dressed the same in white T-shirts and black jeans. Taken maybe ten years before while Andy was in uni with the boy giving his mum a piggy back, Ralph watching with an amused, indulgent expression. All set against a plain white background. All of them laughing. All of them so alive.

Rob let out a low moan and let his head fall into his right hand.

Andy. God.

Silence filled the room. It was a feature of this house and this place. No passing cars. No street noises. No trains. He could hear nothing but the sound of his blood pumping in his ears as he breathed in and out, slowly.

A soft knock on the door made him look up. He stood, pretended to be unpacking and said, 'Come in.'

Fran stood on the threshold. She'd put on some ballerina pumps and stuffed a comb in her hair to hold it up. But her anguish hadn't changed. Nor had her predilection for sweaters with extra-long sleeves.

'Rob,' she said in a shaky voice before stepping in and grabbing him in a hug. He couldn't return it, not properly. Not with one arm still in a sling.

'Fran, I'm so—' he began and even her name seemed weighed down in apology.

'Don't. Don't say anything. Nothing will change it,' she blurted.

'But I'm so sorry.'

'God, Rob. He's dead.'

He managed to half-hold her with his good right arm and let her cry big shuddering sobs. For almost three minutes that's all he did. She felt thin through her sweater. Never big, she now reminded him of a frail bird. Eventually, her sobbing subsided and she pulled back. 'Thank you. I needed that. I came to tell you I'm making coffee.' She held out her hand to reveal four coffee pods.

'I don't think I can face—'

'Not in the house. Here, just you and me. I promise not to ask you anything because the police will have asked you already and you'll tell me when you're able to. Let's just sit and talk. About normal stuff. For the last two days all anyone has talked about is Andy. I want to be normal for ten minutes. Just ten minutes because if I don't I think I might wither away and die.'

'Sure,' Rob said. 'But I need to freshen up. I'm a bit ripe. I was going to tape up the bandages.'

'I'll help you once we've had an Americano. How about that?'

Rob sighed. 'Okay. Thanks.'

They sat in a little kitchenette – she was pale as snow, Rob, bloodied and dirty. Fran made coffee using the Nespresso machine. The Gearys had stocked the fridge with milk and there was even a frother for cappuccinos.

Fran took a sip and reached a hand to hold on to Rob's good arm. 'Andy told me about Hannah.'

Rob dropped his eyes to the teaspoon. He stirred the coffee though he'd put no sugar in it. He didn't want to talk about Hannah, but Fran pressed.

'When did you two—?'

'About three months ago.'

'Oh, Rob.' It seemed almost impossible for Fran to look or sound any more unhappy than she already did, but somehow she managed it. 'I didn't know. What happened?'

'The Canada thing didn't come off.'

'But you were both going?'

'That was the plan. She's out there now. I… it didn't work out.'

'Oh, God. Andy didn't say anything about why.' Fran's voice was tight.

'Probably didn't want to upset you.'

'Where was it she got the job?'

'Vancouver.'

Fran shook her head. 'We were there in the summer. It's beautiful.'

'So Andy said.'

Fran kept staring at Rob as if she didn't believe him. 'But you had that engineering job all set up, didn't you?'

Rob stayed silent.

Fran sat back, unable to stop herself from voicing her shock. 'I was wondering why she wasn't here now. She'd have been the first to—'

Rob cut her off. 'Look, Fran, I don't want to talk about it. Not now. Not ever.'

'I was only—'

'I know you were.' Rob cut her off, his words quick and harsh. He exhaled loudly, shook his head in apology. 'It's too raw for me, Fran. Please.'

Fran looked stricken. The 'let's try to be normal for five minutes' act had evaporated and the confused, hurting fiancée was back, all tear glands firing.

'I'm sorry,' she whispered. 'I'm sorry. I didn't mean to—'

Rob squeezed his eyes shut but forced them open to contemplate this frail, hurting woman. 'It's fine. You weren't to know.'

Misery engulfed Fran again. She screwed up her face forcing a tear down her cheek which she stroked away with the pads of three fingers. The skin beneath looked red and raw. 'I'm trying to understand, but I can't. I can't. Why would anyone want to do this, Rob?' Her voice came out as a pleading whisper again.

He wanted nothing more than to turn away and not do this now. He needed a shower and to be alone for a bit. But he couldn't. He'd avoided answering the police's questions, but he couldn't do it here. Not in front of Fran.

'I know why,' he said in a low whisper.

Fran frowned, blinking away the tears. 'What?'

Rob looked up at her, his anguish a mirror image of Fran's. 'I wish you didn't have to find out, I really do. But it's too late now.' He sucked in another ragged breath. 'I know why and I know who.'

'What… what are you talking about?' Fran asked. She got up from the chair, staring at him. 'How… how do you know?'

Rob heaved in a deep breath and let his lungs empty once more before speaking. 'Did Andy ever tell you what happened to us when we were fourteen?'

———

SUPERINTENDENT SION BUCHANNAN always looked like he'd wandered into a primary school classroom whenever he was in the SIO office. The tiny space at the back of the Incident Room hardly gave Warlow room to swing a feline and he was not a tall man. The Buccaneer, on the other hand, was a giant. A little stooped now and creaky after his rugby playing days, watching him lower his frame into a tiny plastic chair made Warlow wince.

'Back or knees?' asked Warlow.

'Both. And hips and neck.'

'Isn't there a song about that?'

The Buccaneer made his eyes into slits. 'Yeah, go ahead and laugh. You wait, it's going to catch-up with you one day.'

Warlow shook his head. 'I spent all my playing days avoiding getting caught. You lot in the scrum were only there because you loved jumping on top of someone else or kicking each other until you bled. Never saw the attraction of rucks and mauls myself.'

'Ah well, different game these days. Neither of us would last ten minutes unless we put on another three stone of bulk. Speaking of health issues…' The Buccaneer let the question hang.

It hovered there for a while, looking for somewhere to land until, reluctantly, Warlow fielded it.

'I'm fine. Next check-up is in two months.' He thought, but didn't add, *so long as I keep taking the tablets.* In fact, there was only one tablet but two drugs in combination. To make life easy. Though it had not been to start with. The vivid dreams that came with them hadn't helped. But things were better now.

'You know you can pick the phone up any time, Evan.'

'I do.'

The Buccaneer waited two seconds, but with nothing else forthcoming from Warlow, gave up and nodded. He'd been at some Heads of Department meeting upstairs and was checking in. Warlow was relieved when he swapped personal concern for the case at hand. 'Any progress with Geary?'

Warlow puffed out his cheeks. 'Bits and pieces. Someone tried to run over DC Harries in the woods, and we've recovered Andrew Geary's drinks bottle from a petty thief in Burry Port who was pretending to be James Hunt the night Geary was killed.'

Buchannan sneered. 'James Hunt? Christ, that's a blast from the past. Not a reference many people on your team is going to understand. When was he Formula One Champion, the seventies?'

'I was using the name more in the context of rhyming slang.'

It took the Buccaneer just two seconds to grin. 'Ah, not on the list of future community leaders then, our petty thief.'

'Aaron Key is a lying little turd,' Warlow said with a nod.

'You don't like him for the killing?'

Warlow wrinkled his nose. 'I don't like him full stop. But no, not for the killing. I'm about to let him go. I thought he was lying about seeing a motorbike in the woods that night, but I'm reconsidering my opinion there since someone on a dirt bike put young Rhys on his arse.'

'He's okay though, right?'

Warlow let out a quiet little laugh through his nose. 'Bruises only. Both arse and ego. He'll survive.'

The Buccaneer nodded. 'I'm going to speak to the press soon. And Geary, the father, is a friend of the Assistant Chief Constable. Why they've asked me to do the preliminary press statement. It'll be all yours after this.'

'Pressure?'

'No.'

Warlow waited, unconvinced, until the Buccaneer capitulated.

'Well, nothing more than the usual. I've told her we have our best team on it.'

The DCI grinned. 'But then you said she'll have to make do with us until they arrive, correct?'

'Took the words right out of my mouth.' Buchannan stood up, knees creaking.

Warlow stood too, if only to avoid a crick in his neck now that Buchannan was upright. Even then the height discrepancy was almost laughable. Warlow offered up one last piece of advice. 'Once there's something tangible we can chomp on I'll let you know. Go with, "A local man is helping police with their enquiries," for the press.'

'Can I say his name is James Hunt?'

Warlow shook his head. 'No, but you can say that he is one.'

CHAPTER SEVENTEEN

EVERYONE WAS BACK in the Incident Room when Warlow walked out of the office a short time later and he could sense the lull. They needed something to gee them up.

Rhys was dressed in jogging bottoms and a sweatshirt having showered off the forest mud and sent his suit to the cleaners via an emergency call to his dad.

'You'd make a fine leisurewear model, Rhys. Has anyone ever told you that?' Warlow said.

Rhys looked up. 'No, sir. Thank you, sir.'

'What you wearing tomorrow, wetsuit and snorkel?' Catrin remarked.

'You can go off people, you know.' Rhys pretended to be affronted. A pretence that failed miserably because he blushed a bright red.

Warlow walked up to the Gallery and stared at the photos, lingered a little on Key's, before removing it and repositioning it right at the bottom.

'Should we let him go?' Gil asked.

Warlow turned to Catrin. 'Nothing else at his place, was there?'

She shook her head. 'I am glad to report that there

were no signs of female company either, sir. If there had been, I think I might have had to claim a sick day because I would be throwing up.'

'Then yes, let him go,' Warlow told her. 'We won't charge him over the bottle. But I hope we've handed those car parts over, have we?'

'We have, sir,' Catrin replied.

'Good. Can't stand the idea of the little sod getting off unscathed.' Warlow turned to face the room 'Right,' he said. 'Rhys, kettle on. Let's see where we've got to. Catrin, where are we with Geary and his laptop?'

'I've made a bit of a profile, sir.' Catrin glanced around at the other team members. 'I've emailed you all but there's a paper copy here.' She stood up and walked to the Gallery and pinned the report underneath Andrew Geary's photo. Not the crime scene horror shows or the post-mortem death shots, but the one of him looking alive and well from his LinkedIn profile. 'I'm still not into the encrypted files but I've spoken to tech support and I'll hand the laptop over to them once I've finished with it. But I've accessed most of it, I think.'

'Anything of use?' Jess asked.

'A lot of his emails are work related,' Catrin explained. 'Or at least directed at people where he works. From what I can tell he has another work laptop but that's in London. I spoke to his fiancée and she said that he only ever used it for work. In fact it's a rule of employment that it's used for nothing else.'

'Anything contentious apart from these encrypted files?' Warlow asked.

'No. As I say, he was planning a trip to Thailand with some people we haven't traced yet.'

'Not with his fiancée?' Jess asked.

Catrin shook her head. 'All male by the looks of it. And previous emails suggest they go twice a year.'

'Didn't Ralph Geary run a business out there?' Warlow turned to glance at the image of Geary Senior.

Catrin grabbed another piece of paper off her desk and scanned it quickly. 'Ralph Geary's company is based in Bangkok, yes.'

This was interesting background but not terribly useful. Warlow kept probing. 'What about his London connections?'

Catrin nodded. 'I've spoken to his manager and to some people he worked with. They're all devastated. At least that's the impression I got. He was a party animal according to his male colleagues. A more reserved response from the women. My feeling is Andrew played the field a little before he got engaged.'

'What about afterwards?' Gil asked.

Catrin shrugged.

'So he's a bloke,' Jess said. Warlow glanced at her, but there was no rancour. She was simply stating the obvious. Any personal baggage that Jess harboured after the recent separation from her husband got left unceremoniously at the door when she was in this room.

Besides, Andrew Geary *was* a bloke. A thirty-something, in a well-paid job in London, bloke. He knew the type well. The last time Warlow had been to visit his son Tom in London, he'd been the oldest man in most of the pubs they'd visited by a long chalk. The Smoke was for the young.

Rhys walked back into the room and Warlow fired off a question. 'What about his phone?'

Rhys nodded. 'The PIN was his date of birth. I'm in. Most of the photos and emails are just as Catrin found on the laptop. He's got loads of apps. I can't access his banking app or anything that needs a separate password. But I'm working my way through.'

'Fine. And you can give Catrin a hand with the laptop when you're done. Two minds and all that.'

Gil grinned and glanced at Jess. 'We can only hope you don't get run over between here and the kettle this time.'

Rhys took the bait. 'I didn't see him coming, sarge. I think he might have had a stealth mode on that bike.'

Catrin shook her head and mouthed, 'Stealth mode,' as her eyes went to the ceiling.

Warlow smiled. 'Right. What about Hopley?'

Catrin got back to business. 'Same age as Andrew Geary. Went to the same school and they became friends there. Hopley spent summers at Journey's End between the ages of thirteen and seventeen. That's where they got to know the woods and the trails. Hopley went to Durham University to do engineering. Broke up with a long-term girlfriend three months ago. She was Canadian and moved back there. He was meant to have emigrated, but he didn't. He was going to be Andrew Geary's best man and he organised the stag do they were about to go on.'

Warlow nodded, but from her expressions she hadn't finished. 'Yes?' he prompted her.

'There is one odd thing. Neither Hopley nor Andrew Geary have any convictions but Hopley's record did flag up a caution from 2004. Issued by us locally.'

'Aren't cautions supposed to be spent after a couple of years?' Rhys asked.

Catrin turned to him and recited. 'Cautions are spent immediately. A cautioned individual can answer no in an interview when asked about cautions or convictions and they're filtered off the Disclosure and Barring Certificate after six years. Well at least some of them are.'

'Someone's been busy,' Rhys said, in a 'you-swot' tone.

Catrin sent him a defiant glare.

'But they stay on our records, don't they?' Gil asked.

'What was the caution for?' Warlow asked before Gil's question was answered.

Catrin glanced down at her notes. 'Abduction of a girl under sixteen.'

No one spoke for a good ten seconds as they exchanged glances around the room.

'That doesn't sound good,' Rhys said.

'I'm digging into it,' Catrin explained.

'What about Geary's record?' Jess asked.

'I'm digging into that, too.'

Warlow folded his arms and turned towards the Gallery again, prowling back and forth in front of it. 'So what we have is a lorry load of bugger all.'

'We've got a biker in the forest who tried to run me down,' Rhys chipped in, framing the statement as more a question than a statement.

Warlow pivoted. 'And what exactly do we make of that?'

Jess shrugged. 'Maybe we disturbed a kid who was in there with no permission.'

'Or no licence,' Rhys added.

'Or it was the Beast of Brechfa on wheels,' Jess muttered.

'The what?'

'Old wives' tale thing, sir,' Rhys explained. 'A what do you call it, ma'am?'

'A totem.'

'A totem,' Rhys continued. 'In the forest near where the bike came from. It's BS, sir. Just kids pretending they're in the Brechfa Witch Project remake.'

'That's the film where they all end up standing staring at a wall, isn't it?' Gil asked.

'That's the one,' Catrin said.

'Bit like half time in the bog at an International in the

Principality Stadium, but with less splashing and the ammoniacal reek,' Gil observed.

Warlow shook his head. 'Lovely analogy, Gil.' He turned back to the DC. 'You don't think that the motorbike links in anyway?'

Rhys shook his head.

Warlow glanced at Jess for her take.

She mulled over her response before answering. 'Do I think that a rogue motorcyclist is hiding out in the forest and just so happened to run over Rhys as we turned up? No. I think we spooked a kid who should not have been there. The link is that dirt bikers use the forest.'

Warlow turned back to the Job Centre. 'Back to the crime scene. Where are we with the DVLA and motorbikes of the dirt bike type?'

'I've got a list,' Catrin said. 'It's long.'

'Talk to Traffic. Ask if we can whittle it down by make, or engine size. I don't know. But they will.'

Rhys checked his watch and got up. 'I'll fetch the tea.' He stopped halfway to the door and turned back, a half apologetic look on his eager face. 'I thought about being a police motorcyclist once. Fancied being on one of those unmarked bikes because they can really shift.' His expression took on a faraway look.

Jess looked at him almost pityingly. 'You've obviously not seen someone come off a bike doing a hundred and twenty, have you?'

'No, ma'am. Avoided that.'

'Not something you want to see more than once in your career,' she told him. 'How Traffic deal with it, I do not know. The two I attended needed a wheelbarrow to pick up the bits.'

Rhys's grin faded into a grimace.

'Don't worry, Rhys,' Gil said. 'You'd never pass the interview for Traffic in those togs. You have to look good in leather. Now, as you rightly observed, tea has brewed so chop-chop. I've brought in a selection of *biscuits*,' Gil used the French pronunciation. 'Which are in this receptacle on my desk. If you see anyone pilfering or trying to remove this tin, you have my permission to arrest them.' He picked up a large box with "HUMAN TISSUE FOR TRANS-PLANT" written on the side. 'Psychological deterrent,' he said in answer to the question everyone wanted to ask but didn't. He handed the tin to Rhys. 'Selection on a plate, please. We will award prizes for artistry and I always count the contents so if you nick a cheeky bourbon, I'll know.'

'Yes, sarge,' Rhys said.

Warlow turned to the Gallery one last time. 'What would help is the murder weapon,' he muttered. 'Nothing from the crime scene, I take it?'

Gil shook his head.

'Jess?' Warlow turned to the DI for her opinion on the state of play.

'We work with what we can for now. Chase up the bike angle. Man the phones once we receive a curated list of owners.'

As if by magic a phone rang. Gil answered it and started writing something down on a pad.

'Catrin,' Warlow said, 'Get Rhys to talk to Traffic about the bikes, you dig in to this Hopley caution thing. See what comes up.'

'On it,' she turned back to her screen and keyboard. Warlow saw Jess smile. Catrin was one of the good ones. Professional and keen.

'Hang fire for now with that, Catrin,' Gil said holding up a piece of paper. 'Believe it or not, Hopley and Fran Dee are downstairs in reception wanting to speak to you, DCI Warlow.'

CHAPTER EIGHTEEN

Rob Hopley had wanted to drive with his injured shoulder, but Fran Dee insisted on bringing him in. They sat in a meeting room at Dyfed-Powys HQ. Warlow deemed the interview room where they'd quizzed Key unacceptable. They'd chosen an empty conference room instead as this was a more relaxed affair, though from the haggard expression on Rob's face you'd never think so.

Warlow and Jess sat across from Rob on one side of a table that accommodated ten. Fran Dee sat on Rob's side a little further back. In the room at his request.

'I think it's only fair Fran hears all this,' Hopley explained when Jess queried it.

'How are you feeling?' Warlow asked.

'My shoulder aches a bit, but the pain killers work okay. They gave me some of the good stuff.'

Washed of the blood and grime that had stained his skin and clothes in hospital, Rob Hopley looked more presentable. He'd abandoned the sling but rested his left forearm on the table for support. When he moved it, an involuntary wince creased his features.

'What can we help you with, Mr Hopley?' Jess asked.

'You said if I thought of anything, I should let you know.'

'We did,' Jess said.

Warlow inched forward in his seat. Rob kept worrying at a loose fold of bandage on his left arm.

'Okay,' Warlow said. 'You have our attention.'

Rob sighed. 'I doubt this will be a surprise to you, but in case it is, Andy and me, we were cautioned by Dyfed-Powys police over something that happened when we were fourteen.'

'The both of you?' Jess asked.

Rob nodded. 'After your visit to the hospital I began to think. I've tried to put what happened then behind me. It was a stain on our copybooks. Fact is I've tried hard to forget all about it. But then when you asked it made me wonder. Because I didn't recognise it to start with. The glade I mean. Probably because trees have grown or been chopped down. It wasn't until I thought it about it later in the hospital that I realised it must have been the same glade.'

'You're talking about 2004, yes?' Warlow said, making sure Hopley knew they were aware of his record.

Rob shot him a glance, nodding. He looked like he might throw up at any moment. '2004. Two stupid kids who knew it all. Kids who should have known better.'

'What happened, Mr Hopley?' Jess said.

Rob dropped his eyes. 'It was a stupid, horrible thing to do.'

'Start from the beginning,' Warlow said.

Rob took a deep breath. It shuddered as he exhaled.

'That summer I'd gone down to Journey's End for the last couple of weeks of the holidays. The second year in succession. Summer term always broke up early as they do in public schools. A good few weeks before the state schools. So, early summer, we'd go on holiday with our parents separately, or at least Andy did. I hung around Slough. But the last two weeks of August I'd come down here and we'd ride our bikes or go fishing. Everything's close by. The coast isn't that far away. But we didn't do much beach stuff because it meant we'd have to go with Ralph and Celia. We preferred being on our own. So we'd take a packed lunch and go off exploring. It's an amazing place, the forest.'

Warlow waited. Rob was easing himself in. Preparing, it looked like, for a bumpy ride.

'We'd been out all afternoon,' Rob went on. 'Riding around. We'd seen no one but a handful of other riders and a few walkers. We had these half masks we wore under our helmets and goggles to protect our mouths from dust and mud. Mine was a replica of a skull, but Andy had a good one. A zombie mask, with half the nose missing, big bits of flesh hanging off with burnt skin and google eyes his dad brought back from one of his trips abroad. Scary under a bike helmet and goggles. We thought it was funny and the masks always drew stares, especially when you came across someone unawares.'

Jess couldn't hide her distaste. Rob read it and shrugged. 'What can I say? We were idiots. We'd been up and down the trails a dozen times by mid-afternoon that day when we rode into the glade and there they were. Babes in the woods. Two kids. Much younger than us. A boy of ten and a girl of six. The Daniels kids. Later we found out that they lived on the edge of the forest somewhere. They'd lost their mum and their father wasn't doing so good. A farmworker who couldn't be at home in the day and spent most evenings drinking cheap cider. The kids, Tristan, and Iona, were left to their own devices. Of course we knew none of this when we found them. This stuff all came out later.' Rob paused and looked up, his eyes flicking between Warlow and Jess.

'I honestly don't know why we did what we did, but I expect we thought it would be funny in that way kids do without any awareness of consequences. The Daniels were lost. We had no idea where they lived. The girl, she was pretty upset, the boy, Tristan, he was petrified. Mainly because of what his dad might to do when he found out he'd got his sister into this mess. But a little bit because of us. The masks didn't help.' Another regretful sigh. 'They were grotesque to say the least. We rode down to them. Iona was hiding behind her brother. I took my mask off. So did Andy. But I could see that Tristan was unhappy. In a different way to his sister. I mean she was scared of the monster masks; he was scared because we were bigger boys in a kind of Lord of the Flies way I suppose.'

Rob paused, squeezed his eyes shut, and then opened them again, as if he was trying to un-see the memory replaying in his head. 'I'd like to believe it wasn't my idea. But we decided it might be funny to mess about. We played hide and seek with them. It was stupid and cruel, but I can only think we got caught up in the idea. We made Tristan hide his eyes and count and we took Iona to hide.'

Once more Rob took a breath in and swallowed. The movement looked somehow painful. As if something sharp or big wouldn't go down. Warlow risked a glance at Jess. Her expression remained unreadable, but he could guess what might be going on behind it. She was a police officer and a mother after all.

'Andy found a place. A fallen tree with lots of broken branches. He told Iona to hide in there and not to say anything.' Rob dropped his head. 'I know I should have stopped him. I know what I should have done. I saw him put that mask back on before he went under those branches and that was bad. He shouldn't have done that.' Rob shook his head. 'Then we rode off. Just left them there. This ten-year-old scared kid being told what to do by older kids he trusted now looking for his sister in the forest. Andy wanted to get up higher so that we could watch what happened. We rode for maybe five minutes, but when we got to the ridge there was no sign of Tristan. We waited. Not long. Ten minutes at the most. But he must have wandered off in the wrong direction. We went back to Iona but by then we couldn't remember exactly where she was. We looked for ages, but we didn't find her. We yelled her name, yelled both their names. But they didn't answer.'

The loose fold of bandage on Rob's left arm had expanded thanks to Rob's worrying at it. He smoothed it down, only to pick it up again a few seconds later. 'I wanted to go to the police, but Andy said we'd get into trouble. So we waited. We did nothing and waited for two hours. Eventually a man came. We found out it was the kids' father. This desperate, frantic red-faced man, calling and calling. We said we'd seen them earlier that day and showed him where.' Rob dropped his head again and for a long beat he said nothing. When he spoke his voice croaked. 'The worst thing of all was that he was grateful. He thanked us. I wanted to tell the truth, I really did, but Andy said to wait. Daniels called the police. It triggered a huge search, and they found the boy a mile away, calling his sister's name. It took them four more hours to find Iona. She'd crawled out of the fallen tree and wandered off. She was by a stream. Just sitting there, lost.'

Fran Dee had a hand up over her mouth. She looked pale and sick, like she might throw up.

'We were kids, but that's no excuse. When Tristan Daniels told them what had happened, Andy wanted us to keep on lying. His word against ours he said. But in the end Iona clinched it. She was only six. But when she saw us, all she did was scream.'

Rob shifted his good hand up away from the bandage

to knead the flesh of his forehead, as if rubbing might erase all the terrible memories he'd relived in the telling.

'I didn't take Iona in to the space under the fallen tree but I heard Andy whispering to her. He told her to stay quiet, that's what he said to me. But I think he might have said something else. Told her something to frighten her. Whatever he said made her terrified of us both. In the end, the police believed Tristan. My parents were out of their depth. They came down, but it was Ralph who took charge of everything. It would have been much worse for us if he hadn't helped. He convinced the police not to charge us. We accepted a caution instead. Went over my head at the time, but I know it's on my record. You'll find it if you look.'

'We already have,' Warlow said.

'Is that why you're telling us. Because you knew we'd find it?' Jess asked. She kept her voice even, but Warlow sensed the effort it took for her not to show any emotion.

Rob shook his head. 'Lying in hospital I realised it was the same place. The same glade we'd found the Daniels kids in. So then I wondered… what if someone saw us two days ago? Someone who knew us from before.'

'You think it might be one of the Daniels kids?' Warlow's pulse ticked up. They wouldn't be kids anymore, that was for sure.

'You asked if there was anyone I could think of who might want to do Andy any harm. If I was Tristan or Iona Daniels, I might want to. If I was their father I might want to.'

'Did Andrew ever tell you any of this?' Jess turned to Fran.

Fran's pale face crumpled. 'No,' It emerged as a kind of moan. 'Until Rob told me an hour ago I had no idea. It sounds awful.'

'The Caution was for abduction of a girl under the age of sixteen,' Jess said.

'I know how that sounds. But it was only hide and seek.' Rob kept his eyes on the DI's face. 'That's all. I swear to God. And if I could take back that day, tear up the masks, take the kids back to where they lived instead of... I'm sorry. I've been sorry every day since.'

Warlow waited but there was no more. Jess asked a few questions but they already had the report. In light of Hopley's statement, they needed to move things along. When another silence appeared, he stood up, signalling the end of the discussion. 'Thanks for coming in and being so candid, Mr Hopley.'

Rob looked over and locked on to the DCI's face. 'In a funny way I hope to God I'm wrong about this.'

CHAPTER NINETEEN

THE TEAM SPENT the next few hours with heads down in the Incident Room. Gil took charge marshalling the troops. Rob's statement needed following up and priority given to finding out what happened to the Daniels' family. Mid-afternoon Warlow called a halt to watch a live broadcast from the crime scene where Superintendent Sion Buchannan was about to deliver a statement. They gathered around a TV, bunched together, tallest at the back.

The cameras had set up outside the police cordon at the edge of the glade. The wind was up and the superintendent stood self-consciously leaning into the breeze with the cordon tape flapping behind him. This was to be a prepared statement only. There would be no questions.

'If that's a syrup of figs on his head, I hope he's super-glued it on. *Mawredd*.' Gil said.

Jess sent Catrin a sideways glance. Something she'd done since DS Jones had arrived. His tendency to pepper his language with Welsh oaths was disconcerting. Not that she was a prude but not understanding what they meant was a worry, in case she used one herself. Now she'd check with Catrin to make sure it wasn't anything vile or too profane. So far, the worst he'd come up with was *Iesu Grist* – no translation needed – *cachu* – shit, and now *mawredd*.

Catrin leant across to whisper. 'Quite safe, ma'am. Blimey comes closest, I think.'

'It's his own hair.' Warlow replied to Gil.

The Buccaneer's tie began flying up and around his face as the wind caught it. He quickly smoothed it down and started speaking.

'The tie looks like a demented spider's leg dancing about like that.' Rhys craned his neck for a better look.

'Someone should have given him a tie pin,' Jess said.

'I hope he's anchored down with a guy rope,' Gil added.

On screen, The Buccaneer cleared his throat.

'The night before last, an emergency call was placed near to this location. When units responded, they found one man badly injured, and a second man fatally wounded in what can only be described as a very violent and unprovoked attack. Both the dead man and the survivor were assaulted by one assailant on a motorcycle. The attack took place in darkness. Relatives have been informed and we can reveal that the deceased is Andrew Simon Geary, aged thirty. Dyfed-Powys police have launched a full-scale murder enquiry and we would appeal for anyone with any information they might consider useful to come forward. Mr Geary was—'

Buchannan halted mid-flow as his wind-driven tie found its way into his mouth. He swept it away with a huge hand and furiously spat a crumb of lint out before continuing. 'Mr Geary was riding cycle trails on the day prior to this vicious attack. We'd like to talk to anyone who believes they saw him that day or were aware of any motorcycles in the vicinity of Keepers' car park on the night before last. Please contact the action line. Thank you very much.'

'*Arglwydd*, that thing's alive.' Gil flinched, as the tie

caught the Buccaneer one in the eye causing everyone in the room to either wince with vicarious pain, or hoot with laughter.

'Think it's possessed?' Jess asked.

The superintendent turned away, swatting again at the offending item of clothing and muttering a couple of words that were hardly ever heard prior to the watershed outside of Channel Four.

The hotline number appeared on the screen.

'No mention of James Hunt,' muttered Warlow.

'Who?' Catrin blinked and dabbed her eyes.

'Don't ask,' Warlow said. 'But brace yourselves for the calls.'

'What calls?' Rhys asked.

'The crazies.' Catrin explained and turned to her monitor. 'I've already seen an article online with the title, The Beast of Brechfa.'

'What?' Warlow growled.

Catrin pulled up the online article. Warlow read it in silence, leaning on Catrin's desk with both hands and slowly shaking his head. As well as the lurid headlines, there were images. One a replica of the totem Rhys had snapped a photograph of in the woods. The other an unidentifiable shape.

Warlow squinted at the screen. 'And we are supposed to believe that this beast is some kind of being that lives in the forest and hunts down innocent walkers and campers?'

'What, like a Yeti or a Bigfoot?' Gil asked, peering over Warlow's shoulder at a very blurry image of the vaguely biped figure under what looked like a shaggy car blanket taken in half light on a long lens through dense trees.

'All that's going to do is pull the weirdos in by the dozen.' Jess shook her head.

'Anybody can put anything on the internet though.'

Rhys ran a hand through his hair. 'I don't really think there is a beast.'

Once more the room fell silent as everyone turned to stare at the DC.

'Did you know they've removed the word gullible from the Oxford English Dictionary?' Catrin turned her earnest face towards him.

'No they haven't.' He snorted, but the mild bunching of his brows hinted at a smidgen of doubt.

Gil put him out of his misery. 'Of course they haven't. It was naive they took out.'

'Really?' This time, the surprise in Rhys's voice was undiluted.

'Oh my God. Of course there's no beast.' Catrin threw Rhys a searing glance. 'A nerd sitting in his—'

'Or hers,' Rhys interjected. 'Sexist alert.'

'—bedroom somewhere wrote this, making it all up as they go along.'

'So tell me what is real,' Warlow said.

Catrin flicked off the page and stood up, notebook open.

'Traffic have got back to me on the bikes. They reckon it's unlikely to be anything more than a 125cc, so that's what we should look at. They gave me a few makes to try. I've reduced the numbers of owners within fifty miles. It's still a big list, though.'

'But smaller than it was?' Jess asked.

'Yes. I've got some bodies manning the phones.'

'Good. That's progress.' Warlow turned to the most junior member of the team. 'Rhys, tell me something useful.'

'Geary's phone, sir.'

'What about it?'

'We've been able to get into it, so the tech guys have

cloned it already. But there's an app on it called Reperire. That's Latin for find. It's basically a retrieval app.'

'English?' Gil asked; eyebrows raised.

'Helps you find things. At least the things you've listed and tagged with a locator device.'

Warlow frowned, willing to give the young DC the benefit of the doubt for a moment but wondering how much of a garden path meander this might end up being. 'Such as?'

But the DC was keen if nothing else. 'There is a list. Keys, bottle, wallet…but it's easier if I show you, sir.'

Rhys stood. At the back of the room bits and pieces of evidence sat on a table, logged in by the evidence officer. Rhys put on some gloves and removed the phone from the clear evidence bag, opened the app, and held it up so that everyone could see the screen. Gil fished out some glasses. Warlow needed to visit an optician, too, but got by with squinting his eyes. A list appeared on the phone screen. Wallet, car keys, bike bottle, house keys, BK. Rhys pressed a button and a new screen appeared with a directional red arrow that was pointing to their left. Rhys turned his body and the phone until the arrow pointed straight ahead. He started walking towards the back of the room as the phone beeped. A noise that grew with each step Rhys walked until he reached the evidence table and picked up the sealed evidence bag containing Geary's drinks bottle. The tone became a single note. He brought the bottle back to the team and held it so that the base was uppermost.

'See that little square stuck to the dimple in the bottle's base, that's a tracker device. Geary has one on this bottle and his keys, according to the app.'

'So the phone tracks them?' Gil asked.

'It does. It has a two-hundred-foot search radius. Still, it means that Geary never lost his keys. And he would have found his bottle if he'd dropped it in the forest and back-tracked.'

'That's useful,' Gil said, clearly impressed. 'Amazing what they can do these days.'

'Can it help us find the murder weapon?' Warlow asked.

Rhys's face fell. 'Murder weapon isn't on the list, sir. Only car keys, house keys, bike bottle, wallet, and something called BK, but nothing under murder weapon.'

Catrin shook her head.

Warlow pursed his lips. 'So, apart from this wonderful app, anything else of actual use to us on the phone?'

'Not yet, sir,' Rhys said and walked back to replace the bottle on the evidence table a little crestfallen.

'Excellent work though, Rhys. Keep at it.' Jess smiled at him.

Rhys turned and smiled back. 'Thank you, ma'am.'

'I've been digging into the Daniels family,' Jess said. 'There's a lot buried there.'

She walked to the Gallery at the front, once more taking the initiative. Warlow approved and waited for the DI to continue which she did, pointing out a yellow arrow recently added to the map.

'Hopley was right. The Daniels lived in a woodsman's cottage. The mother, Bet Daniels, died when the little girl, Iona, was three, and her brother, Tristan, seven. Iwan Daniels worked for the forestry part time, sometimes also as a farm labourer. The children went to school, but absenteeism was a problem. Social services were well aware of the situation, but until the episode involving Hopley and Geary, theirs was a watching brief.'

'Sounds tough,' Warlow said.

'Stark contrast between the Gearys and the Daniels, certainly,' Jess agreed.

'What about the caution?' Gil spoke up.

Jess picked a sheet up from her desk. 'When it comes to the actual incident, from what I've read, though there was no evidence of any physical wrongdoing, there was genuine concern things might have got out of hand.'

Warlow's mind was churning. He knew what got out of hand meant. Everyone did. Situations like Hopley described, interactions between younger and older kids, were two a penny on streets and schoolyards. They flared up and fizzled out to nothing. But in the isolation of a forest, rarely but harrowingly, things could turn nasty. He doubted there was anyone in the country over forty who couldn't recall a much-broadcasted CCTV camera still of a little boy walking hand in hand with an older boy through a shopping arcade in 1993. Proof, if anyone needed it, that bad things could happen in the blink of an eye.

'But Hopley and Geary didn't harm the younger children.' Catrin folded her arms and perched against a desk.

'Physically, no. Hopley's description is pretty accurate,' Jess continued. 'No one came out of it well. They cautioned both Andrew Geary and Rob Hopley, despite pressure from the father who wanted them to be punished for scaring his daughter and wasting police time.'

'What happened to the Daniels family?' Gil asked.

Jess glanced down at the sheets she held. They were words on paper but Warlow sensed that they made for difficult reading. 'The father faced a lot of criticism. But the social service reports showed no intervention. Tristan went through school, left at sixteen, followed in his father's footsteps. Farm work, labouring, scaffolder. Looks like he's had quite a few jobs.'

'What about the girl?' Warlow asked, guessing the answer was not one he would relish hearing.

Jess made a clicking noise with her cheek. 'Not such an easy passage into adulthood. She was forever in trouble in school. Reports of self-harming, petty theft, drugs. These days she'd have been in counselling before you could say Adolescent Mental Health Initiative. Maybe they tried, I don't know. But in 2014 she attacked her father with a knife. He wasn't badly injured, but she was arrested and sectioned. She did it again in 2016 after they released her. She's now serving a twelve-year extended sentence at a medium-secure unit in Bridgend.'

'*Mam fach*,' Gil muttered.

Jess threw Catrin a glance. She mouthed back, *My goodness, sort of.*

'Where's the father now?' Warlow demanded.

'Died in 2017. He was found at the cottage. The post-mortem says he bled to death from ruptured oesophageal varices. Whatever that is.'

Warlow knew. He had insider knowledge on that one. 'It's something alcoholics get. The liver scars up, back pressure causes the veins in the oesophagus to balloon. Sometimes they burst.'

The look on Rhys's face was enough to tell the DCI they all understood. He had no intention of elaborating on how he knew.

'And the son, Tristan?' Warlow asked.

Catrin responded this time as she flicked through some pages in her notebook. 'His registered address is the cottage.'

'Have we checked with the DVLA to see if he has a motorbike, or at least a licence?'

'None registered,' Catrin replied.

'Hmm,' grunted Warlow. 'Right. Then that's our afternoon set out for us. Rhys and Catrin, get out to the Daniels' property and check out if this bloke is our Evel Knievel. See what you can find out. He will have seen our lot all over the forest, so it'll come as no surprise to see you call. If he's there, play it cool. Ask him if he saw anything of Geary and Hopley on the day of the attack. Get a feel for how he reacts and then come back here. If he isn't there, have a look around and find out what you can.'

'On it,' said Catrin.

'DI Allanby and I, in the meantime, have the dubious pleasure of visiting The Oglan Clinic.'

'The madhouse,' said Jess.

'Not very PC, Detective Inspector.' Warlow waggled an eyebrow.

Jess shrugged. 'Still a sodding madhouse. I can't wait.'

CHAPTER TWENTY

It was M4 all the way to Bridgend, then right on a road parallel with the river to the site of the old asylum.

Warlow drove, Jess sat in the passenger seat, answering texts.

'Molly says hi,' Jess said.

'I was meaning to ask you. What can I get her for looking after Cadi?'

Jess laughed. 'You're kidding, I hope. Having the dog with her is more than enough of a treat. It's hardly a chore.'

'Still, I'd like to get her something. To say thanks. I was thinking some kind of voucher. I mean money is better than something useless she'll never use.'

Jess inclined her head. 'Money's good. She'll never turn that down. But she won't turn her nose up at anything you give her. She likes you.'

Warlow let out a derisive snort. 'She likes to insult me.'

'She's sixteen. It's the same thing.'

Warlow huffed out some air. 'Boys are easy. I know about boys. I always defaulted to sport, and that usually sorted them out. Tickets to a match or new boots. The away-colours shirt of whatever team they were supporting. Uncomplicated.'

'There's still a child inside that feisty teenager, don't forget,' Jess said, as if she was reminding herself. 'And as for the insults, she feels betrayed by the one man she loved. Her dad. For the moment, all men are targets.'

Warlow toyed with taking this conversation further, but thought better of it. Jess had made no secret of the fact that she'd separated from a husband who, also a police officer, had played hide the truncheon with a fellow officer who was not his wife. Worse was that he'd done so in a workplace environment. An insult to injury act that merited a disciplinary hearing and sanctions from the Greater Manchester police. There was no going back after that. Manchester's loss. Dyfed-Powys's gain.

'How would she react to a book?' Warlow asked.

Jess thought and then nodded her agreement. 'That's more personal. She'd like that.'

'Okay, then a book it is. From our chats, I know she's an Avengers fan. So would you say she's into fantasy or sci-fi?'

'Fantasy definitely. But nothing soppy.'

'Right. I'll have a think.'

Jess opened the file she'd brought with her and read the first few paragraphs before exhaling loudly. 'Iona Daniels is only six years older than Molly. When I read about what she was doing at sixteen, I said a silent prayer of thanks that me and Molly's battles are all about clothes and how soon driving lessons can start. Not drugs and alcohol. I can't help but feel for the dad. Fate dealt him a shitty hand.'

'Sounds like he did his best,' Warlow said.

'Until Geary and Hopley turned up.' Jess compressed her lips together.

'Agreed,' Warlow muttered. 'I don't like the sound of that one bit. Still, best we don't prejudge talking to her.'

But he hadn't read the report. And the look he kept seeing on Jess's face every time she glanced down at it told him it wasn't exactly the script of *It's a Wonderful Life*.

The Oglan was two storeys of orange brick in the middle of a scattered complex of sombre grey granite. The green, four-metre-high surrounding chain link fencing highlighted the difference even more.

Warlow parked up. They showed their warrant cards at the reception desk, but protocol demanded they shed themselves of anything that might be weaponised or stolen and made use of afterwards.

Warlow talked to a nurse consultant who knew Iona's case and he suggested they meet in a seminar room.

'It is only an informal chat, isn't it?' The nurse, whose name badge read Simon, asked.

'Absolutely,' Warlow answered. 'Informal.'

Iona was in jeans and a hoodie. She was small, thin, no make-up, her shoulder-length mousey hair tucked back behind her ears. She sat watching Warlow with an intense look. They'd set the room up for a lecture with six rows of chairs five across. Iona sat at the rear. Warlow pulled a chair out at the front and sat facing her. Jess did the same.

Simon sat quietly at the end of the first row, trying hard to be unobtrusive.

'Iona, I'm DCI Warlow, this is Detective Inspector Allanby. Thanks for agreeing to talk to us.'

The woman in question had one knee drawn up with her foot on the chair, hands clasped over her shin. She rocked gently as she listened. Warlow took the rocking as an acknowledgement of what he'd said.

'We wanted to talk to you about what happened in 2004.'

The rocking stopped.

'Do you read the newspapers?' Warlow glanced at Simon who shrugged by return as if to say she did but probably didn't want to admit to it.

'Something happened in Brechfa Forest a couple of days ago.' Warlow tried again. 'We wondered if you could help us with that?'

'How?' The reply came as muffled, rasping words spoken into her knee. 'I wasn't in the woods two days ago. I'm never in the woods.'

Nicotine had yellowed Iona's fingertips. They were the dirty ochre colour that came with roll-your-owns smoked down to the last half inch. Warlow wondered what the rule was about smoking here in the clinic. He resisted the urge to tell her to sit up straight with difficulty.

'We know that,' Jess said, taking the reins. 'It's just that—'

'Was what happened in the woods a bad thing?' Iona's eyes were down, staring over her drawn-up knee at the floor.

'Yes. A terrible thing,' Warlow replied.

Iona rocked again. This time, a hum accompanied it.

Warlow glanced at Simon again. He turned his eyes on Iona. There was a momentary impasse until the nurse gave a reluctant little nod as permission for Warlow to continue.

Warlow decided on plain speaking. It risked a backlash, but he didn't think that skirting around the issue would help. 'We know that the boys who made you play hide and seek should not have done what they did. Not to anyone. Certainly not a six-year-old.'

A long pause followed. Finally, Iona came back with more, barely audible, muffled words. 'Did the bad thing that happened this time happen to a little girl?'

'No,' Jess said.

Iona's rocking speeded up. The answer seemed to please her.

'Iona, what did the boy who made you hide say to you?' Warlow asked.

Once again, the rocking and the humming stopped. Iona's head came up, baring a confused, almost irritated expression. 'I promised I wouldn't tell anyone.'

Jess sat forward and dropped her voice. 'This is important, Iona. More important than the promise you might have given to the boy.'

Iona hugged her bent leg and buried her head behind it. After half a minute, she looked up at Warlow and shook her head. 'Not a boy. He was something else. An It. I promised It. And It said if I told then It would come back. For a long time afterwards, when I was alone I would see It. Never when the others were around—'

'The others? You mean your brother and your dad?' Jess probed gently.

'They never saw It. But I did. At the edge of the garden. In the woods. Once, It looked in through the window…' She inhaled and let it out in a series of jerky exhalations with her eyes closed. 'I told once, and It did come.' She pulled up the hoodie's sleeve. Scars criss-crossed the inside of her forearm. 'In my dream It came. That's how It showed me what to do with a knife. I won't tell again.'

Jess sent Warlow a side-eyed glance. They'd been expecting this to be difficult. But Iona seemed to be in a worse state than either of them had anticipated. The DI, however, pressed on, determined to learn as much as she could. 'The boy who made you hide, what's his name?'

Iona's face dropped towards the floor, the words mumbling out again. 'It wasn't just a boy. It pretended to be a boy.'

Jess took the baton again. 'The boy who did this to you was the one the bad thing happened to. Do you know anything about that?'

Iona flinched. 'I don't go to the woods. Not anymore. Did It... did something happen to It?'

'Someone died.'

Iona's face came up, animated for once. 'Did It die?'

Warlow nodded. 'The boy who hid you. He died.'

The rocking knee started again. Iona buried her face so that her entire head started moving in time to her leg.

'Iona,' Warlow said, gently.

When she looked up the next time, she was smiling, A sly, shy smile. 'I do know.'

'Good,' Jess gave the girl a bright, encouraging smile. 'Tell us what you know. She took out her pocketbook and found a pen.

'It made me use the knife on my father. It made me set the fire. I hated It then. But afterwards, I asked the woods to do a bad thing to that boy because that boy was hiding It.'

Jess glanced at Warlow. He shook his head and Jess clicked her pen shut and closed her book.

'Your brother, Tristan, he comes to visit you, doesn't he?' Warlow asked.

Iona shook her head. When she spoke, it was into her knee again and Warlow strained forward to hear.

'He knows not to. He knows It is waiting.'

Warlow felt something roil in his gut. Not because of what she was saying, but because of the reason she said it. He couldn't prove anything, of course not. But he'd come across the mad and the bad throughout his career. The bad deserved the full weight of his derision. But nothing chilled him more than a victim of circumstance, or brain chemistry, or lousy genes who couldn't tell right from wrong. It all fell apart there. Without that compass, as with Iona, all bets were off. Unpredictability was no defence, he knew that. But it was hardly prosecutable either.

They thanked Iona and left her. But before they went

back to the car, Warlow had one question for Simon. 'She's clearly very disturbed. Is there any evidence that what happened to her in those woods might be a contributory factor?'

Simon raised his eyebrows. 'Oh, it's more than that. We think it's likely that a childhood trauma like she suffered was the trigger. Who knows if any underlying tendency existed? You can't tell that in childhood, of course. But we've seen severely traumatised patients before who then end up very disturbed. She was only six when all this happened. Most of the analysis we've been able to do traces all her troubles back to that one incident. She'd already lost her mother, remember. Being alone without her brother and father in those woods, being frightened by someone wearing a mask...' Simon pressed his lips together for a long beat. 'Who knows what damage that might have done. She might have got through it with some family and professional support. Both were sadly lacking.'

'And there is no way she could have got out of here and travelled to West Wales two nights ago?' Warlow asked.

'No possibility,' Simon said. 'We lockdown everything at 9pm.'

'Does her brother visit?' Jess asked.

'He does. But they don't speak. He only wants to ensure she's okay so he stays out of sight. It's sad.'

They thanked him and Warlow gave him his card. 'In case she remembers anything else that might be of use.'

Neither Jess nor Warlow spoke for the first ten miles of the journey home. The DCI broke the silence in the end. 'Geary had a lot to answer for.'

Jess was looking out of the window, lost in thought. She turned back in response. 'What did you make of the whole Stephen King thing. The It reference?'

Warlow shook his head. 'Who knows. If the medics at

the Oglan can't work her out, I'm buggered if I have a theory.'

'Referencing popular culture might be her way of understanding or rationalising what Geary did.'

'That stuff is beyond me,' Warlow said.

'I suppose he was just a kid.' Jess's words were an explanation of sorts, but they lacked conviction.

'Agreed. But I'd like to think one of my boys, in the same situation, wouldn't have been a tormenting little bastard.'

'Sounds like they deserved the caution, though.'

Warlow mulled that over, running his tongue across his fillings until something appropriate came to him. 'If you ask me, they deserved a lot more.'

CHAPTER TWENTY-ONE

BEFORE SETTING OFF FOR THE DANIELS' property, Catrin downloaded and printed off a section of the Ordnance Survey map for the area and marked their destination in red. When Rhys had asked why she was bothering – because they both had phones, didn't they? – she reminded him that lots of these out of the way places played havoc with communication signals.

He'd shrugged at that. 'Mr Warlow likes things printed off, too.'

'Paper doesn't need a signal, as he rightly says.'

They left the car at the turn off outside a gate that hung off its hinges. A point marking the entrance to Ffrwd Y Dderwen, the Daniels' property. Someone had placed an enormous boulder three yards inside the entrance to deter vehicles, and a wonky, faded Private Property sign had fallen over next to it. Either side of the track was scrub and reedy grass. The forest started about twenty yards from the edge of the track and from that point extended in all directions.

'Hah, the inevitable muddy patch,' Catrin said, as they

turned down the track towards a damp bottom where run-off from the adjacent hill had pooled into brown puddles.

'Why inevitable?' Rhys asked. The early rain had blown off and the sun was unseasonably warm on their backs.

Catrin picked her way through a boggy patch. 'Isn't there always one wet patch on every hike you do? In the driest July or the frostiest winter, there's one patch guaranteed to get your boots filthy.'

Rhys looked down at his feet. He'd learnt his lesson on his jaunt around Keepers with DI Allanby, and now wore walking boots with his trousers tucked into his socks. Catrin, being Catrin, had brought purple wellies.

'Never thought about it.'

'That's probably because you can step over most things with those legs. How tall are you again?'

'Six three.'

The DS stopped and looked up with disapproval. 'Hang on, the last time I asked it was six two.'

'I don't know why, but I've added an inch since last summer. My mother said I'm doing too much training. Thickening my bones.' He sent her a sheepish look.

'You cannot still be growing. It's unnatural. You need a scan or something.' She shook her head and began skirting the worst of the water.

Rhys followed Catrin to the wet patch, but took a toe-ended gamble and found a stone in the middle of the puddle to step on and jumped the rest of the way onto drier ground.

'Hilarious,' Catrin said, fending off a bush that was trying to claw her face as she pushed around the edge.

They swatted flies and dodged puddles for another ten minutes. On the map it looked to be a good one and three-quarters of a mile up and down hike. 'Can't be much farther.' Rhys swatted away a horse fly. 'Just around the next bend, I reckon.'

And it was. At least, what was left of it.

It looked as though a fire had done its best to ravage one-half of the place and the roof, or what was left of it, sagged down, with the rusted edges of the corrugated sheets that had once kept off the rain hanging out into space. To the right, the remnants of the whitewashed long-house walls still stood, reflecting the sunlight. There was still glass in the windows of the far right and the door adjacent firmly shut. But where the fire had been, two walls had crumbled revealing the blackened remnants of the room's contents.

'Bit of a mess,' Rhys said.

'Bit of a derelict mess if you ask me. I don't remember reading about any fire.' Catrin kept her eyes on the floor to avoid stepping in something left by a deer she'd likely regret.

They took a stoned track where grass grew between the tyre trails left by vehicles long since past. The path led them to the front door.

'Worth knocking?' Rhys asked.

'No harm, I suppose.'

'Best we do. It's the polite thing.' Rhys stepped forward.

Catrin shook her head. Here they were, miles from anywhere, and DC Rhys Harries was concerned about being polite and doing the right thing. And, like a favourite, loyal old dog, you couldn't help but love him for it. She smiled. One of a kind was Rhys Harries.

He was taller than the door and his knock caused both door and surrounding frame to rattle. Must have been a draughty old place when someone lived there.

After the second attempt Rhys turned to her. 'No one here,' he said.

'You don't say?' Catrin sent him a smile with too many teeth showing.

She walked to the side devastated by fire and stood at the edge of the crumbling wall. Inside, the flames had done a lot of damage, scorching everything. Still, she could make out the remains of a metal wood-burning stove against the far wall, its tubular chimney reaching up and through the rusting roof. The remains of bits of furniture, the leg of a chair, the corner of a table, lay scattered over the damp floor. To the right of the fireplace, a doorway, still with half a door intact, but with a charred bottom half, stood shut.

It was a dark and sad building now. Whatever life there had been here had died with the fire. Or perhaps had begun to decay with the demise of Mrs Daniels all those years ago.

'Let's have a look around the outside first,' Catrin said, not wanting to rush inside through that burnt door.

Grass and weed had grown through what might once have been a vegetable garden, but a rough crazy-paving path remained around the edge of the building's walls. They followed it to a couple of dilapidated outbuildings at the rear. These had not been obvious until they rounded a corner. Both had tin roofs. One looked sturdier, made of breeze block with an ancient generator taking up most of the space inside, fuel cans stacked against the back wall and a metal door that creaked rustily when Rhys yanked it open. A strong smell of kerosene oozed from the interior.

The second was a wooden shed. Its door had long gone, and the contents comprised of rusty farm imple-ments: hand scythes, pitchforks, spades, barrels. But at the rear, in shadow so that only the very back of one wheel was visible, two rusting carcasses of old motorbikes.

'Look at these,' Catrin said. She took out a torch and sent a beam of light into the cobweb infested corner. One bike looked like something from a museum, with thin wheels and rusted springs. Nothing like the sleek machines that wind up and down the A40 on a Sunday in the summer. Bikes ridden by middle-aged men from the Midlands that were the bane of her Traffic-cop boyfriend, Craig's life.

'Someone was interested in bikes,' Rhys said.

'These are ancient though.'

'Yes, they are. No plates either.'

They poked around a bit more but found nothing of interest.

Rhys took a walk around the perimeter of the property. 'Nothing else here except for a couple of paths leading off through the woods.'

Catrin joined him and inspected the well-worn footpaths. 'This is used. I wonder if it was one of these that the kids took when they got lost.' She peered into the dark under canopy of the woods.

'They call that the understory,' Rhys said.

Catrin frowned. 'What?'

'The layer underneath the canopy of the forest. Where water drips through. It's a great name. I mean, if only it could tell us, you know?'

For a moment, Catrin toyed with letting fly another sarky comment, but she didn't. Not this time. Rhys sometimes deserved the ribbings he got; what good was being constantly nice to people when the people you dealt with – the criminals at least – had nothing but hate and disdain to throw back at you. Such was a copper's lot. But sometimes Rhys's inherent wonder at the world deserved admiration instead of a bucket of cold water. Catrin judged this to be one of those times.

'Right,' she said, 'no point wandering off down one of these. Might as well look inside the house, agreed?'

They retraced their steps to the burnt side of the

house, to the charred remnant of door that led into what, from the outside at least, looked like the bit that had survived the flames. But once they got through the door into the hall beyond the burnt room, it was clear that they'd been mistaken.

Fire had taken out the narrow staircase and the walls here too were scorched and soot stained. There was no access to the upstairs and Catrin had no interest in clambering up there over fire damaged joists, anyway.

It was only the farthest room from where the fire had taken hold that retained any semblance of what it might have looked like before.

The room was small, with a sofa and an armchair now stained with damp and mould. A darkly varnished table sat to one side with four tucked in chairs. Another fireplace, this time with an open grate and a chimney place set into the far wall. A small TV stood on one corner, a dresser in the other.

Rhys knelt and opened the dresser cupboards.

'Empty,' he said.

The small kitchen in a lean-to at the rear had similarly been stripped of its content, apart from some old cutlery in a broken drawer under the sink. But even these had chipped faux bone handles.

'Well, I think it's safe to assume no one lives here now.' Catrin turned on a tap and got nothing but a weird hiss of air and a trickle of rust from the pipes.

Rhys went back into the living room. To the TV and the little table next to it, still with the remote sitting on top of a pile of newspapers. He knelt again – his default position in a house this small – and riffled the papers.

'Hang on,' he said, gingerly removing a little pile of glossy magazines from under a fold of newspapers. He held them up for Catrin to see. 'These are a lot more recent.'

Catrin stepped forward and peered. The magazine had a one-word title: "MOTORCYCLE"

'There's one here from 2018,' Rhys said. 'When did the old man die?'

'Twenty-seventeen.'

'Unlikely to be his then. Unless of course his ghost is still here.' Rhys's eyes drifted to the ceiling.

A chill ran through Catrin. She didn't like these old, abandoned places. Too many corners to hide in. Too many shadows. Too many bad memories soaked into the walls. 'Yeah, well, it'd be a very special kind of ghost that could go to a newsagent and hand over money for a magazine because I doubt anyone delivers out here.'

Rhys's eyes eventually drifted down. 'Yeah, I suppose so. Probably Tristan's.'

'You don't say,' Catrin said, enunciating every word with an added glare. 'Put that in an evidence bag and let's get some photos of the place and the bikes out back. And then, Sherlock, we can get back to the office in time for a cup of tea and maybe one of Gil's *biscuit*.' She adopted his affectation of pronouncing the word in French.

It was all the incentive Rhys needed.

CHAPTER TWENTY-TWO

IT WAS late afternoon by the time everyone reconvened in the Incident Room. Warlow and Jess hit early afternoon traffic and it had taken them longer than expected to get back.

The good news was that Gil had a tea and biscuit array already set up. By the time the two senior officers had their coats off, there was a mug of steaming brown liquid in front of each of them.

Gil held court. 'I'm still finding my way around peoples' preferences, but I noted that you, sir, went straight for the Hobnobs yesterday. Catrin's a chocolate finger girl, and—'

The conversation ceased as Rhys choked on his mouthful of tea.

'Sorry...' he croaked in the middle of a coughing fit. 'Couldn't help it. Must have gone down the wrong way.' He'd gone a dusky red. Partly from the constriction of his bronchial tree and partly from being the only one who'd seen any innuendo at all in Gil's remarks.

Catrin was giving him an impassive dagger stare, knowing full well that the innocent 'chocolate finger' quip had floated his schoolboy-humour boat. 'How old are you.' she chided him with a prissy shake of the head while trying not to laugh herself.

'—and DI Allanby,' Gil continued, 'Eats half a custard cream and discards the rest.'

'I'm conventional when it comes to biccies,' Jess said. 'But disciplined with it.'

'What about the boy with the filthy mind here?' Catrin nodded at Rhys.

Gil shook his head. 'Eclectic tastes aka. a bloody hoover. Finishes whatever's left behind as soon as my back is turned. *Anifail.*'

Rhys held out both hands palm up, pretending to be insulted at being called an animal in Welsh.

Warlow took a slurp of tea and said, 'For that affront on good taste you're up first, Detective Constable Harries.'

Rhys brushed tea droplets from his trousers, stood up and, while his face faded to a healthy pink, recounted his and Catrin's fruitless visit to the Daniels' property, emphasising the fire and the magazine from 2018.

'It literally is in the middle of nowhere. First thing to say is that someone has blocked the access road to Ffrwd Y Dderwen—'

'What does it mean, the name?' Jess asked.

'The brook near the oak,' Rhys answered.

'Very poetic.'

'Doesn't look like it belongs in a poem at the moment though.' Catrin slid a laptop around so that the others could see the images of the building and its surroundings.

'No evidence at all of recent occupation?' Jess asked.

'No.' Rhys answered. 'As DS Richards said, it's abandoned. And it's registered as an empty property with the council, too. Looks like Tristan Daniels got an exemption from paying tax after the fire.'

'So abandoned, but not quite, is that it?' Warlow asked.

Rhys nodded.

Catrin spoke up. 'The DVLA still have Tristan Daniels registered at that address but there was no sign of habitation.'

'No need for a forensic unit to go out there and give it the once over?' Warlow asked.

Catrin shook her head. 'Waste of time.'

'But at least we know from the magazines that Tristan Daniels was interested in motorbikes,' Gil said, munching on a bourbon.

Warlow absorbed all this information. His next words were a question. 'So where does Daniels live now?'

Catrin went to the Job Centre and pointed to his name written in capitals 'I've actioned the CID help we've been allocated to ring around the local farms. See if they can come up with something. He does casual labour and farm work. With any luck, someone local should know.'

'Good idea.' Warlow gave her a nod. Once again, he was impressed with the DS's initiative.

'How about you, sir?' Rhys asked. 'What was Iona Daniels like?'

'Very damaged goods.' Warlow shook his head and recounted his and Jess's visit.

'Wow, so she thinks something is making her do stuff,' Rhys said. 'That's way weird.'

'It is,' Warlow agreed. 'But it's also her watertight alibi. She may have been capable of doing that to Andrew Geary and Rob Hopley judging by her previous, but it most definitely wasn't her. Unless she can bloody well fly.'

Rhys glanced around at the others before settling back on Warlow's face. 'On a broomstick, you mean, sir?'

Everyone paused, analysing what they'd just heard and hoping it was merely a lame attempt at humour and not, in any shape or form, a genuine question. Luckily, Rhys turned back to look at his own screen and missed the incredulous stares.

Gil put on one sterile blue glove, waited until everyone had taken a biscuit, and rearranged those that remained into a pleasing regular pattern, Hobnobs in the middle, custard creams and chocolate fingers alternating as a fringe around the edge. There were no bourbons left.

No one said anything because no matter how much derision they thought the act deserved, DS Jones was the biscuit provider, so why rock the boat? Even so, Warlow couldn't resist just the one little quip. Though he was careful to couch it in vaguely complimentary terms.

'Nice work, Gil. I can see it on a plinth at the Tate.'

'Don't mock.' Gil adjusted the last couple of biscuits and shuffled his chair back to his own desk. 'Besides, while you lot were out gallivanting, I did some more digging around Andrew Geary's record. His Disclosure and Barring Service record makes for interesting reading. By that I mean squeakily uninteresting. I can't find any caution on his records.'

'What?' Catrin's head snapped up from her monitor and she hurried over to Gil's desk.

Warlow sat forward. 'You're sure about this?'

'Yep. I've been staring at the bloody screen for hours. I've sent you all copies.'

'But why would Hopley lie about something like that? Something so easily checked.' Catrin stared at the screen over Gil's shoulder.

Warlow weighed up the question. It was a good one. 'Haven't we been through this already. Don't cautions fall off the records with time?'

Catrin answered. 'I spoke to someone in CPS, sir. Cautions are a bit of a minefield. Mostly, they're issued in circumstances where the crime is low-level, and to first-time offenders. It's an out of court disposal avoiding the need for a charge. But it also implies acceptance of guilt by the person cautioned.'

'So less serious than convictions?' Rhys asked.

Catrin nodded. 'Yes, but the implications are that the record for caution can be kept by us for future use and referred to in future legal proceedings. And form part of a criminal record check. After six years, they're filtered from an adult's record. In other words, they drop off – so long as the caution is filterable.'

'Is that what's happened?' Rhys asked. 'It's been filtered off Geary's record.'

'And if it's true, why not Hopley's?' Jess asked.

'That's where it gets interesting.' Gil offered the rearranged plate. No one took anything. Except Rhys, much to the sergeant's displeasure as registered by his mock scowl. The DC transferred the biscuit to his other hand and started back for another, only for the plate to be snatched back out of reach. '*Trachwant*,' Gil said.

Catrin mouthed the word, 'greedy,' to the inquisitive Jess while Gil continued the caution explanation. 'Not all caution-able offences are filterable. Some are too serious. So, you may ask, if they're that serious, why bother with a caution in the first place?'

Rhys opened his mouth before shutting it again, realising it was full of biscuit.

'That is a question for the big-nobs in wigs, not for me. All I know is that abduction of a child under sixteen is not a filterable caution,' Gil explained. 'It's stayed on Hopley's record for that reason. If Geary was cautioned, too, then it should still be on his.'

Warlow sat back, took another slurp of tea and let the cogs mesh. 'Something isn't right,' he said eventually. 'I can smell it.' He turned to Rhys. A quick motion, like a striking snake. 'What about that laptop?'

Rhys swallowed hastily. 'No joy, sir. It's with the tech

guys now. They think they might get into those encrypted files, but they couldn't say how long it would take.'

'Get back on to them. Tell them it's a priority.'

His head flicked to Catrin. She met his gaze unflinchingly. 'Chase up Tristan Daniels. Find out where he's holed up.'

Warlow finished his tea, stood up, and turned to Gil. 'Good work. Ask around. Check if anyone remembers the case. I don't but I'm sure some of the old lags will. You may even know one or two on account of your... seniority.'

'That's below the belt, that is,' Gil said.

Warlow tilted his head towards the biscuits. 'Keep on stuffing your face with those and you won't be able to do yours up.'

Gil turned a disappointed face towards Rhys and nodded towards an open pad on his desk. 'I hope you're taking note of these slurs, DC Harries. Ageism and body image-ism are what I've counted so far.'

Rhys started writing. 'How do you spell image-ism?'

'You don't,' Catrin said, taking the pen out of his hand.

'I notice you did not turn down a Hobnob, DCI Warlow,' Gil said.

'You know the rule, never turn down the offer of refreshments. It might be the last thing you ever eat.'

Rhys watched the exchange between his two senior officers. 'Should I write that down, too?'

Catrin handed back the pen. 'Yeah, you should.'

Coat on, Warlow turned to Jess. 'Eaten half your custard cream yet?'

The DI held up the remains of the biscuit.

'Good,' said Warlow. 'I fancy a trip to Journey's End.'

CHAPTER TWENTY-THREE

WARLOW RANG the FLO from the car.

'How is everyone holding up?'

'Waiting for news. Like always in these situations, sir.' Mellings' voice remained subdued, as if she was trying not to be heard. The sound of a latch opening followed almost immediately.

'Warn them we have nothing new to tell them, but we wanted to clear a few things up. I also do not want Hopley in on the chat. The Gearys and Fran Dee only.'

'I'll get that organised right away.' Her voice was normal now and Warlow guessed that she'd gone outside to take the call. It spoke to Warlow of a difficult atmosphere in the house. When he asked, Mellings confirmed it.

'Most of the time you can hear a pin drop. No TV. No radio. All they do is sit there, waiting. I'll be glad when this one is over, sir.'

The young PC was waiting to let them in when they arrived a short time later. She stepped outside as they pulled up.

'All as arranged. The Gearys and Miss Dee are in the

living room. Mr Hopley is in his room over in the guest block.'

'Good.' Warlow scanned the well-kept property. Everything tidy and in its place. Ralph Geary was a man who enjoyed control.

Mellings glanced over Warlow's shoulder at the car. 'No DC Harries?'

'You know Rhys?'

'I bump into him occasionally. I'd heard he was on your team.'

'We left him holding the fort,' Jess explained. 'But I'll tell him you were asking after him.'

The FLO smiled. It came close to dazzling. But then she was back to business and showed them in. She'd set up the Gearys on the sofa. Ralph, dapper in pressed shirt and raspberry slacks, Celia in a dress over thick tights. Fran Dee looked even more pale than previously, still with her sleeves over her hands and split-knee jeans, huddled with her legs up on an armchair.

Warlow took a seat next to Jess at a small table and watched as the DI put her phone on the table and started up a recording app. The Gearys watched her every movement as if she were performing some kind of close-up magic.

'Thanks for agreeing to see us,' the DCI said. His words drew their glances.

'Do you have news?' Celia Geary couldn't help herself. The words seemed to burst out of her.

'As I said, Celia—' Mellings began, but Warlow put his hand up to stop her. This was his gig.

'It's okay PC Mellings.' He turned to address Celia Geary directly. 'I can understand your concern. Us turning up here like this is bound to trigger some anxiety. And what I want to talk to you about might seem strange, but something's come up in the course of our enquiries—'

'For God's sake man, spit it out.' Ralph Geary had frowned when Warlow started talking. Now his brows were almost knitted together.

'Two-thousand and four,' Jess said. Geary's gaze switched to the DI.

'Two-thousand and four? What does that mean?' Celia asked.

'That was the year that Andrew and Rob were cautioned, am I right?' Jess posed this as a simple question with a yes or no answer. Making it as easy for them as possible.

Ralph Geary blinked at her, his anger evaporating in shock.

'A caution,' Warlow said. 'For something they did wrong.'

'Hang on a minute. Wrong is a bit strong,' Ralph protested. 'They were just kids.'

'Fourteen,' Jess said.

'Still kids in law,' Ralph replied sharply.

'And the caution was for abduction of a girl under the age of sixteen,' Warlow said, slowly, emphasising the age.

Ralph shook his head. 'She was six. They played hide and seek. Played a game.'

'A game that went badly wrong, unless I am mistaken,' Jess said, deliberately adding the formality.

'It did. But still only a game. Your lot went completely over the bloody top. They wanted to take the boys to court, for God's sake. Over a game.' Ralph delivered the last sentence with a throaty laugh. As if it was the silliest thing anyone had ever heard.

'I don't think Tristan and Iona's father thought it much of a game,' Jess protested.

Ralph looked as if he might leap out of his seat. He'd gone a deep shade of aubergine.

'So you all settled for a caution,' Warlow said, directing his question at Celia Geary.

She nodded. 'It seemed the better option.'

'At the time?'

'The boys were due back to school a week after it happened. We, that is Rob's parents, and us, wanted it settled. Not have it hanging over them. So, after taking advice, we opted to accept a caution,' Celia explained.

'By advice you mean legal advice?' Jess asked.

Celia sent Ralph an uncertain glance. His cue to rejoin the fray.

'I spoke to a couple of solicitors I knew. Nothing formal.' He spoke gruffly. The sentences like staccato bursts. 'Why are you even asking us about this? What on earth has what happened all those years ago got to do with —' Ralph's words froze in mid-bluster, his mouth hanging open as an idea formed and took root.

But his wife stole his thunder. 'You don't think what happened to Andrew had anything to do with back then, do you?'

'We're looking at this from all angles, Mrs Geary,' Warlow replied.

Celia nodded, but Ralph continued to stare.

Warlow looked across at Fran. She watched the Gearys with a calculating expression.

'Then it's a bloody odd angle if you ask me.' Ralph barked out the words. He was getting angry again, which, of course, he was perfectly entitled to do. But who was he getting angry with, Warlow wondered.

'Agreed.' The DCI nodded. 'Especially as the caution has been expunged from the PNC and Andrew's Disclosure and Barring Certificate.'

'So?' Ralph's reply bordered on the belligerent now.

'So, abduction cautions such as these are not filtered off the records. Not normally.' Jess gave Ralph one of her special smiles. The kind that showed off a lot of her very good teeth, and about as friendly as a dirty scalpel. A scalpel she twisted with the added, 'As you well know.'

Ralph deflated and made do with a sigh. 'We gave Dyfed-Powys a little nudge. When Andrew got to twenty, the time when the caution should have filtered off, we learnt it wouldn't be. Some nonsense about it being of significant interest and not eligible. They wanted it to be a permanent stain on his record. He hadn't started applying for jobs at that point, but he would be within a year. We sought more advice.'

'What advice?' Jess asked.

'Bloody expensive advice, that's what.' Ralph grunted out the words. 'We got a QC to write to your lot arguing that it was not proportionate to retain the caution. She used a human rights argument. Clever woman and worth every penny. I mean, it could have stopped Andrew going abroad, getting visas… who knows what else. What if his job took him to Australia or the USA? He'd have to declare that caution. For a bloody game gone wrong.'

'So, you got it expunged.'

'We did. Yes.'

For the first time since Warlow had walked in, Fran Dee spoke. 'Why didn't he tell me?' She glanced at Ralph when she spoke.

Celia answered, her mouth turned down at the corners. 'Oh, Fran. Why would he? He wasn't proud of it. It was something he'd tried to wipe off the slate.'

Fran flicked a glance at Warlow. 'But perhaps not everyone accepted that wiping off. That's why you're here, am I right?'

The DCI returned her gaze with his own impassive expression. 'As I say, we're looking at all the angles. We have to.'

Ralph's frown kept his brows crumpled. 'They never

touched the boy or the girl. Frightened them a bit, but never touched them. From the way your lot reacted, you could have sworn they'd as good as horse-whipped them.' He shook his head before continuing. 'I don't even know why we're talking about this. I mean, it's years ago. It's been long forgot—' Once again, the words died on his lips. 'Oh no. Don't tell me it's that Daniels girl. That little psychopath. It's her, isn't it?' Ralph lunged to his feet.

Warlow didn't move, but there was steel in his voice. 'Have a seat, Mr Geary.'

Celia Geary snaked up a hand and pulled her husband back down to the sofa with a shake of her head. 'Sit down and listen, Ralph. Please.'

'It has nothing to do with Iona Daniels,' Jess said. 'We can be completely certain of that.'

'How?' Ralph sneered. 'How can you be completely certain?'

'Because she's locked away in a secure unit with a curfew and lights out at 9pm.' Warlow uttered the statement in a low voice heavy with meaning.

'Good. I hope they throw away the bloody key. She became feral you know. Set fire to her own house, stabbed her own father.' Ralph blustered. Finally, he sat down next to his wife.

Jess continued. 'As I say, we are not suspecting Iona—'

'But I suppose there's still that brother of hers,' Ralph said. 'I've seen him around. Avoid him like the plague, as does everyone else. It isn't him, is it?'

'We're not at liberty to discuss details of the case, Mr Geary,' Jess told him.

'There is one other thing, though.' Warlow shifted in his chair and changed tack. 'We saw Andrew liked to visit Thailand.'

Ralph nodded. 'Understandable. Though again, I do not see its relevance.'

'Indulge me, Mr Geary,' Warlow urged.

Ralph sighed. 'I had an office there in Bangkok. Lots of security for their Royal Family's distant relatives. Lucrative work. I'd go out on security details and Andrew might come with me. Once or twice a year since he was twenty. He'd go off to the beaches, I'd go to meetings. He got the bug.'

'We saw he was planning another trip.' Jess glanced at the recording app on her phone, making sure it was running.

'With his mates.' Ralph nodded. 'They liked to go down to Vietnam sometimes.'

'Has he ever taken you?' Jess asked Fran.

'Everywhere but.' She added a wistful sigh. 'I'm not complaining. We did a bit of the west coast of the USA and Canada.' A smile flickered as memory flared and just as quickly died. It didn't take long to realise that those summer memories with Andy would be her last.

Warlow stood up. 'Right. I think we have what we need for the moment. Thanks for your time, everyone. That's all been very helpful.'

'How?' Ralph asked. He held both hands out. 'I'm all ears. Take your time. We'd all like a glimpse into the brilliant detective's thought processes here, wouldn't we, Celia?'

But Warlow didn't have to answer.

'An investigation like this is highly complex, Mr Geary,' Jess explained. 'Often it's not until we've explored a particular avenue that things become clear.'

A good one as platitudes went. Good enough to shut Ralph Geary up anyway, thought Warlow. But it wasn't Ralph that drew his gaze as he and Jess stood to leave. Celia Geary had done a Procol Harum. Turned truly a whiter shade of pale. She'd pivoted in her seat to stare at her husband, and her expression was not one of concern for a loved one. It was something else. Something feral.

'Mrs Geary—' Warlow began. But before he'd finished, a wail escaped Celia's lips. It started small and grew into a curdled scream as she finally found the words to hurl at him. 'I told you. I told you it was a mistake. We should never have accepted the caution. Never. He needed help—'

'Celia!' Ralph's voice doubled in volume. 'For God's sake, get a hold of yourself.'

Celia reacted as if she'd been slapped. She jerked and looked around as if seeing the room and its occupants for the first time. Her eyes widened with fear before her head fell into her hands. 'God, oh God, oh God. My Andrew... my Andrew... my Andrew...'

Warlow exchanged a look with Jess. To her credit, Mellings immediately went to Celia and took her out into another room. She didn't object. Whatever fight there had been in her seemed to have leeched away with that wail.

Ralph Geary sat rigid, looking flushed and unrepentant. 'I'm sorry. You'll appreciate how hard this has hit her,' he muttered, without making eye contact with the officers.

'Think nothing of it,' Warlow said. 'It's a difficult time for you both. We understand.'

'Do you?' Ralph said, his head snapping up as the vitriol returned. 'Well, why don't you bloody well do something about it and find out who killed my son.'

They showed themselves out. But instead of heading for the car, Warlow stopped three yards from the door and looked around. 'Where exactly are these guest rooms?'

CHAPTER TWENTY-FOUR

THE CALL CAME ten minutes after Warlow and Jess had left for Journey's End. Catrin took it with Gil and Rhys busy at their screens.

She turned away with the phone to her ear.

'Nice of you to call.'

She'd dropped her voice in an attempt at avoiding being overheard. To that extent it failed miserably as Rhys poked his nose up over his screen to look at her. A feat, given his enormous frame, he had no difficulty in achieving.

'Do you mind?' Catrin said, hand over the receiver.

'That's Craig, isn't it?' Rhys grinned, knowing he'd caught her.

'What if it is?'

'Personal calls.' Rhys tutted. 'You know what the boss says.'

'Craig is in Traffic. He's responding to my request for assistance—'

'I bet he is.' Rhys dropped his chin and raised his eyebrows.

Catrin took her hand off the mouthpiece and said, 'Let me ring you back... yes... yes, it is... I will... I'll tell him.'

She put the phone down and rounded on the DC.

'Craig says they'll be looking out for your car. One mph over the limit, and bang, you're for it.'

Rhys looked immensely pleased with himself because of how miffed Catrin looked. 'Never,' he said with an exaggerated shake of his head. 'I'm law abiding, me.'

'You remind me so much of my cousin Osian.'

'Smart and good looking is he?'

'No, he's ten.'

The phone went again mid-bicker. Catrin picked up once more and shimmied to the end of her desk, away from Rhys.

The DC extended his long neck around his monitor. 'If that's Craig again, tell him I—'

'Shush,' Catrin waved a finger to shut him up before reaching for pen and paper and scribbling something down. She spent a long time listening to the caller and muttering a series of yeses. The scribbles filled half a page. 'Can you send me the coordinates, or, better still, the photos? Great... much obliged... Thanks.'

'God, get a room you two,' Rhys whispered, his grin even bigger.

Catrin shook her head. 'That was not Craig. It was one of the DC's from downstairs. She got lucky with calling a farm called Bryndu. They've been employing Tristan Daniels on and off for a couple of years. And they know where he lives.'

Rhys blinked, the grin fading. 'Where?'

'They're sending a photo.'

'Why not an address?'

'There isn't one.' Her phone pinged and she opened up the image that downloaded. She showed it to Rhys over the top of their screens. The DC stared at an aerial shot of the forest with a numbered B road nearby.

'That's Pant y Dderwen.' Rhys jabbed a finger at a point on the screen.

'And that,' Catrin said, pointing a few inches away towards a rough red circle, 'Is our man.'

She rolled her chair over to Gil who looked at the photo and mumbled, 'Could be anywhere.'

'We know where it is, Gil. That's not the issue. I want to go back out there.'

'Great. But that's a lot of forest and it's a small field.' Gil said.

'It's a field half a mile away from where we were today. That,' she pointed again at the circle, 'Is a caravan.'

'Think we should, sarge?' Rhys asked. He'd got up and loomed over the two sergeants.

Gil adopted an expression that caused his mouth to turn down in contemplation. He looked at the phone and twisted it from vertical to horizontal. You could almost hear the cogs whirring. Finally, he made up his mind. 'Why not? Evan wants you to find Daniels. Besides, you're driving me nuts, the both of you. It's like having the grand-children to stay. Go on, bugger off. And play it cool.' He raised a wagging finger and changed into Welsh for a take-it-easy warning. '*Cam bwyll*. You heard what the DCI said. Don't spook the bugger.'

'I'm driving.' Catrin leant forward to glare at Rhys.

'You always drive,' Rhys complained.

'Privilege of rank.' Catrin got up and grabbed her coat.

They were still arguing as the door to the office closed behind them. Gil watched and breathed a sigh of relief.

Half an hour later DS Richards and DC Harries stood on the same spot they'd stood in that morning in front of the ruin of Ffrwd Y Dderwen. Catrin had the image up on her phone and was trying to orientate it.

'Looks like it's northeast from here.' She tilted the phone back and forth in her hand.

'Must be one of the paths we saw last time around back,' Rhys said.

'Okay. Lead the way, KemoSabe.' Catrin gestured with a held-out hand.

Rhys hesitated. 'Who?'

'KemoSabe. What the Lone Ranger called Tonto.'

'TontWho?'

Catrin sighed. 'Craig's into Westerns. Django, Deadwood, The Hateful Eight. The Lone Ranger isn't one of my favourites, but he liked it.' She made a face, 'Johnny Depp, you know. But Tonto was a tracker. Comanche I think.'

'So you want me to be the tracker?'

Catrin glanced at the sky. It was overcast but still bright. They had maybe an hour's daylight left. It was only half a mile to the caravan on the map but they hadn't moved during this conversation.

'Second thoughts, you be the Lone Ranger, I'll be Tonto.'

'Okay.' Rhys sounded dubious.

'Hi Ho Silver! Away!' Catrin said.

'That's a song my mam and dad dance to at weddings.'

'No, it isn't.'

'It is.'

'No. You're thinking of 'Hi Ho Silver Lining'. Jeff Beck.'

'Okay.' Rhys pitched his agreement with an added dollop of condescension.

Catrin responded with a little grunt of frustration. 'Right,' she said, knowing she was very much rowing against the tide here. 'How about we forget the cowboy thing and get on with it.' She strode forward.

'Lead on Mulan.'

Catrin had taken three steps but stopped without looking round. 'That's not... it's a different culture... nothing remotely...' She closed her eyes, breathed in. No, it wasn't worth it. 'Yeah, good. I'll be Mulan. Let's go.'

Behind her, Rhys started singing the dwarves' work song from *Snow White*.

'Hi ho! Hi ho!'

Catrin put her head down and kept walking.

They took the second of the two paths into the trees, one that seemed to point in the right direction on the compass. Within ten steps, they were under the dense canopy of evergreens, with moss and desiccated dead branches underfoot, but at least there was a path to follow. Though it was nothing more than a foot-wide strip where the moss and grass had thinned from traffic and the pine needles sparser. They negotiated a couple of fallen trees, but neither of them spoke. The woods seemed to demand silence. Reverential, like a chapel or a cathedral.

What wind there was wafted the high tops of the canopy above, sending down a sibilant message. But there was no physical sense of the breeze here deep on the floor of the wood. Here it was silent.

Like walking through the ranks of a petrified army, thought Catrin.

These were new trees but in an ancient wood. School had taught her the Arthurian legends about sleeping legions waiting for a call to come back to life. They'd sounded like nonsense to her then. Since then, *Game of Thrones* had made the screen. Irrelevant fairy tales they may be, but now, here, deep in the forest, it wasn't so difficult to believe that something else might be here.

A sleeping beast.

The path wound left and right, up and down until a light patch appeared through the trees. A clearing, probably never planted, possibly a fire break or even a glade, like the one that Andrew Geary had been murdered in.

'I see something,' Catrin said.

And within fifty yards they were upon it. A patch of grass with open sky above, trees all around except where a gate in one corner led to a muddy track which must have been used to bring the caravan to this spot.

The vehicle sat in one corner of the clearing, starkly incongruous, like an alien spaceship on a strange planet. It had a curved front end and a more upright back. Breeze blocks and railway sleepers firmed up the surface for parking and blocked the wheels. Blue water pipes snaked towards the gate and beyond. It wasn't a big vehicle, just two windows and a door. Rough stock fencing with wooden posts and wire made up a perimeter against deer or whatever else lived in the wood. Behind it, to the left, the forest was but a few yards away. Behind the rear of the caravan, some twenty feet in under the canopy of trees, a small shed had been erected.

'My bet is an outside toilet,' Rhys said.

'If you want to find out, be my guest.' Catrin scrunched up her face.

They stepped out into the open space and walked around the fencing which enclosed a twenty-five-metre square patch with the caravan at its centre.

'Whoa, look at this.' Rhys pointed to something on the far side of the caravan. A rough wooden shelter housing a bicycle and, next to it, a yellow, mud-spattered dirt bike.

'Bingo,' Catrin whispered. 'Evel Knievel indeed.'

'Well done, Tonto.' Rhys grinned.

Catrin returned it. 'Never mind The Lone Ranger and Hi Ho Silver, we have a very dark horse here and his name is Tristan Daniels.'

CHAPTER TWENTY-FIVE

JESS EXCUSED herself to make a quick phone call while Warlow took in the surroundings. Everything looked groomed and polished, the walls power-washed clean of moss and lichen, the gravels weed free. The paintwork refreshed, all the windows clean.

Jess talked for no more than a minute and joined Mellings as she walked them across the crunchy gravel to the tastefully remodelled stable block. An FLM renovation, as an old friend would have called it. A friend who'd shared some bad cases with Warlow when he'd been in the Met and who took great delight in educating those who asked what FLM meant.

'A fucking lot of money,' she'd say. That officer, who clearly had a way with words, was now a superintendent in Birmingham with a special interest in media and communications.

A curtain twitched as they approached the block and the door opened before Warlow could knock.

'Mr Warlow,' Rob said. 'What are you doing here?'

'Crossing as many t's as is possible,' Jess said.

'Quick word?' Warlow framed it in a half whisper, implying it was pretty important.

'Of course.' Rob stepped aside to let the police officers in. Jess entered, but before he crossed the threshold, Warlow turned and thanked the FLO in a low voice. 'Thanks, uh, what's your first name?'

'Gina, sir,' she said with a smile that would win a lot of hearts and break a lot of others.

Rhys had better get a move on, thought Warlow.

'Okay, Gina. Ears open, eyes wide. Okay?'

She nodded and turned on her heels.

In Hopley's apartment, Warlow didn't bother sitting this time, but Jess accepted the offer of a seat.

'What can I do for you?' Rob asked.

Warlow took in the tasteful decoration before fixing his gaze on Hopley. 'This is a heads up. I thought you ought to know that we've just had a chat about the caution you and Andrew received.'

Rob missed a beat. 'Oh?'

'We have no choice,' Warlow explained. 'If it's material to the case. You understand.'

'Sure. All I was trying to do by not involving them was spare Ralph and Celia that extra bit of pain.'

Warlow nodded. 'Understandable. And we're pleased you brought all this to our attention. But the main reason I wanted to talk to you is that we could find no sign of a caution on any of Andrew Geary's records.'

Rob laughed. A sudden expulsion of air that stopped abruptly when he realised there was no punchline. 'What?'

'This is news to you?' Jess asked.

'Is this a joke?'

'No joke, Mr Hopley.'

Rob stared at the DI, his mouth working but with no words emerging.

Warlow stepped forwards. 'Are we to assume that this news is as much of a surprise to you as it was to us?'

'I don't understand. We were both cautioned. We were both at the police station. Andy and me.' Rob's earnest confusion left his mouth gaping.

'We know you were,' Jess said.

'But what you didn't know is that Andrew had his caution expunged,' Warlow added.

'Expunged? What does that mean?'

'It means,' Jess explained, 'That there is no longer any record of that caution on Andrew Geary's history.'

A series of expressions seemed to flash across Rob's face in rapid succession. Confusion, shock, bewilderment. 'How?' he whispered.

'Expensive lawyers, from the sound of it,' Warlow said.

Rob collapsed into a chair, staring at something on the engineered oak flooring invisible to everyone but him, blinking until he finally looked back up. 'I had no idea you could do that.'

'And Andrew hadn't told you?' Jess had her notebook out, pen in hand.

'No.' The confusion of before was yielding to something like relief. 'Wow, but that's… I mean knowing that is…' He shook his head as if to clear it. 'What we did was bad. I know that. They were just kids. We shouldn't have frightened them. It's a shit thing to do. And it's hung over me all these years. To think that I could wipe it off the record is…' His head drifted up towards the officers. 'Why the hell didn't he tell me?'

'That's something you're not going to get an answer to.' Jess said.

Rob's face became suddenly slack as the implication of her words sank home.

'And you've had no contact with Tristan Daniels since you've been down here?' Warlow asked.

'None. I didn't even know he was still around.'

'What about his sister? Did you know about her?'

'Know what?' Once again, Rob's face searched both Warlow's and Jess's expressions, looking for clues to what they were leading to.

Jess filled him in. 'She went off the rails. Drugs and alcohol when she was a teenager. And ended up attacking her father. Psychotic episodes, so the docs say.'

More slow blinks and a frown from Rob. 'That's... I had no idea.'

Warlow had one last question. 'Did you ever go with Andrew to Thailand?'

'No. Never. We talked about it, but for some reason or other it would always be too late for me to organise, get time off, you know. He loved it, though. Ralph had an office there.'

'He did,' Warlow said and let his eyes fall to the bandages on Rob's arm. They seemed less obtrusive than he remembered. 'How're the arms?'

'On the mend, thanks.'

'Good. You'll be staying around for a while?'

'For as long as you need me,' Rob said.

———

'So, what's your take?' Warlow sat back in the passenger seat as Jess gunned the engine of her Golf and drove around the little tree at the centre of the turning circle in the neat courtyard at Journey's End.

'For one thing, abduction is a bloody heavy-handed label for what seems to have been a fairly minor offence. They were kids.'

'Agreed.' Warlow clicked home his seat belt. 'We wouldn't do that today. Abduction shouldn't even be caution-able. Someone taking another person without their consent deserves a bloody hammer. But it doesn't sound like that's what happened here.'

'No.' Jess slowed down as she turned into the lane leading out of the property. 'Whoever ran the investigation felt the boys needed a lesson.'

Warlow nodded. 'A lesson they would have to live with. Unless you got rid of it with money and a sharp lawyer.'

The car slowed to negotiate a couple of deep puddles. 'Bit mean of the senior Geary not to have told Rob Hopley, though. I mean, if they were spending all that money, surely adding his name to a letter petitioning Dyfed-Powys to have the caution removed would not have cost a lot more.'

'Is that how it's done?'

Jess kept her eyes on the pot-holed lane. 'The phone call was a chat with a lawyer I know in Manchester. She's big in human rights. That's the sort of argument that's used. They try to persuade forces to delete cautions by issuing judicial review proceedings. It's a slow and laborious process apparently.'

Warlow shrugged. 'If it worked for Geary then I see no reason it wouldn't work for Rob if he tried now.'

'Something like that wouldn't be cheap, though. My Manchester lawyer friend doesn't get out of bed for less than two hundred and something an hour.'

'Jesus. Why don't they just put a mask on and hold a bloody gun.'

Jess snorted.

Dusk was an hour away as they turned out of the lane and onto tarmac road, but a golden rim of evening light lit up the sky in the far west beyond a bank of dark cloud, filling the world with afternoon light.

Something shot into the air off to their right, causing Jess to swerve the car before righting it.

'What the hell…'

'Stop the car!' Warlow said.

The car screeched to a halt. 'What's wr—'

Warlow was out of the door before Jess finished the sentence, staring up at the drone that, on being found, banked up, and away into the sky.

Warlow cupped hands around his mouth and yelled. 'Right, where are you? Come out now or you will regret it? My name is DCI Warlow. I can get thirty pissed-off Uniforms here in ten minutes. Believe me, you do not want them poking under hedges to find you.'

The drone banked right and descended fifty yards up the road.

'I know you're there, you bastards,' yelled Warlow. 'This is a police investigation. It is illegal to fly drones within fifty metres of a vehicle not under your control.'

Somewhere out of sight, a car engine started and the squeal of tyres taking off at a rate of knots in the opposite direction met Warlow's ears. Jess had her window rolled down and a grin on her face.

'I think they got the message, Evan. Along with the rest of the county.'

'Bloody vermin,' Warlow muttered. 'I swear if I see another drone at a crime scene I'll shoot the sodding thing down.'

'With?'

He was too angry to not answer and so said the first thing that came into his head. 'The lasers from my eyes.' He stood in the road, looking around, desperate for something else to yell at.

'I think I saw a windmill a couple of miles back. All you need is a lance?'

Warlow swung around ready to react to her quip, but common sense prevailed when he registered her stifling a giggle. 'Point taken,' he said. 'But you'd better keep the Quixotic references to us two. I don't want to have to explain where La Mancha is to DC Harries. He has enough trouble with Bristol and Birmingham.' He threw himself back into the car.

'One day he might surprise you.' Jess grinned as she drove off.

'Rhys? Oh, he surprises me every day. For example, today's revelation was how he tied his shoelaces on his own.'

Jess, still smiling, shook her head. 'He's alright.'

'Of course he is. His heart's in the right place. Just a foot higher than everyone else's. He's set for a stellar career. I mean he can do joined up writing for a start. That's more than many a sergeant I've come across.'

Jess shook her head. 'Were you always this crusty?'

Warlow sent her a sideways glance. 'Me, crusty? Nah. Soft as suet pudding in my younger days.'

'I don't believe that.'

'You should. Meek as a lamb I was. Geese were never booed. Trouble is that all melted away by the time I'd attended my second murder scene. Or was it my second traffic accident? Doesn't really matter. Take your pick.'

'But you do like some people, don't you?' She threw him an amused, mildly desperate glance.

'That's a big question,' Warlow mulled it over. 'People, in my experience, are overrated. Most are on the whole polite, even nice until something comes along that might give them an advantage over someone else. That's when nice buggers off on holiday and leaves naughty, or down-right shitty at home to look after the silver. So, not so easy to like on the whole.'

Jess chuckled.

'Of course, you get the odd decent one.' Warlow added the afterthought, but only after some considerable delib-eration.

'Are you in that bracket then? Decent?'

'I try. And family is different, obviously. My kids get the benefit of the doubt because of genetics. Other family members, on the whole, I like, or like-ish. Although the previous Mrs Warlow is the exception that proves the rule.'

Jess sent him a questioning glance, but he waved it away with a held-up hand and a little shake of the head before continuing. 'That's a can of worms for another day. But the boys, my boys, are fine. And colleagues are different, too. They're wading in the same neck-deep cesspool as I am. On the whole, they pass muster because we all smell the same crap day in, day out. So family and colleagues I can put up with. Most other people, I can take or leave. Preferably the latter.'

'My God, cut you in half and there'd be a circle spelling cynic all the way through.' Jess kept her eyes on the road, but her grin hadn't slipped.

Warlow adopted a prim tone. 'I find it helps not to expect too much from people, let's put it that way. Present company excepted of course. Trusting people is the last thing a DCI needs.'

They'd reached a better road. This one had lines down the middle splitting it into two lanes and everything. Jess turned on to it and headed back towards HQ. She laughed softly. 'Good to know you enjoy your work, Evan. And there you were six months ago contemplating retirement.'

'Not contemplating it, living it.' Warlow corrected her.

'Exactly. I still can't get my head around that.'

He turned back to look at the road. At least once a week, Jess sneaked in little 'why did you retire?' questions. Warlow was an expert at spotting them before they could develop into anything serious. 'I can see you're angling, Inspector, but I'm not taking the bait.'

'Why is that I wonder?'

'Some things are better left not discussed. One day, maybe. But today is not that day. Now, let's get back to thinking about the Gearys. Has anyone checked Fran Dee's travel arrangements on the day Andrew Geary died, I wonder?'

Warlow took out his phone and sent a quick text to Gil asking that very question.

CHAPTER TWENTY-SIX

'Oy!' The voice came from their left, from the woods near the outhouse. Catrin and Rhys turned as one to see a man standing there. He wasn't tall, not compared with Rhys, but then few people were. She took in the brown camouflage jacket, dark trousers, long hair, and bearded face. Barely recognisable from the photos she'd pinned up on the Gallery. But it was him. No doubt about it.

'Mr Daniels. Tristan is it?' she asked, going for jaunty pleasantry in tone.

'You're trespassing.' Daniels stated the obvious, but with a touch of menace attached.

'Mr Daniels,' Rhys said, 'I'm DC Rhys Harries, this is DS Catrin Richards. Sorry to disturb you—'

'You're trespassing. This is private land.' He repeated the mantra, his voice rough, heavily accented, rising and falling as anger built.

'We just wanted to ask you a few questions, that's all,' Rhys said.

'Questions, is it? Oh yeah, I know all about them.'

'Okay, good. That's good. Maybe you heard about

what's happened. Seen the police helicopter about the place?'

Daniels didn't answer. Instead, he glared back at them, his eyes unreadable in the shadows of the trees.

That was when Catrin noticed his right hand held something under a dirty piece of canvas. Hidden, but she immediately clocked it was long and straight and thin.

Rhys stood in front of her. Keen to engage, de-escalate the conflict. He'd done all the training. *Keep your voice steady, ask questions, listen, paraphrase if need be.*

'I see you've got a motorbike, Mr Daniels. Registered vehicle, is it?'

Catrin blinked. Inside her head a voice was screaming. *No, Rhys, No. Wrong approach. Wrong question.*

She had three seconds to assimilate these thoughts before Daniels lifted his hand and what it was holding, up. It looked odd. It had a bend in it for a start. Not much of one, but an angle that made it not entirely straight.

Not a stick then.

Something else. Something slightly weighted.

Rhys's eyes dropped to what Daniels was holding. He froze.

'This is my place,' Daniels said. 'My place. No one comes here. You shouldn't have come here. Big bloody mistake.' He brought whatever was under that canvas up to waist level and held it snugly against his hip, pointing the end at Rhys Harries's chest.

'Turn around and walk back the way you came.'

'Tristan,' Catrin said, 'This is not a good idea. Threatening a police officer—'

'You've got no right to be here. I don't have to speak to you.' Harsh words through gritted teeth.

'All that is true, but pointing a—'

Daniels stepped forward. 'Shut up. Shut up, turn

around, and start walking the way you came. Single file. And don't worry, I'll be right behind you.'

———

GIL FILLED Warlow and Jess in on what was happening when they got back. Explained about Catrin getting a call about Daniels' whereabouts and how she'd been keen to follow it up.

'No holding those two, is there?' Jess grinned.

Warlow phoned Catrin for an update, but she didn't answer. He thought nothing of it at first, remembering how patchy reception was out there in the dense woods. He'd give them fifteen minutes and try again.

Gil stuck a cup of tea in his hands as Warlow sat down to write up his impressions from the informal interviews that day. It helped, much as he didn't enjoy the process. What emerged from his assessment of those that he'd spoken to, from Iona Daniels to Celia Geary, was that whatever had taken place in that forest sixteen years ago had left a dark stain on a lot of lives. Dark enough for Ralph Geary to have striven to wash it out of his son's life like so much soiled linen. Dark enough to have destroyed a struggling family. Dark enough to have driven at least one member of that family over the edge.

Warlow was not a great believer in fate, and under that big umbrella he included coincidences. That the murder had taken place in the same glade screamed significance from every tussock of grass, swaying tree, and lichen-covered rock.

There had to be a link and the sooner they got eyes on Tristan Daniels the better.

6pm came and went.

He wandered over to Jess's desk. 'Why don't you go

home. Make sure that daughter of yours is looking after my dog properly.'

'What about you?'

'I'm hanging around. I want to speak to Catrin when she gets back.'

'Okay,' Jess said. 'You going to get your head down in the back room?'

'Probably.'

'A couple of cushions off the sofa in the coffee room make an acceptable mattress if needed.' She clamped her lips together in a sympathetic smile.

Warlow nodded. He already knew that. But it was gratifying to learn that Jess had got the "T-shirt". 'I doubt I will. Once they're back I'm off home.' Though he spoke the words they had a hollow ring. 'Nothing else to do here now.'

Jess grabbed her coat and left but only after having an assurance that they'd contact her if anything changed. Warlow wandered back to the office with Fran Dee still on his mind as an unchecked box.

Gil had rung the friend she supposedly had been going to stay with and confirmed that her story held water. But Warlow was left wondering how late Fran Dee could have left it before leaving London and still get to the woods at Brechfa at the time Andrew Geary was killed. It made little sense as a theory, but it was a thought. He wasn't convinced; the motorbike angle made it a complete fantasy. Still, she could have parked somewhere to avoid road cameras and done the last leg by train. It needed checking. He fired up the computer to look up when the evening trains from Swansea to Pembroke Dock got in.

Seven, then eight, then nine came and went.

No sign of Catrin or Rhys.

But Gil was still in the Incident Room.

'Why are you still here?' Warlow asked, when he walked through to find the sergeant still staring at a screen.

'Same reason you are. I let them go. I want to make sure they're okay. *Diawled bach.*'

Little devils indeed, agreed the DCI, translating Gil's oath automatically in his head. 'No phone calls or texts?'

'No.'

Warlow opened his mobile and sent Catrin another message. Did the same with Rhys's number. After five minutes more of staring at the phone and willing it to ping, he turned again to Gil. 'And they said the caravan was how far from the Daniels' property?'

'Half a mile at the most Catrin said.'

Warlow massaged the back of his neck. Sitting staring at a computer screen always made him stiff. 'What's her boyfriend's name again?'

'Craig Peters.'

'See if you can get him on the phone.'

While he waited, Warlow walked to the Gallery and stared at the satellite image of the forest and the old Daniels' place: Ffrwd Y Dderwen. 'What is it you're not telling me,' he muttered.

Gil called over to him, phone held up in his hand. 'Craig Peters,' he said.

Warlow took the handset. 'Craig, Evan Warlow. Now listen carefully. Do you and Catrin share things on your phone? Music, that sort of thing?'

'Uh, yeah.'

'Find my phone app?'

'That too.'

'Are you sober? Can you drive?'

'Yeah.'

'Where are you. At home?'

'Yes.'

'Where is that?'

'Tumble.'

'Good. Can you meet me in HQ car park in twenty minutes and bring your phone with you.'

'What's this about?'

'We need to find Catrin's phone.'

Craig laughed. 'Don't tell me she's lost it.'

'Has she lost it before?'

'No. She doesn't lose things. Got it nicked once, but we got it back. Has she lost it though?'

'Something like that,' Warlow said and decided not to expand the explanation. Best to leave Craig in the dark for now. 'Twenty minutes, okay?'

———

GIL AND WARLOW were waiting for the Traffic officer when he arrived in a red Jaguar XE. Obviously, a Traffic officer who took his work home with him. He was a rangy lad, much younger and taller than Warlow; much, much younger and fitter than Gil. Par for the course on both counts.

Warlow introduced himself.

'I know who you are, sir,' Craig said.

'Of course, the Llyn Llech Owain case. How could I forget.'

Craig grinned.

'Did you check your phone for where Catrin's is?' Warlow hadn't asked him to do this, but if he'd have been in Craig's position, it would have been the first thing he'd done after getting a phone call from a senior officer asking about your detective girlfriend's phone.

'Yes. It's in the middle of nowhere. What's this about?' Craig's open face registered a vague suspicion now. When he'd arrived, he'd assumed that this had all been his girl-friend's doing. But doubt was creeping in.

'Quicker and easier we explain in the car,' Warlow said. 'Alright if we go in yours? You are the trained driver, am I right?'

'The Jag's not a pursuit vehicle,' Craig said half smiling.

'Doesn't matter. You drive.' Warlow started walking towards where Craig had parked. Better that he was occupied when they explained what was going on. He was less likely to panic that way. Warlow took the passenger seat, Gil in back.

'Where is she then?' Craig asked, as they pulled out of HQ. 'Why isn't she coming with us?'

'She's meeting us there,' Warlow said.

'And where is that?'

'Wherever her phone is.'

'What?' Craig asked.

'I want you to listen to what I'm going to say now but concentrate on your driving, is that clear?' Warlow said.

'Yes, sir.'

Warlow half turned to face Craig and spoke calmly and succinctly. 'We don't know where Catrin or Rhys Harries are. They went out to look for a suspect hours ago. We haven't heard from them since. Her phone is receiving text messages, but she's not responding. But we can find her phone with yours, correct?'

To his credit, Craig didn't slam on the brakes, or yell, or scream. He threw Warlow the one glance to make sure that this was not some kind of elaborate wind-up. The look on the DCI's face was enough to dispel that thought in an instant. It was then that Warlow saw Craig's eyes widen and his breathing speed up as fear made his adrenals spurt.

'We should be able to, yes,' he said.

'Right,' Warlow turned back to face front. 'Now, show us how fast this thing can go.'

CHAPTER TWENTY-SEVEN

THEY'D COME equipped with torches but the way was treacherous. Trips and stumbles seemed to happen every twenty yards.

At least the rain was holding off.

They used Craig's phone as a direction finder, but within a hundred yards of leaving the road where they'd parked the Jag, Gil was cursing his inappropriate footwear.

'You didn't say this would be a bloody cross-country run,' he muttered when his foot splashed into a puddle. Again.

'We'll get Rhys to clean them when we find the little bugger.' Warlow deliberately chose the word when, not if. He could sense Craig's anxiety in the way the younger man pushed the pace.

The torch beams picked out shapes on the track. Once, Gil stopped and pointed to where two yellow pinpoints of light stared back at them through the trees.

'Deer,' Craig said.

'Or a fox,' Warlow added. 'Not human, that's for certain.'

Bushes and trees loomed out of the darkness as they

picked their way along with the torchlight lighting up the path. Warlow's socks squelched as he walked. But Catrin's phone lay somewhere ahead of them and a wet foot was the least of his worries.

They sensed, rather than saw, the clearing when they arrived at it. But when they moved in closer, Warlow noticed the dark shapes of buildings outlined against the already inky sky and felt a sudden coldness in the open air above them. Warlow's torch picked up the blackened, burnt-out, side of the house. Gil's alighted on the doorway into the better, preserved side.

At Warlow's instruction, they turned off their torches and stood together in a huddle, speaking in hushed whispers. There was still some light from Craig's phone and its locator app. It illuminated Craig's face, rendering it drawn and anxious as he studied the screen. 'It's here somewhere. Within twenty yards.'

'Try ringing it,' Gil said.

Craig's fingers moved across the screen. The men listened.

'It should ring,' Craig said.

But they heard no ringtone.

'Maybe it's on silent,' Gil offered.

'Then it should still vibrate,' Warlow said.

'I can hear something.' Craig tilted his head, zoning in. 'Yeah, definitely a buzz.'

Gil turned to Warlow. 'Can you hear anything?'

The DCI shook his head. 'Younger ears.'

Craig walked around the side of the building. Warlow and Gil followed, torch beams back on but aimed in a tight circle at their feet. The Traffic officer got to his knees, parting the grass with one hand, patting the ground with the other. 'Here. I've found it,' he said, his voice a triumphant whisper. 'Face down, on silent. No wonder she isn't answering,' he tutted.

'I doubt that's an accident,' Warlow said. 'My guess is she dropped it deliberately. So it wouldn't be found if she was asked to give it up.'

Warlow looked back at the house. Something red flickered at a top window. A flame, or a moving beam. Red for someone who wouldn't want their vision disadvantaged by the excess stimulation of a white light. In case they had to make a run for it.

'Time we revealed ourselves, agreed?' Warlow looked around.

Craig and Gil nodded.

'Go on, Craig, you do the honours.'

Craig stood up. 'This is the police! Make yourselves known!'

His voice shattered the silence. Several things happened at once. Shouts and banging started up to their left. It came from a breeze-block building with a shut door. Behind him, Warlow saw the glimpses of red in the upstairs room dance wildly.

'Craig, is that you?' Catrin's voice, surprised and relieved, muffled but identifiable.

'Craig, we're here. Over here.' Rhys's voice followed by fists thumping on a metal door. Gil and Craig moved towards the sound, but Warlow grabbed Craig's arm.

'She's fine. I need you with me. Gil can manage.'

For a second it looked as if he might object, but something in Warlow's face brought the PC into focus.

Warlow pointed a finger. 'There's a light on at the top. We've spooked him. Let's spook him some more. I see only two ways in or out. You watch the side that's burnt. I'll go to the front.'

Craig glanced over to the generator house where Gil was attending to the door, but as soon as Warlow moved, he moved too.

All semblance of subterfuge had evaporated with

Craig's call into the night. No sense in subtlety now. Warlow banged on the front door. 'Tristan, we know you're here. Come out now. This doesn't need to get any worse.'

From inside something metallic slid. *A ladder*, thought Warlow.

He banged on the door again.

'Tristan. It's the police. Don't make this hard for us.'

There came the slap of feet on a floor. Some awkward banging. 'Tristan!' Warlow yelled.

'Oy!' Another shout, this time from Craig. A grunt, a squeal. A lot of swearing.

'Fuck off! Get off me! This is my house!'

Warlow ran around the building. Craig had his knee on the back of a struggling body. A face-down head under a mass of black hair whipped back and forth.

Rhys, Catrin, and Gil were hurrying through the dark towards them. All intact, all keen to help.

Rhys knelt to help quell the writhing Daniels, not being too gentle about it either.

'Lie still,' Rhys ordered. 'Lie still or this will not go well for you.'

'Lost your phone again, I see,' Craig said through gritted teeth, grinning at Catrin.

'She lost nothing,' Warlow said. 'Let it go and kept it on silent, If I'm not mistaken. Quick thinking, Sergeant.'

Catrin nodded.

'Rhys, you in one piece?'

'Yes, sir.'

'Right, someone get the uniforms out here and let's get the ball rolling.'

————

It was almost midnight by the time Daniels was arrested and taken to Ammanford station to the custody suite.

Warlow decided not to interview immediately. Daniels had been drinking and they had twenty-four hours to play with. Best to give him time to sober up and give Povey's crime scene ants a chance to crawl over the property and the caravan.

But Warlow wanted to know about what had happened to Catrin and Rhys. No point letting this wound fester. They sat in the Incident Room for a debrief, fresh tea in mugs. Craig Peters included as a special guest.

Catrin did most of the talking. Rhys sat, subdued.

'He came out of the woods holding this thing in his hand. It was covered up. I…' she glanced at Rhys, 'We, assumed it was a weapon.'

'Weapon?' Warlow asked.

'A gun. I knew that the senior Daniels had a shotgun licence. I wasn't sure what happened to the gun when he died.'

Warlow nodded. 'An informed decision then.'

Gil had his phone out. He'd taken some snaps of the generator house, the door, and some discarded material found on the outside. 'Is this the canvas you saw?'

Catrin studied the image. 'Could be. But we need to get you a better phone with a decent camera, Gil.'

Rhys was staring at his mug. 'He frogmarched us to the generator hut, shut the door, and locked it.'

Gil had other pictures. Of what had been jammed across the door to lock it. A foldable shovel, three or four feet long with a thin, extendable handle that looked suspiciously like the barrel of a shotgun. 'This may be what he used. The canvas bag was on the floor beneath it.'

'Not a gun, then?' Rhys said.

'You weren't to know that,' Gil said.

'I do now.' Rhys looked crestfallen. 'I think it was the shovel he had under the canvas. I think he held it at the blade end and pointed the handle at us. I should have—'

'No you shouldn't.' Warlow's words emerged sharper than he'd meant them to but full of feeling and urgency. 'You assume that it's a gun until proven otherwise.'

'But he tricked us with a bloody shovel,' Rhys had reddened, his expression sour. 'I wondered about it. I wanted to—'

Warlow shook his head. 'Don't even think about that. You had no way of knowing that wasn't a gun. Did he say it wasn't?'

'He didn't say it was,' Catrin said.

'No,' Warlow spoke in a low rumble. 'But you assumed, rightly, that it could be. And if it had been, and Rhys had played the hero, I could be on the way to the Heath for another dose of Tiernon with you two lying on slabs. Neither of you take any blame for anything, is that clear?'

Rhys looked up. It was obvious he'd been expecting a dressing down from Warlow. Or at the very least, some derision from Craig. But the Traffic PC had gone very pale on hearing Warlow's words.

'Get home, Get some sleep. I want us here at eight thirty, Daniels in the interview room by ten. Now finish your tea and bugger off,' Warlow said.

He stood up, still holding his mug, and walked out to the SIO room, with one look back as he got to the door.

The others stood clustered around Gil's phone, staring at the photos he'd taken.

No one was laughing.

The last thing Warlow saw before he shut the door was Craig Peters shaking Rhys Harries's hand with as earnest an expression as he had ever seen. In his face, Warlow read the lines of a man who had just woken up to realising what might have been and was grateful to a fellow officer for having taken the right course of action.

Gil clapped the DC on the shoulder, too. For good measure.

Sometimes, doing nothing was as good as doing everything.

Warlow sat and let out a huge exhalation of breath. He'd never say it to the two young officers but that had been a close thing. The kind of situation that could go south at the drop of a hat. All it took was a sudden silly movement, or the wrong word spoken, or the wrong gesture made. And it would have been his fault.

And yes, it wasn't a gun. But it could have been.

He'd sent them there. The buck stopped with him. These were the moments that scared him. More than any violent encounter. More than poison pen letters and threats from the Geoghans. His own safety was something he at least had control over. But concern over others coming to harm in the course of doing his bidding was the real burden of command. Warlow recognised that this fear was, in its way, a healthy one. If he ever lost it, ever abrogated the responsibility of his decisions, he'd walk out and never look back.

Some of his colleagues hid behind the need to get things done. Bringing offenders to justice got them out of bed in the morning. It drove Warlow, too. Yet, the greater good argument never sat easily with him. Crime was society's bane, and the police had a job to do, but top of his list was always protection of life and property.

Always.

His watch read five minutes to midnight. He had eaten little all day and he was bone tired. He thought about the sofa pillows and shook his head.

No. He'd go home to his own bed and get some sleep. Or at least try.

CHAPTER TWENTY-EIGHT

RAIN STARTED SPITTING at his windscreen as he crossed the county line into Pembrokeshire. A nice welcoming drizzle that hissed up from the back tyres of the cars in front and never seemed to clear no matter how hard the wipers swished. Spray turned the street lights and oncoming head-lights into moving starbursts. Not a pleasant journey.

He opened the door to silence. No swishing tail. No padding paws. Cadi was at the Allanby's.

It felt odd being in the cottage alone.

Ffau'r Blaidd.

Of course that had given the team much merriment when Rhys had told them all. Warlow the lone wolf's lair. But the name wasn't Warlow's choice. The old shepherd's hut and its surroundings were on ancient maps. Someone else had given it the name. From a time when wolves really posed a threat. Who the hell was he to think about changing it? And to what, anyway? Journey's bloody End?

He'd not had any human company stay there since he'd moved in, but it was the first time there'd been no other living creature there with him. He wondered if Cadi thought similar canine thoughts lying in a bed in a strange house.

'She'll be fine,' he muttered.

He made some toast and jam, and it barely touched the sides. Still hungry, he stripped off in the laundry room and took a quick shower. Ablutions completed, it should have been nothing more than a matter of course to get his head on a pillow and throw the light switch for sleep to come. But too much had happened that night for that particular fairy tale to come true.

Besides, his medication would undoubtedly have something to say about it. One of the side effects of the stuff he took was vivid dreams. And there'd be more than enough to fuel them tonight.

Head on the pillow, bedside lamp on, he stared at the ceiling, going through what the case had thrown up and what he hadn't got answers for. Talking to Tristan Daniels was the big one. Tomorrow's centre piece. But there were one or two loose ends that needed a stick poked at.

Geary's laptop loomed large. He wasn't expecting much, but an encrypted file remained a corner piece of the jigsaw that had metaphorically fallen under the sofa and until it was found and slotted into place, the picture would be incomplete.

Then, of course, there was the murder weapon. Wasn't there always? Since the attacker rode in on a motorbike, it seemed more than likely he'd brought the weapon with him and taken it from the scene. If they could find that they'd be more than halfway there.

Warlow shifted to lie on his side, listening to the rain on the roof, wondering if his team were lying awake too. They'd made progress but a great deal more to do remained. And, as always with random thoughts, Jess Allanby's question popped in. The one about why he'd given up the job in the first place.

In the dark, Warlow allowed himself a dry smile. There were good reasons why some people retired. And, huddled outside Ffrwd Y Dderwen this evening in the dark, not knowing what had happened to two officers under his care, were exactly the reasons the responsibility of the job got too much for some.

All completely understandable.

Everyone was a grown up in the police force. You didn't have to join, but if you did, then you signed up to interacting with the worst that modern society could offer. And if you entered the fray so be it. The training was supposed to make you better prepared than the average punter and Warlow had no problem with putting himself in danger. Yet some people couldn't handle the violence, others the stress of command.

Neither were the reason Warlow walked away.

His reasons were insidious and invisible. Ones no one could see or feel. Not even Warlow as yet. Real enough though. They'd not disappeared just because he'd rejoined the force. They were simply locked away until…

From somewhere outside in the night came the almost human scream of a fox. It didn't bother him; he was used to the noises of the countryside. But soon the call was answered. A fainter call further away. A hunting pair then. He counted the seconds, waiting for the squawk of a terrified chicken, or the mewling of a cat. Noises that meant that the foxes had found some prey.

But this night stayed silent.

And so, grateful that nothing had died on his watch, DCI Evan Warlow drifted off to sleep.

His dream was a shocker. He was on a plane and being asked to get off. The flight attendant kept telling him this was the address he'd given the booking agents. One on the outskirts of Perth in Western Australia. If he didn't deplane now – jump out in other words – he'd miss it. But he hadn't told his eldest son, Alun, he was coming. What if they'd gone out for the day? How would he explain turning up out of the blue? What about a parachute?

A recurring dream fed by the guilt he felt at not having visited for so long.

Not having visited at all, in fact.

First there'd been the cottage to build, now the job again with all its time-sucking attributes. His subconscious took its revenge by making him jump out of a plane from thirty thousand feet. A cheap flight, too. Parachutes were extra. Bastards.

The phone's ringtone pricked the balloon and jerked him out of the dream at a little after six in the morning. He reached for the mobile with a fumbling hand.

'Yeah,' he grunted, opening one eye to note that night had not yet given way to morning outside.

'Evan, sorry to wake you,' Povey's voice came through amidst a background of other voices.

'What's up?'

'We're at the Daniels' place. I'm outside the caravan under a tent. The weather is crap.'

'Thanks for the update.' Warlow flicked on the bedside lamp.

'I know it's early, but before your day begins, I thought you ought to see something.'

'Not the director's cut of Bambi, by any chance?'

Povey laughed. 'Anyone ever told you to consider stand-up, Evan?'

'No.'

'Good. If anyone does, you have my permission to strangle them before the suggestion gains any traction.'

'What have you found?' He opened both eyes.

'No, this is not anything I can explain over the phone. By the time you get here it'll be light. Then you can see and judge for yourself. I'll text you directions to the nearest access point. You'll still need to walk through the forest and a field. I suggest you bring some wellies.'

―――――

HE MET Povey at seven thirty-five on the soggy grass outside the fenced-off area surrounding the caravan. In the grey morning light, the sight of light-blue suited techs walking through the trees lent a surreal air to the scene. The forensic service changed suppliers occasionally and white Tyvek had morphed into baby blue.

'We've started examining the pathway back to the main house. Not much there, but there's a lot to see here.' Povey's breath plumed into the air.

'Okay. lead on.'

'Here.' She walked to a tent where a fold-up table had been set up and poured him a coffee from a thermos flask before topping it off with hot milk from another.

'Christ, it's like the bloody Holiday Inn. Any chance of a croissant.'

'Sarcasm this early in the morning is likely to lose you many friends,' Povey said. She held the cup while she waited for him to slip on some plastic overshoes.

He took the proffered cup, sipped it, and nodded. Warm, wet, and not half bad. He said as much as he followed Povey out, walking around the cordon they'd set, until they reached where the bikes were parked.

'The tyres on the dirt bike match those found at the scene. We've done a preliminary but we're going to take it to the lab for further testing. See if we can get an exact match.'

'Any sign of blood on the bike?'

'No. Not yet. But then he's hardly likely to have been on it when he attacked Geary.'

Warlow nodded. The same thought had occurred to him. 'But his clothes would have been in contact.'

'True.' Povey slid her hood down. Her nose was red from the cold. Warlow suspected his might be, too. 'But he might have washed the bike down,' she added.

'Have you found any clothes?'

'Lots. And I would not hazard a guess from just looking. You'll have to wait for spot testing. But it's inside the caravan itself I want you to see.'

It wasn't uncommon to find caravans like this in isolated spots in and around farms. Cheap, mobile accommodation for farm hands doing temporary work when it was needed. They generally looked the worse for wear and badly kept. But not this one. This one had no moss on its walls, no grimy windows. Not even any grease marks around the door handle. This one was virtually spotless.

'New?' Warlow asked.

'No, fifteen years old. Bought from a second-hand dealer in Llandysul.'

They'd marked another path to the vehicle and Warlow carefully followed in Povey's steps. The caravan door stood open to reveal the tiny space inside. Barely room for two. Warlow handed over his cup and took the gloves Povey held up in its place. He slid them on while the crime scene tech stepped aside for Warlow to go in. A mat had been laid just inside the door and this was where Warlow stood to survey the home that Daniels made for himself.

He knew instantly why Povey wanted him to see this. If the outside was spotless, the inside was immaculate. Not only tidy but furnished. Not expensively, not ostentatious, but comfortable and individual. Curtains on the windows, covers on the seats, both in materials of a pattern that Warlow doubted very much were something the caravan manufacturer had provided.

The table and wheel-back chairs in the middle of the tiny dining area didn't suit the small space and would not have looked out of place in a farmhouse kitchen. And then there were the photographs on the walls and on the table. The space really was tiny; Warlow could take one step and almost be at the table. But he didn't. He needed to respect the evidence. Instead, he shuffled to the end of the mat and leant forward to study the images.

The Daniels family from twenty and some years before. The four of them. Mother, father, son, and daughter. A quick glance around revealed no pairs. None of the grown-up children or the parents alone. All the photographs in frames, and all depicting a time before fate had trodden on them with its size fourteen hob-nailed boots.

Warlow glanced to the left into a little galley kitchen and beyond that a made-up bed with more photos on the walls.

Povey spoke from behind him. 'More like his grandma's parlour than a killer's lair, right?'

'But then there's no blueprint for one of those, is there,' Warlow answered. 'A killer's lair.'

'Bloody spooky if you ask me.'

'I presume you've searched it?'

'Not yet. We've concentrated on the surrounds. We'll be in here next. I wanted you to see it first.'

Warlow took some photos on his phone, then he stepped out and took back the coffee. 'So no murder weapon?'

'No.'

'When will you make a start here?'

'As soon as you leave. Should be able to get back to you by lunchtime.'

Warlow nodded his approval. It hadn't rained yet but more was forecast by mid-morning. He ought to get out of

Povey's way. But he took a moment to peer around at the trees that enclosed the caravan on all sides.

'Why do you think he chose here as opposed to parking it on the cottage grounds?' Povey asked, sensing his thoughts.

'Perhaps because he wanted to remember a life once lived and couldn't do it surrounded by all the nasty stuff. The dark memories that the house held.'

Povey sighed. 'At least you've got him in custody.'

'We do. They told you about how we found him?'

'Close call that.'

'Hmmm.' More a grunt than a snort. 'Time we found out what he has to say for himself, I think.'

Povey nodded. 'Rather you than me on that one, Evan.'

CHAPTER TWENTY-NINE

WARLOW PHONED Gil from the car.

'Everyone in?'

'They are. All wondering where the big cheese is?'

'Have they tried the giant freezer?'

After three, long, suspicious seconds, Gil asked, 'Why are you in such a good mood?'

'Because I'm turning out of Maccy D's on the Pensarn roundabout with an egg McMuffin in hand, having already been to Daniels' caravan for a chinwag with Povey. What better way to start any day? I'm sending Catrin some photos. Get her to post them on the Gallery. I'll be there in ten minutes.'

'You'll have had your coffee then.'

Warlow pulled up at the roundabout lights. 'Yes. But a mug of tea won't go amiss. Get Rhys on the case. He owes me at least that for scaring seven different colours of excrement out of us last night.'

'No sooner said. I might even stretch to a breakfast Hobnob.'

'You old charmer, you.'

By the time Warlow walked in the photos were already

posted up. Rhys handed him a mug of tea. Warlow took a sip, sucked air in through the mouthful like a sommelier and swallowed, keeping his eyes slit in concentration before nodding sagely.

'Not a bad effort. We ought to put you in mortal danger every week if this is what comes out of it.'

Rhys's attempt at laughter was half-hearted. 'I can't tell if you're being serious half the time, sir.'

'Good. All part of the training. Bullshit detection 101.' Warlow shrugged off his coat and stood in front of the board. 'I'm pretty sure you will have brought DI Allanby up to speed with an account of last night's entertainment.'

Catrin and Rhys nodded. Both with equal amounts of guilt on their faces.

Jess leaned a hip against a desk, arms folded, ankles crossed, looking miffed. 'You should have rung me.'

Warlow shook his head. 'No sense you losing sleep over it. I lost enough for the both of us. But if it makes you feel better, next time the kids balls it up, it's all yours.'

Rhys looked at Catrin, pointing to himself and then at her, mouthing, *Kids?*

Warlow considered both junior officers. 'This is a team piss-take. It's allowed. It's the price you pay. The truth is we draw a line under what happened here and now. As I've already said, you both did exactly the right thing. As for your bruised egos, hawk it up and swallow it down. Understood?'

Catrin and Rhys nodded. Catrin with an added expression of distaste at Warlow's word choice.

Behind them, Jess smiled.

Gil said, 'I thought the hawk it up and swallow bit was a bit visceral if you ask me. *Ych a fi.*'

Jess nodded in agreement. No translations needed for *ych a fi* which did an excellent onomatopoeic job.

Warlow shrugged. 'Right. While you lot have been

enjoying a nice chinwag in this temperature-controlled office environment, I've already been out on site. Povey's team are going over the caravan but from what I've seen, it says more about Daniels' mental state than any psychiatrist's report.' He turned and tapped the images that Catrin had posted. Were it not for the plastic walls and the caravan windows, they might have been zoning in on a typical Welsh farmhouse kitchen.

'Is he trying to relive the past, sir?' Catrin asked.

Warlow inhaled and held his breath while he considered the question. 'Recapture it, I'd say.'

'Reason enough for Daniels to lose it then on seeing the two people who scared the permanent daylights out of his sister?' Gil posed the question.

'There is that.' Warlow nodded without looking away from the images. 'Has he been fed?'

'Bacon and two eggs.'

'Solicitor there?'

'Just arrived.'

'Good.' Warlow walked towards the photograph of the room in the caravan, his eyes never leaving it. 'Then let's go over the plan of attack. Let's ease in nice and gently.' He pivoted back towards the team. 'Catrin, you're about the same age as his sister so why don't you and Jess have first crack. That means the four of us go up to Ammanford, Gil stays here to man the fort.'

———

IT WAS a half an hour journey to Ammanford along the A48 before heading east through Capel Hendre and Tycroes to the town itself. They'd shut the old station and moved to another featureless red-brick hangar on an industrial estate in 2001. A functional and characterless building, but one with more modern facilities.

At around ten o'clock in one of the purpose-built inter-view rooms, Catrin pressed the button on the dual tape recorder, waited for the long tone to end and did the preliminaries by the book.

'This is an interview with, state your full name please.'

'Tristan John Daniels.'

'State your address, please.'

'Ffrwd Y Dderwen, Brechfa, Carmarthen.'

'State your date of birth, please.'

'Eighth of August 1994.'

'I am Detective Sergeant Catrin Richards. Also present is Detective Inspector Jessica Allanby and Mr Daniels' legal representative. State your name for the record, please.'

'Sheena Briggs, solicitor.'

In the observation room, Warlow watched as Catrin stated time and date where they were and explained that she would give Daniels a form at the end of the interview explaining the procedure for accessing the recording. Then she cautioned him. So far, so squeaky.

Jess was sitting back from the table, letting Catrin take the lead as they'd agreed.

And so the dance began.

'Mr Daniels, can you tell us what you know about the death of Andrew Geary?' Catrin asked.

'Nothing.' Daniels sat, arms folded, face solemn. Next to him, Briggs, who was not a small woman by any stretch of the imagination, sat, eyes down on the pad on her knees, her clothes rustling alarmingly every time she moved.

'But you know Andrew Geary?'

'I met him once a long time ago.'

'But you knew he was dead?'

'I heard.'

'And where were you the night he died?'

Daniels hissed out some breath and shook his head.

'For the record,' Catrin said, 'Mr Daniels has not answered.'

Annoyed, Daniels looked up. 'I was at home. In the van.'

'Can someone confirm that?'

Daniels shook his head. Next to him, Sheena Briggs wrote something down.

Outside in the observation room, Warlow, Gil, and Rhys watched on the monitor.

'What time did you get back to the caravan that evening?' Catrin asked.

'I've been milking at Bryndu. Left there at about seven. They'll tell you.'

'They have. And how did you leave?'

'No comment.'

'We know you left on your motorcycle, Mr Daniels. We have two eyewitnesses from the farm.'

'No comment.'

Catrin wrote something in her notes. Daniels watched her with his chin downturned. 'And did you go directly back to the caravan?'

'No comment.'

Jess had a closed file on her desk. It was mostly full of crap she'd grabbed off the desk to bulk it out, but there were two items of interest in there. And it was these two photographs she took out and placed face up on the desk before sliding them towards Daniels.

'On the left is an image of the tyres from the dirt bike found in the shed outside your caravan. On the right is an image of imprints of tyre marks taken from the ground at the site where Andrew Geary was stabbed to death. They are a match. Do these tyres belong to your motorcycle, Mr Daniels?'

'No comment.'

'We have a witness who saw you on the bike that night, Tristan.' Catrin used his first name.

'No comment.'

Jess sat back but left the photographs where they were. Catrin leant her elbows on the desk. A smooth transition. Like clockwork. Catrin began again. 'You say you met Mr Geary once. When was that?'

'No comment.'

Catrin nodded. 'It's not something we need you to confirm because it's on the record. We know you met him in August 2004. That's when Andrew Geary and Rob Hopley were cautioned for taking and hiding your sister, is that correct?'

This time Daniels stayed quiet.

'Is that a no comment?' Muttered Rhys from behind Warlow in the observation room. The DCI said nothing.

'We've been to see Iona,' Catrin said.

On hearing his sister's name, Daniels, who had been slouching back, lifted his head up to glare at the sergeant. 'You need to leave her alone. She has nothing to do with this. You'll only upset her.'

Catrin shrugged. 'We don't want to bother her. We know she isn't well. But if you won't answer our questions, Tristan, what choice do we have?'

'She don't...'

Briggs leant in to whisper something in her client's ear. Whatever it was she said, Daniels didn't seem to like it. But he sighed and hunched back down into sulking-child pose.

'Iona remembered Hopley and Geary. She remembered a lot. But sometimes her answers aren't quite... straightforward,' Catrin said.

Daniels' mouth became a thin slash.

'She told us Geary had frightened her. Threatened her. Coerced her into silence.'

'Shut up.' Daniels' lips hardly moved when he spoke, but the threat was obvious.

'She's getting to him,' Rhys said. Someone opened the observation room door and motioned to the DC who left with an apologetic shrug in response to Warlow's annoyed glance. But within two seconds Warlow's eyes were back on the screen.

'You're making this difficult for yourself and for us, Tristan,' Jess said, reasonableness personified. 'Threatening two police officers last night does not look good on the charge sheet.'

'I didn't touch 'em.'

'It's an implied threat. You had what might have been a weapon in your hand—'

Daniels blew air out of the side of his mouth. 'It was a bloody shovel.'

Jess nodded at Catrin. She shuffled some papers and read something out. 'An imitation firearm means anything which has the appearance of being a firearm, whether it's capable of discharging any shot, bullet, or other missile. An imitation firearm is treated as a firearm for purposes of considering an offence.'

'It was a bloody shovel,' Daniels said again, slowly and with emphasis.

'Hidden under a piece of canvas and pointed at us as if it was a gun,' Catrin's eyes were brittle bright, fixed on Daniels. 'And then you locked us up in a shed full of fuel. Hardly the actions of an innocent man, Tristan.'

Briggs looked up. 'Do you have a question, Sergeant?'

'I've done nothing wrong,' Daniels said.

Briggs frowned. This wasn't in her script. She leant in again. Her clothes rustling like a Christmas parcel as she moved. Tristan flinched away. 'No comment, yeah, I heard you.'

'I did nothing wrong isn't the same as I didn't do

anything.' Jess eased forward. 'We know you were there,' she tapped the photos. 'Hard evidence. Tell us what happened. Did you lose your head? Who could blame you for wanting to hit Andrew Geary after what he did to—'

Daniels exploded forward, his chair screeching back across the floor. 'You have no fucking idea what that bastard did to us.'

Briggs, panic stricken, leant in once more. But Tristan rounded on her, glowering 'Shut up for fuck's sake.' When he turned back towards Catrin and Jess, he was trembling.

'Those bastards scared my sister. Scared a little girl to death. She was only six and I... I was scared too. Too scared to stop them. Too scared to protect her. My own sister.' Anger and frustration twisted his features, distorting his face into a mask of despair.

'We know. Iona told us about It.'

Tristan squeezed his eyes shut as if the word was a dagger into his heart.

'Tell us what happened the other night, Tristan. Just tell us the truth.'

His eyes shot open. 'The truth? Since when were you lot interested in the fucking truth. Don't make me laugh.' He shook his head again. 'Nothing happened. Nothing.'

Rhys tiptoed back into the silent observation room. He crept forward and tapped Warlow on the arm.

'Not now,' growled the DCI.

Jess was pressing Daniels now. Trying to wrong foot him.

'Were you in the forest two days ago on your bike, Daniel?'

'No comment.'

'Did you attempt to run my colleague, Detective Sergeant Harries, over?'

'No comment.'

In the observation room, Rhys spoke again. 'Sir, we've

just received Alison Povey's preliminary report on the caravan and Ffrwd Y Dderwen. You wanted me to tell you as soon as it arrived.'

Warlow threw him a look.

'Sorry, I—' Rhys puffed out his cheeks.

'Don't apologise. Right, let's look at it.'

CHAPTER THIRTY

WARLOW STOOD in the corridor and read Povey's preliminary report for the third time before picking up his mobile and punching the video camera logo under her name. She answered on the fourth ring and her face appeared on the screen, non-Tyvek framed for once. Short hair, glasses, minimal mascara. A different Povey, this one in a lab coat with a name badge.

Warlow balanced the phone on the inside of a window frame so that she could see him without the world spinning crazily. Which is what usually happened when he tried to hold the damn thing for a video call.

'I know what you're going to say, Evan, but I can't change it. I can't put anything in there that we haven't found.'

'But nothing? I mean… nothing at all? From what you and Tiernon said the killer should have looked like a bloody accident in a ketchup factory after the attack.'

'We've found no weapon, no blood, and the bike has thrown up nothing. Covered in mud and deer crap, but forensically, clean as a whistle.'

Warlow's sigh was a long and a deep one. 'Could he have buried his clothes?'

Povey gave him a defeated look. 'You've been to the forest. It's huge. That's like asking could there be fish in the sea. The answer is yes, of course he could. But we've found no sign of the earth having been disturbed. What we did find are pits where he's buried his own crap, but that doesn't count, other than to cause two of my techs to threaten resignation. But there is no evidence that he's tried to wash down the bike either.'

Warlow turned his head away to look out of the window at the huge Lidl next door.

'We both saw that crime scene, Evan,' Povey said. 'You know how much blood there would have been. Impossible that the perpetrator was not contaminated.'

'Hopley said it was too dark to describe what Daniels was wearing.'

Povey nodded. 'We found some clothes in a locker. A helmet and over-trousers someone riding a dirt bike through a muddy forest might wear. Stuff you'd clean once a month when it gets too stiff to pull over your legs and arms. Nothing there. Nor on the helmet, goggles, or bike. No sign of bleach, no puddles from a hose down. Because there would be if he'd tried to wash anything. He has running water from a farm a mile away.'

A pause followed. A big and pregnant one. Twins. Triplets even.

'I mean, you've got him in custody,' Povey added. 'Do you think he's a sophisticated enough killer to think all that through. Is he a plotter?'

Plotter. Grand word that, thought Warlow. A word that implied planning, which in his experience, happened rarely in murder. Especially in a dark wood where you would not have foreseen coming across your victim. Plotting needed forewarning so that you set a plan in motion. But to kill and get away with it you probably needed a five or even six warning, a cool head, and a ticket to Bolivia. You wouldn't try to hide away in a caravan in the middle of a Carmarthenshire forest and pretend a shit shovel is a shotgun when the police come round. That showed as much planning as an inkblot. From what he'd just seen in the observation room, Tristan Daniels failed to qualify as a plotter on all counts.

'But people are still on site?' The words sounded more needy than he wanted them to.

'They are and still looking. Still photographing. But we're pulling out today. The rain has wiped out anything incidental.'

'So there is still some hope?' Warlow aimed for irony but got nowhere near and ended up sounding desperate.

'There always is until the morbidly obese cisgender starts her aria.'

Warlow frowned, worked – or was it woked? – out what she was trying to say, nodded at her grin, thanked her, and rang off. He trudged back to the observation room where Rhys was still making the room live up to its label.

'Forensics found anything useful?' he asked, as Warlow entered.

'Fanny Adams.' Warlow sighed. 'What about here?'

'We're back into no comment territory. Little Miss Whisper has Daniels back on track.'

'Right. Time to shake the tree then. Rhys, call a break and offer Daniels and his representative some tea or a soft drink while I have a chat with Catrin and Jess.'

———

TWENTY MINUTES LATER, they were back in the interview room, this time with Warlow at the helm and, for a change, taking the reasonable policeman role. One he wasn't that used to, but needs must.

'See, the thing is, Tristan, we know you were there,' Warlow began. 'You've seen the photos, the tyre marks. We've got brilliant people who will swear in court that these imprints are from the bike on your property. But you don't have a licence, do you?'

'I don't need one.'

'Because you only ride the bike in the woods, right?'

Daniels didn't answer, but his little smirk did the talking for him.

'Fine. We can let that one go. Who did you get it from by the way?'

'Friend of mine. Works as a *gwas* over in Peniel.'

'*Gwas*?' Jess asked.

'Farmhand,' Warlow explained. 'We need to get you on that Welsh immersion course, Inspector Allanby. *Gwas*, just like Tristan here.' He smiled at the prisoner. 'Cash only I expect. No paperwork.'

Daniels shrugged.

'Say we let all that go. That leaves us only with, what was it, DI Allanby?'

Jess took out a sheet of paper from her file and read. 'Threatening behaviour, kidnapping two police officers, and murder.'

Warlow whistled. 'Not much change from a fiver there, Tristan.'

'It was only a sh—'

'A shovel, yes. But a jury won't see that. They'll see you deliberately cheating and lying all the way through this interview.' Warlow turned to Jess. 'How many years is that, Detective Inspector Allanby?'

'Thirty plus.'

Warlow nodded. 'That's a long time.'

Daniels' face flushed. 'I did nothing to those two.'

'So you keep saying. But what that really means is you did something, isn't that right?'

'No comment.'

'The person I'm most worried about is your sister. I know you visit her. Maybe you're the only person who does. But you can say goodbye to all that when you're inside. And she's going to feel even more betrayed than she does now. Losing her mother, then her father, and now her only brother. But if you cooperate, we can arrange something. A supervised visit perhaps.'

Daniels growled out another denial. 'I've done nothing wrong.'

Warlow shook his head. 'She won't understand that. She'll think you've forgotten her. And I know you love her, Tristan. I've been in your caravan. Seen the photos. Nice place by the way.'

Anger flared in his eyes. 'You have no right.'

'We have every right. And we'll keep looking and probing and turning everything upside down until you tell us the truth.'

Briggs began to lean in, but a look from Daniels stopped her in mid-rustle. A significant feat given the gravitational forces involved. Warlow could feel the mental rumbles, the deep stirrings of a dam cracking.

Half a minute of silence went by until the first trickle of words came out as a mumbled phrase from Daniels' mouth.

'She told no one all of it.'

Warlow steepled his hands and leant forward, elbows on the table to show Daniels that he had his undivided attention. 'All of what, Tristan?'

'All of what happened.'

They had to strain to listen. Warlow wanted to tell Daniels to speak up, but he held his tongue, not wanting to disrupt the moment.

'He had this mask on,' Daniels said. 'A horror thing. And he said some things to her. Things a little girl shouldn't hear. Things she didn't understand, not then. But she did later. When she was old enough. He said he'd come back and do all those things to her if she ever told anyone. So the only one she told was me. And I had to explain it to her. As best as I could because I was only ten. But I knew what he meant.'

Next to Warlow, Jess opened her mouth, but he waved his hand under the desk to quell her. This was no time to stop the flow.

Daniels' mouth looked hard and bitter. 'Kept all that inside for years. Me and her. I lived with it, but it poisoned her. Poisoned her against my father and the world. My mother would have killed Geary if she'd been alive. My father... my father had no idea what to do or how to do it. He was only glad that she hadn't been touched. But she had.' Daniels tapped his head. 'In here.'

'What happened two nights ago, Tristan?' Warlow asked.

Daniels looked up into Warlow's face with an expression of undisguised disdain. 'I saw them in their fancy get up. Like a pair of big bloody kids on their shiny bikes. I saw them but they didn't see me. I've been riding these woods for years. I know all the trails. I recognised them because they've been back once or twice over the years. Always laughing, always with the best kit. As if what happened meant nothing to them. And then they pitch up in their posh bloody gear just a few yards from where I was. Laughing and joking, like they didn't have a care.

'I watched them ride to the glade and then something broke inside me. They even set up camp where... where it happened. I couldn't help myself. It was as if they were rubbing my nose in it. They set up camp and then left the tents to watch the sunset.' He snorted. 'A bloody sunset, I ask you. Walked up the glade and through the trees to the hill like a pair of stupid kids. I waited until they'd gone and then I rode in and all over their expensive tents and bikes. I don't know why. It was as if all those years of pain wanted to find a way out. I didn't try to hide it. The bike was loud and they saw me so I rode off. It was almost dark then. I didn't want to see them. I hated them but I never wanted to speak to them because I was too scared of what I might do.'

'So you rode off?' Warlow asked.

'I rode off and left the bastards to it. I ruined their bikes and their shitty tents but I didn't touch either of them and that's the God's honest truth.'

CHAPTER THIRTY-ONE

THEY WENT over it a dozen times, but each time Daniels stuck to his story. He signed a statement to that effect and went back to the cells. At five o'clock, Warlow got Catrin to apply for a twelve-hour extension of custody.

On the way back to HQ at Carmarthen, Warlow rang Povey again on the off chance they'd found something and got the same answer as before.

Zilch. Sweet FA. De nada.

The team reconvened in the Incident Room to dissect Tristan Daniels' statement.

'How do you see it, Gil?' Jess asked.

'I don't buy the trash the tents story. Hopley's version of it has a more truthful ring.'

'What about the lack of blood?'

Gil shrugged. 'He's a farmhand. They have overalls for the muck work. More than one pair. He may well have worn something like that and, realising what he'd done, thrown it into a stream. Christ, thrown himself into a stream, or buried the clothes and the murder weapon. We'd never know.'

'The murder weapon,' Warlow muttered. 'A bloody big knife with a serrated edge. Where is it?'

Rhys, who'd been studying his screen, pivoted in his chair and said, 'Umm, I may have something on that?'

Something moved in the pit of Warlow's stomach and everyone turned towards the DC.

He looked up at them as blush faced as ever. 'The techs I've been liaising with finally opened the encrypted files on Geary's laptop and sent it over. I've been looking at it for the last ten minutes. There's some weird stuff on here.'

'Porn?' Catrin asked.

'A bit, though I've seen a lot worse. There's other stuff...' Rhys's voice sounded odd. 'The tech guys said I should be careful.'

'Careful?' Catrin repeated.

But Rhys didn't answer directly. 'There are photos of massage parlours in Bangkok specialising in teenage girls. But there's hunting stuff too and a section on knives.' He looked up, his boyish face troubled. 'It might take me a few minutes to go through all this.'

'I'll give you a hand,' Catrin said.

'Me too,' Gil said.

Rhys nodded, relieved.

'Okay, twenty minutes?' Warlow said.

He sat with Jess and a fresh cup of tea. The HUMAN TISSUE FOR TRANSPLANT box was raided and they munched a biscuit while they waited for the rest of the team to comb through the files.

'What's your honest opinion of Daniels?' Warlow asked after a while.

Jess arched her back and tilted her head until a couple of clicks seemed to ease the tension. 'Not sure what to make of him. Like his sister, he's damaged goods. Less damaged maybe, but still damaged.'

Warlow picked up a folder and leafed through the photos Povey had sent over. 'The caravan was something else. He's attempting to recapture a better time.' He picked out a snap of a polypropylene bulk bag taken on the perimeter of the site with a local builders merchant's logo on the side. These usually came on the back of lorries and held eight hundred kilos of sand or chipping. Warlow had ordered and emptied his fair share during his cottage renovations. But this one did not contain sand. It was full of bottles. Mainly beer, but the odd cheap vodka bottle as well. 'Looks like he's following in his father's footsteps.'

'So he was a powder keg, and the spark comes along in the form of Hopley and Geary. But the important question is do I think we've got enough to charge him?'

Warlow sighed.

Jess shook her head. 'There's always the unregistered bike and what he did to Catrin and Rhys. But as for the murder, I'm not sure the CPS would go with it.'

She was right and though these were not the words he wanted to hear, Warlow was grateful for her saying them because they mirrored his own feelings on the matter. And powder keg was probably the best description he'd heard of a mind like Tristan Daniels'. There were others that might fit. Tinderbox or volcano, to name but a few. But powder keg, given the ferocity of the attack that had killed Andrew Geary was the best. It suggested a conflagration. And to stab someone twenty or more times required quite a bit of fire in the veins.

It took longer than twenty minutes for Geary's file to be dissected. Jess eventually drifted back to her desk and after half an hour Warlow stopped looking at his watch. No point hassling his team. They were doing their jobs as quickly as they could. These things took time. But he couldn't help jumping up when he was finally called.

'Sir,' Gil announced.

Warlow rejoined the others. The three of them were huddled around Rhys's desk. All wore serious, troubled expressions. Like they'd smelt something bad.

'Not a list of his favourite sitcoms then I take it,' Warlow said.

'No,' Rhys answered. 'We think you should look through it yourself, sir, at some point. But there's some bad hunting videos on there. Animal stuff that I wish I hadn't seen. And some videos from the massage parlours… you know the score.'

'You mentioned weapons,' Warlow said.

'Andrew Geary liked guns and knives. Lots of photos. One looks to be of interest,' Gil said.

Rhys swivelled the laptop around and Warlow gazed at several photographs of a black hunting knife with a serrated edge.

'There's a sequence of him packing this away in a suitcase and then unpacking the suitcase with a backdrop of a London skyline,' Catrin said,

'You mean he carried this around with him?' Jess asked.

'It looks like it. There are more photos of him on hiking trips and on the bike with the knife in his hand. Seems it was part of his outdoor gear.'

Warlow felt a tingle dance over the back of his neck. 'Get a photo of that to Tiernon. Ask him if it fits the bill for the murder weapon.'

Rhys nodded.

'If it does, how does that help?' Gil asked.

Warlow stood up, brain fizzing. 'What if he had it when Daniels rides in like bloody Clint Eastwood on a motorbike. Being the macho idiot that he is, Geary has it in his possession when the attack happens. But Daniels is well protected. Helmet, heavy riding gear. What if Geary is disarmed in the altercation, or drops the knife and Daniels picks it up, I don't know. Either way, Daniels gets hold of it. Once it's in his possession he does the deed and then takes the knife away with him on the bike.'

The team sat, mulling it over.

'Alternative scenarios?' prompted Warlow.

'Could be that someone else had the knife all along,' Catrin said.

Rhys looked around at the others for clarification. 'Like who?'

'You mean Fran Dee?' Jess asked.

Catrin shrugged. 'She lived with Geary. She, of all people, might have known about it.'

'I thought she travelled down the day after everything happened?' Rhys piped up.

Catrin walked to the Job Centre and tapped a sheet of paper. 'No. She was on the way to a girlfriend's house for the weekend. She was on the road. We still need to find out if and where her car was flagged on ANPR.'

'What about the motorbike?' Jess asked. 'How do we explain that if you put Fran Dee in the frame?'

'We can't,' Warlow mused. 'Not yet. We have the tyre match but Povey also told me that those tyres are bog-standard. So not necessarily Daniels' bike. All we can say is that the bike at the murder scene had Yamaha tyres, as did Daniels'.'

'It's a bit of a stretch, sir,' Gil said. 'I don't see Fran Dee on a bloody big dirt bike.'

'No, neither do I. But stranger things.' He stood in front of the team, looked at his watch, and glanced out of a window at the growing darkness. 'Okay, I'm going to call a halt to things. Forensics need a bit more time, and now that we have a possible murder weapon, I'm going to suggest extending the search from the glade along all cycle tracks to the Daniels' property and the caravan. Get the dogs in and metal detectors.'

Gil made a noise like a small horse. 'That's going to take a lot of manpower.'

'It is. But we have no choice. Daniels could have got rid of it anywhere along that route. We'll see if he'll cooperate with showing us his supposed route home. We need to look at all possibilities.'

'What about Dee, sir?' Catrin asked.

'Dig into her background. Any links with motorcycling. Any reports of stolen dirt bikes in the area.'

'I know she cycles. There's photos on Geary's laptop of her and him out and about,' Rhys said.

'Good. So, she can handle two wheels. Right, go home and get some rest. We'll start this in the morning.'

'What about you, sir?' Gil asked. 'You staying or going?'

'Thought I'd call in to Journeys End just to see what Fran Dee knows about Andrew's interest in knives and Thailand again. The FLO has an inventory of what Andrew Geary left in the house whilst he and Hopley were on the bike trip?'

Gil nodded. 'Nothing about a knife.'

'Want me along?' Jess asked.

'No need. I'll brief you if there's anything worth shouting about.'

Jess nodded and unhooked her coat from behind the door.

'Say hello to the girls for me,' Warlow said.

Jess waved some fingers at him as she walked through the door. 'Will do.'

Warlow reached for his own coat and slid one arm in.

'Leave this until morning, sir. You look like an extra from Dawn of the Dead,' Gil said.

The DCI snorted. 'Well now, as my once teenage sons kept telling me when they'd come in at sod o'clock in the morning, you can sleep when you're dead, Dad.'

Gil responded with a slow nod. 'And as my wife keeps telling me, careful what you wish for.'

CHAPTER THIRTY-TWO

A DIFFERENT FLO opened the door and walked out to meet Warlow once he'd parked up at Journey's End. Older and taller than Mellings and carrying a bit more weight. She flashed her warrant card, gave her name as Chant and explained, in response to Warlow's question, that PC Mellings was on again in the morning. She also had a message from Fran Dee.

'Fran's asked if you'd talk to her in the guest block. Mr Hopley's rooms.'

Warlow's eyes constricted. 'Any reason?'

'I explained you'd prefer not to talk to her in front of the Gearys and she asked if Hopley could sit in. Said she'd feel more comfortable with some support.'

'Support? Why does she need support?'

Chant gave Warlow a brief smile that suggested he knew why. He didn't let on, so she filled in the blanks. 'I think she finds you a little intimidating, sir.'

'Am I intimidating, PC Chant?'

'I'd rather not answer that question, sir.' Her smile didn't slip.

'Good answer. You'll go far. I'll shout if I need you.'

Warlow walked around the main house, past the turning circle tree and knocked on the door to Hopley's stableblock rooms. When it opened, he found Fran Dee for once not dressed in an oversized sweater and jeans but in jogging bottoms, trainers, and T-shirt.

'Sorry to disturb your evening,' Warlow said, as she stood aside to let him in. Across the room, Hopley stood up. Most of the bandages were gone from his arms, as was the sling.

'DCI Warlow,' he said by way of greeting. 'Can I get you anything? A beer? Cup of tea?'

'No thanks. This won't take that long.'

Fran sat down with a nervous smile. 'I hope you don't mind that I've asked Rob to be with me.'

'Your choice,' Warlow said. He preferred they talked alone, but if this proved to be a problem, he could always bring her in. For now, he saw no reason to object.

'How's it going?' Rob asked. 'The investigation I mean.'

'Progressing,' Warlow answered. 'But I can't discuss any of the details. Though that's not true otherwise I wouldn't be here, would I?' His half-smile and attempt at lightening the mood didn't seem to have much effect on Fran Dee, whose impression of a frightened rodent got better every time Warlow saw her. 'I'll get straight to it. We opened up some files on Andrew's laptop. Files that he'd encrypted.'

'Something to do with work?' Fran asked. 'He wasn't supposed to but sometimes he'd take something he was working on—'

'No. Not work. Some videos and photographs mainly. A little bit of pornography.'

Fran Dee frowned.

'You shouldn't be too surprised at that. I'd say if you looked at the internet history of the average male between the ages of sixteen and forty you'd find something. Stimulation addiction, I once heard it called. What do you say, Rob?'

The man in question, clearly thrown by the question, came back with, 'Yeah, yeah, you're probably right.' He proffered a weak grin.

'But that's not what I'm here about.' Warlow took out his phone and scrolled to the photographs of the hunting knife. 'Seen this before, Miss Dee?'

Fran Dee stared at the screen before responding with several rapid, brief nods. 'Yes,' she said in a small voice. 'That's Andy's. He called it his Batknife.'

'His Batknife?' Warlow repeated what he'd heard, waiting for a correction.

But the quick little nods were repeated. 'It sounds crass.' She squeezed her eyes shut for two long seconds. 'One of Andy's childish little jokes.'

'What can you tell me about it?'

Fran folded her arms tight across her chest. 'When we went to Canada we ended up in this huge hunting and fishing shop. And I mean huge. The Pro Bass shop in Tsawwassen in British Columbia. It's where the ferry to Vancouver Island goes from. We had a couple of hours to kill, so we went there instead of staying in the ferry terminal. They had a massive fish tank right in the middle of the shop. I couldn't believe it. The place was gigantic. More like a warehouse than a store. Andy would have spent days there mooching around.'

'He was into hunting?' Warlow asked.

'No. But guns and knives held a certain fascination for him. He enjoyed watching that kind of thing on YouTube. Extreme fishing programmes. Hunting programmes. True crime.' Fran shivered. 'I hate all that stuff. But Andy loved it. In Tsawwassen, he spent a lot of time chatting to a knife salesperson in the Pro Bass place. There was this big promotional sale on. Fifty per cent discounts. So he bought the knife and they shipped to the UK because he didn't want to risk carrying it through customs.'

'What's so special about this knife?' Warlow reached into his pocket for his notebook and peeled it open, found a pen, and made some notes. He had a stab at spelling Tsawwassen and ended up with Sowasen.

'The salesperson said it was a replica of the knife that Navy Seals used,' she dropped her head. 'That was another thing Andy was into: Commandos, Navy Seals, anything to do with the military. Andy liked this knife because the case—'

'The sheath you mean?'

'Yes, that. Lots of extra gadgets. Like a firestarter and an inbuilt sharpener.' She paused on seeing the surprised look on Warlow's face. 'I only know about this stuff because he was like a kid in a sweet shop when he showed me.'

'So he bought this knife in Canada and had it shipped over?' Warlow made some notes.

'Yes. The salesman said they were sending a big consignment to Europe with minimal postage and they'd package it as memorabilia. Less problem with customs that way, so he said.'

'Did you think it odd?' Warlow asked.

'No. It's a boy thing. Andy said he'd use the knife for camping.'

Warlow's eyes narrowed. 'He didn't use it for hunting.'

'Like what. You mean hunting as in foxes, or deer? He didn't do that sort of thing.'

'I was thinking more about his trips abroad. To Thailand. There's a market for illegal hunting in the Far East. Big cats, elephants.'

Fran Dee looked horrified. 'No, no nothing like that. I—'

'Is it illegal?' Rob asked suddenly. 'The knife.'

'Not as far as I'm aware.' Warlow said. 'Carrying it in a public place would be. But owning it, no.' He shut his notebook.

But Fran's knitted brows stayed locked up. 'Why are you asking me about the knife? Has it got anything to do with—'

Warlow nipped her question in the bud. 'It's in relation to something we found on his laptop. Photographs like the one I showed you. When was the last time you saw the knife?'

'I have no idea. Andy kept it in his drawer in our spare room. The one he used to work from home when he needed to.'

'Did he bring it with him on this trip, do you know?'

Fran seemed flustered by the question. 'I don't… he might have. I…'

Warlow turned to Hopley. 'Did he show you the knife, or talk about it?'

Rob shook his head. 'First time I've seen that photograph.'

'Why are you so interested in his knife?' Fran was agitated now.

'Might be a good idea when you go back to London to have a poke around, see if you can find it,' Warlow said. 'We didn't find it with his camping gear. The FLO hasn't found it among his effects here, either.'

Another series of rapid nods. 'I can ask my neighbour. She has a spare key.'

'If you could do that, it would be a great help. Right,'

Warlow stood up. 'Sorry to have disturbed you. But at least—'

'Could it have been?' Fran blurted out the words.

The awkward silence that followed told her more than any denial on Warlow's part.

'Was that the knife?' Fran persisted.

'We're waiting for the pathologist to comment—'

'Was it the knife used to kill him?' Fran insisted.

There was no point in lying. 'The simple answer is, yes. Possibly.'

Fran's hand shot up to cover her mouth.

'Right,' Warlow said for the second time, and meaning it. 'Thanks for your help. I'll be in touch as soon as we have anything concrete.'

———

Chant was waiting for him as he left Hopley's guest room. She looked apologetic. 'It's the Gearys, sir. They saw your car. I think they'd like a word.'

Warlow sighed, but not with any true irritation. He'd expected this. He owed them the courtesy of a quick hello at least.

They were sitting on the sofa as before when Chant showed him in. But the strain of not knowing was taking its toll. That was clear. Ralph's dapperness was definitely in decline. He was jumper-free, and the pressed shirt looked rumpled with an undone button just above the belt line showing a circle of pale flesh. Celia had given up on the dress and wore camel-coloured wide-leg trousers with a wine stain on the thigh, under a white ribbed jumper. She looked drawn with dark half-circles working their way in under her eyes. Her hair looked pushed up on one side too, as if she'd been laying on it.

'Evening,' said Warlow, standing in the doorway.

'Well?' Ralph barked. 'You have Daniels in custody. Have you charged him?'

For a second Warlow considered asking Ralph how he knew. But then, this was a small community. Word spread quicker than wildfire. And he remembered the Buccaneer's throwaway remark about Geary knowing the Assistant Chief Constable. Sometimes there was no escaping the odd funny handshake. Though he didn't want the press getting wind of it, Warlow saw no reason to deny it in the presence of these two, hurting people. 'Tristan Daniels is, at present, helping us with our enquiries. He has not been charged.'

Ralph's hands came up into fists and then fell away again just as quickly. 'Come off it, man. Samuels at Maesteg farm told me he'd seen Daniels on a motorbike someone sold him. Doesn't have a licence. It doesn't take a genius to—'

'But it does take evidence, Mr Geary.' Warlow gave Ralph a warning smile. 'And evidence is what we are gathering at the moment.'

Celia Geary trembled, her hands once again together on her knees, writhing like slow snakes. 'Was it revenge?' she asked.

'Celia,' Ralph chided her.

She glared at him. 'If what happened to that little girl is the reason Andrew was…' Her words tailed off, as if she couldn't bear the thought of using the 'm' word.

'Mrs Geary, I am not at liberty to discuss the details of this investigation as yet.' Warlow said.

But instead of placating, his words galvanised her. 'It must be. What other reason could there be?' she spat.

'We're asking Tristan Daniels questions just as we've asked you. That's all there is to it for the moment.'

Celia's eyes wandered over the room, as if searching for something to focus on. 'I think about it all the time.

Was it me? Was it something I did or didn't do? Too much freedom? Was the school a bad influence? Video games? We let him play so many video games…'

'Celia we've gone over this,' Ralph said tiredly.

'We have gone over this, but we've never found an answer,' she whispered. 'What he did was cruel. So cruel. Frightening her like that. I mean, where did that come from?'

'Damned computer games and films. I blame them. You can't watch your children every minute of the day.' Ralph's words weren't aimed at anyone in particular and Warlow wondered if he'd said them for no reason other than to hear them himself. But his attempt at calming the choppy waters backfired.

Celia frowned. 'Every minute of the day? You spent every minute of the day ignoring Andrew when we were down here.'

'I was working, Celia. That's why we had Rob down—'

'You can't blame Rob.' Celia rounded on her husband. 'Andrew was *our* son. Daniels killed *our* son for what he did to *his* little sister.'

Warlow saw no point in reiterating what he'd already said. He glanced at the dregs of red wine in two large glasses on a table next to Celia. That was one way of escaping. But staying here and listening to this brittle relationship sparking was doing no one any good.

He took a step back towards the door. 'As soon as I have some definite news for you, you'll be the first to know. I promise you that. And I promise you we will find out who did this.'

'Daniels did this,' Ralph muttered darkly. 'Of course he did. You know damn well he did.'

'I'll be in touch,' Warlow turned on his heel and left.

He sat in the car and before driving off, took out his

notebook again. In it, under his badly spelled Sowassen, he wrote.

Batknife – boys' toys or something else?
Andrew Geary a military wannabe.
F Dee knows about knife.
Hunting?

Then he closed the book and drove out for the long journey home to Nevern.

CHAPTER THIRTY-THREE

WHEN HE REACHED THE A48, heading west, Warlow called up his contacts on the infotainment unit – who the hell thought up these names? – on the car's dash and dialled a number.

Jess answered after three rings. 'Evan. How did it go?'

'Fran Dee knew all about the knife. Geary bought it as a present to himself earlier this year in Canada.'

'Did he have it with him?'

'She doesn't know. But his justification for buying it was as his 'camping' knife. Called it the Batknife would you bloody believe.'

'Unfortunately, having got to know Andrew Geary from this case, I can believe it. He sounds like—'

'A bit of an arsehole,' Warlow finished the DI's sentence. 'I had to chat with the Gearys too.'

'How are they holding up?'

'Not well. The Geary marriage looks like a very leaky ship, and the blame game is well and truly underway there. Celia Geary is hitting the claret. Ralph gets angrier by the hour. Didn't even offer me a thimble of tea.'

'It happens,' Jess said.

She was right there. The death of their only son would be the acid test of the Geary's longstanding marriage. He'd seen couples grow stronger as the tragedy forged bonds. He'd also, and more often than not, seen the fragile scaffolding of a relationship collapse like a drunken game of Jenga. And it only took one final shaky piece to bring the whole house down.

'Can you put Cadi on please, I'd like a word.'

'How about you speak to my daughter instead?'

Warlow sighed. 'If I must.'

Jess yelled, 'Molly, it's the police. They want a word with you.'

From far away he heard the irritated reply, slowly getting louder as footsteps descended the stairs. 'Mum, that wasn't funny the first time and it isn't funny the hundredth time.'

'I think it's funny,' Jess said.

A growl of frustration was followed by, 'Hello?'

'You mother is correct. This is the police.'

'You're as bad as she is, Evan.'

'She wouldn't let me speak to my dog.'

'I can put her on if you like. See if she remembers your voice.'

Warlow chuckled. Sparring with Molly was always fun. 'Has she behaved?'

'Of course she's behaved. Chased after a cat on the lane and almost caught it. Well, stared at it as it sat on top of the fence for a while and then ignored it. But the idea was a good one.'

'So she's no bother then?'

'Bother less. She also scared off a creepy Amazon delivery driver who was getting a little bit too cosy wanting me to open the kitchen window to accept a parcel when I've told him before to leave it on the front step. Cadi actually barked at him.'

'She never barks.'

'She did today. Feminine instinct. Girl power. Call it whatever you like. She and I have an understanding.'

Warlow toyed with saying something pithy and then remembered this girl was doing him a huge favour.

'You on the way home?' Molly asked in the gap his hesitation made.

'Halfway.'

'Calling in?'

'No. I don't want to disturb you or Cadi. She's probably settled.'

'Yep. Fed and watered and snuggling up with Mr Snoods who has become her new BFF.'

Warlow had to think of the new set of toys Molly had provided. 'Is that the bear with one eye?'

'It is.'

'Great. Gives me peace of mind knowing she's with you.'

'Any time. Do you want to speak to Mum?'

'No, tell her I'll see her tomorrow.'

He rang off and turned the car towards home.

———

In Ffau'r Blaidd, he made himself an omelette. A three-egg job with cheddar and tomatoes and peppers. Tom had given him some chutney from a local deli that had a kick and a half, and he defrosted a chunk of granary bread to eat with it. A bottle of Primitivo stood open, the cork jammed back into its neck from when it was first opened, and he poured himself the one glass.

He showered, shaved, did all the things he should have done that morning but didn't because he'd run out of the cottage like a mad thing once he'd taken the call from Povey about the caravan. He'd toyed with the idea again of finding an overnight room in Carmarthen, closer to the Incident Room, but a little bit of distance sometimes did no harm. Never underestimate thinking time.

He put the kettle on, remembered that he'd accepted offerings from the HUMAN TISSUE FOR TRANS-PLANT box twice already that day and so decided to forego dessert. While he waited for water to boil for a post work cuppa, he retrieved his pocketbook and flicked it open to re-read what he'd written.

Sowassen.

Batknife – boys' toys or something else?

Andrew Geary a military wannabe.

F Dee knows about knife.

Hunting?

He looked up the ferry terminal and wrote the correct name –Tsawwassen – after crossing out his effort.

Yet what he remembered most about his brief visit to Journey's End was Celia Geary blaming herself for her son being a little shit when he was fourteen and scaring the daylights out of six-year-old Iona Daniels. Something he did because… because he could.

And who understood what really went on in the no-man's land of an adolescent's brain? Where adult responsibility hovered on the horizon and doing things because they simply felt exciting impinged on your every moment. Add that to a rich hormonal mix and it could easily spill over into something a parent like Celia Geary should never have to contemplate.

A child psychologist might understand. A copper like Warlow most definitely not. His role was to pick up the pieces when it all went pear-shaped.

While he waited for water to boil, he strolled out into the extension and stood with the lights off, looking down towards the Cleddau estuary. Thinking time with no distractions. That rarest of commodities.

There came a point in many of the investigations he'd been involved in when he'd reflect on the perpetrator's motivation. What made people do the things they did. Greed, sex, jealousy, revenge. There were as many reasons as there were commandments. But occasionally he'd come across something that rattled even his cage.

Rob Hopley telling him that Andrew Geary had gone back into the dark hiding place under the tree roots wearing some hideous bloody mask, fully intending to terrify a six-year-old girl, made his insides twist. 'We were idiots' seemed a pretty lousy excuse.

The kettle rumbled to a boil and flicked off with three warning beeps. Warlow went back to the kitchen, reached for a mug from the cupboard, threw in a teabag, and poured the water. But all the time he was remembering the look on Jess's face as Tristan Daniels told her what his little sister had endured. Remembered her expression when Iona Daniels had said how 'It' had told her to attack her own father.

Warlow swung the fridge door open and reached for milk. What he wouldn't give now for a big furry head to fondle.

A text message came through from Gil.

Dee says no knife in apartment after neighbour checked.

He made the tea, took it back to the extension, put his feet up and sat, thinking, until his eyes got too heavy to see the lights and he dragged himself off to bed. Though exhausted, sleep was slow in coming. He'd be within touching distance of oblivion when the image of an uprooted tree, or a shotgun, or a black hunting knife fended it away. But in the early hours, his brain gave up the ghost and he drifted off while a wild wind blew fresh squalls in from the Atlantic and rattled at the windows.

A frenetic lullaby he was well used to.

———

His phone woke him at six fifteen.

'Warlow,' he growled.

'It's PC Chant, sir. Sorry to wake you.' She sounded anxious and her tone yanked him from drowsy to awake in a heartbeat.

'I've been up for hours,' he lied. 'Who do you think pokes the birds awake?'

'Something's happened at the Geary property, sir. I rang DS Jones, but he said I should ring you, too.'

'I'm listening.'

And he did. For five minutes while Chant explained the details of the new twist in what was fast becoming one of his least favourite cases.

'So she's in hospital now?'

'Yes, sir. Ambulance left half an hour since. And DS Richards is on her way there, too.' Chant sounded on the verge of tears.

'Good. Thanks for letting me know. Sounds like it's been a tough night.'

'I wish… I keep thinking I could have seen it, sir. Stopped it.'

'That's nonsense and you know it. You're not a nurse, Constable.' Though he knew it sounded stern, sometimes stern did the job.

'Yes, sir,' she said.

He hung up and flopped back onto the pillow, running his hand through his hair, thoughts racing. After two minutes, they calmed down from a gallop to trot.

Fine. Catrin was on the way in. No need for him to show his face at the General. She could handle that. DS Richards could handle just about anything. He might even grab fifteen more minutes…

'Nice try,' he muttered and threw off the covers.

CHAPTER THIRTY-FOUR

THE WORD WARLOW chose to describe the atmosphere in the Incident Room at eight o'clock was sombre. They still had Daniels in custody. Still within their clutches. But Warlow knew they were running out of time. If they were going to charge him, something needed to change.

Something had. But not for the better from where he stood.

People were at their desks, busy, heads down. But there was little or no chit chat. All the energy seemed to have drained out of the investigation. Even Warlow busied himself with a bit of paperwork in the SIO room, but it was a half-hearted effort. Until Catrin Richards breezed in and shrugged off her coat.

It was the signal he'd been waiting for.

Warlow hurried out and confronted her before she'd found the coat hook. 'Well?'

Catrin managed a grim smile. 'She's okay, sir. They're keeping her in, obviously. But she's not in any danger.'

Relief flooded through Warlow. Of course he couldn't be held responsible for what had happened. He had no control over what any one person did to themselves or others. Even so, a thundercloud of guilt had pressed down on him since Chant had called that morning. Now at least a glimmer of light had poked through.

He perched a hip on the edge of a desk. Rhys, Jess, and Gil swung around in their seats, waiting, like him, for Catrin to elaborate.

'Okay, Catrin. Tell us the details,' Warlow ordered.

The DS stood in front of them, neat and tidy and composed. 'I got the call from Gil at around four this morning. Somewhere around three thirty, Ralph Geary got up from his bed to use the bathroom. When he got back, he thought he could smell something. When he flicked on the light, he saw that Celia Geary had thrown up most of the Pinot she'd drunk that night on her pillow. When he tried to rouse her, he couldn't. That's when he found the bottle of Zopiclone.'

'Shit,' Jess said.

'Sleeping pills?' Rhys asked.

Gil nodded.

'She'd swallowed half the entire contents of a plastic pill bottle,' Catrin continued. 'Prescribed yesterday by her GP. About thirty tablets. She'd also been drinking quite heavily that night, too.'

'I saw her,' Warlow said by way of confirmation. 'She was chugging the red stuff like it was going out of fashion.'

Catrin nodded. 'Ralph Geary raised the alarm. The ambulance got there within twenty minutes and rushed her to A and E. I spoke to the doctors. They didn't think she'd taken anything else, other than the booze, so they gave her Naloxone—'

'What's that?' Rhys asked. '

'Standard treatment in opioid poisoning,' Catrin replied. She seemed to know her stuff and Warlow was once again impressed. 'To block some of the side effects. The stuff she'd taken could stop her breathing. Anyway, whatever they did it worked. She was pretty groggy when I looked in on her, but the medics say that she'll be fine. She threw up most of what was in her stomach. If Geary hadn't got up though, who knows.'

Warlow nodded. 'She was in a bad way when I saw her. Close to the edge, I'd say. I spoke to them both briefly. They knew about Daniels being in custody.'

'How?' Gil said.

'It's a small community. They'd put two and two together. Celia Geary said some interesting things though.'

'Like what?' Jess asked.

'Like accusing her husband of maybe glossing over the seriousness of the Iona Daniels episode. She blamed him, and to an extent herself, for her son being the way he was.'

'The way he was?' Rhys frowned. 'What does that mean?'

'Good question,' Warlow gestured towards a set of lurid images on the Gallery. 'The kind of kid who puts on a zombie mask to frighten a little girl. The sort of prat who buys a hunting knife and gives it a name. The sort of addict – and I don't mean drugs – who goes to Thailand to fulfil a certain need.' He told them about his visit to Fran Dee the previous night. Jess knew but he had not updated the team.

'So she knew about the knife?' Gil asked.

Warlow let out a tired sigh and bobbed his head. 'It's possible that Dee or Hopley spoke to the Gearys after I left. I should have warned them not to. We'll need to check that with the FLO. Is she okay by the way?'

Catrin nodded. 'Shaken up. But she'll be okay. DC Mellings is on duty today so Chant can have the day off.'

Warlow slapped the outside of his hand into the palm of the other. 'Something tipped Celia Geary over.'

'Sounds like she was teetering already,' Jess said.

Gil agreed. '*Iesu*, you can't blame yourself for that, sir.'

'No? Maybe not. But it's still on my watch. I should have been more careful.' Warlow took a breath to let his mind settle. 'Where are we with forensics on the caravan?'

Jess shook her head. 'Still the same. Povey says they've found nothing. Not in the van nor on the bike.'

'Damn,' Warlow muttered. They'd hit a wall. Daniels had admitted damaging the bikes and the tents but denied any violence towards Geary and Hopley. And as yet, forensics had come up with nothing. A good defence barrister would point to the lack of any linking evidence to the actual attack as grounds for reasonable doubt. They needed something to move things forward.

Warlow's phone buzzed. He looked at the caller ID and walked through to the SIO room to take the call from the Buccaneer.

'Sion,' Warlow said.

'How is she?' The Buccaneer sounded terse.

'Catrin Richards is just back from the hospital. Celia Geary's as well as can be expected.'

'What did she take?'

'Red wine and Zopiclone. A bad combination but not terminal. What some might consider a good night out in Swansea.' Warlow looked out of the window at the grey morning.

'What a shit show.'

'You'll get no argument from me on that one.'

'Ralph Geary's been tearing into the ACC. She's threatened to have me skewered.'

'It'd have to be a bloody long one, then.'

The Buccaneer let out an exhalation that was a mixture of frustration and acceptance that his anger was both misdirected and inappropriate. They'd known each other for too long to be master and pupil here. 'What the hell happened, Evan?'

'This case is what happened,' Warlow said. 'It stinks.

The Gearys are... complicated. Turns out that Andrew isn't the choirboy they led us to believe he is. There's a possibility we have something on the murder weapon, but nothing definite.'

'What about Daniels... is he singing?'

'He is, but he only knows some of the words. He's adamant he attacked neither of them.'

'You believe him?'

Warlow didn't answer immediately because the question had thrown him. Instead, he offered Buchannan a tidbit. 'We've got him until this afternoon. I'll let you know what I think later.'

'Be nice to get this one squared away, Evan.'

'We'll get there.'

Catrin was still talking when Warlow strode back into the room.

'Tea?' Gil asked suddenly.

'Love one,' Catrin said.

'You must be knackered,' Rhys said to the DS.

'I'm fine.' She shrugged off the sympathy and earned a glance of admiration from Warlow. He'd met all sorts during his time in the force. Officers who would have played the system and pleaded exhaustion as an excuse to go home and rest after such an early start. DS Richards was made of sterner stuff. She was not a whinger. No one in this room was, thank God.

Gil turned to Rhys. 'DC Harries, get that kettle on. We need something to boost these flagging spirits.'

Rhys hesitated but then saw Gil reach for the HUMAN TISSUE FOR TRANSPLANT box and hurried out, knowing there was a biscuit in the offing.

'I've brought in a classic today,' Gil said. 'The much-maligned jam and cream ring.' He addressed the room much as any expert might a group of enthusiastic amateurs. 'The shortcake sandwich has much to recommend it, and we are all familiar with the venerable Jammie Dodger. However, in my humble opinion, a vanilla cream layer complements the strawberry splat at its centre and elevates it to a different level.' He lifted the lid with a flourish.

'You ever considered doing that professionally?' Jess asked.

'Biscuiting? No. Not that much call for it. Besides, if it's anything like wine they'd expect you to spit the damn thing out after you'd tasted it. Bugger that.' Gil tapped a big hand on an ample stomach. 'Besides, I feel I have a greater calling.'

'The only thing that you'll be calling is the diabetes hotline,' Warlow said, before dipping his own hand into the tin.

'Ah, well, that's where you're wrong, DCI Warlow. Blood sugar of a marathon runner, me.'

'You sure that isn't a Marathon bar?' Warlow said.

'We can always have the tea without the confection.' Gil lifted one eyebrow and pulled the box back.

'So tetchy.' Jess looped a finger and yanked the box towards her.

When Rhys arrived with the tea, Warlow took it, bit into a jam and cream ring and pushed off from the desk he'd been leaning on.

He chewed, chased the biscuit down with a slurp of tea and stared at the Gallery. At the murder scene and the woods all around, the marked paths on the aerial map of the glade where Daniels had ridden his dirt bike in and out, and a different one showing where Rob Hopley had staggered out to the road.

It was then he saw the little squares in clearings. Three of them: one at the top of the glade, the other two to the west and east, making a roughly equidistant triangle.

He'd seen them before, he must have, but now was the

first time he realised what they were. He'd even walked under them during his treks to and from the scene and ignored them. But suddenly they were the kindling that lit the fire. He sipped some more tea, letting the idea solidify into something more than a vague thought.

They would do. They would more than do.

'Okay. Listen up,' Warlow kept staring at the images, but made sure his voice was loud and clear. 'What's happened to Celia Geary is bad news. I may have contributed and if I did, that's on me, no one else. But it's also fallout from this case. We all thought that once we had Tristan Daniels in custody, all the pieces would fall into place. But they haven't. We need something else. Something that links Daniels to the killing besides tyre tracks. I'm not one for moping and, thanks to Gil's sugar rush, I'm feeling better already.'

'What are you thinking, sir?' Gil considered the DCI warily.

Warlow was still studying the images and his voice had almost fallen to a whisper. 'I'm thinking phones and apps that let you find things that are lost. I'm also thinking about hides.'

'As in seek? Like what Geary did with Iona and Tristan Daniels?' Catrin asked.

'No. I mean those wooden buildings on stilts that you sit in if you want to shoot a deer.'

'You're going to shoot a deer?' Rhys asked.

'Shooting doesn't always involve bullets, Rhys.'

'I don't follow.'

Warlow turned to look at his team with a wolfish smile before his gaze landed on the DC. 'I know you don't. But the first thing I want you and DS Richards to do is to go back out to Journey's End with Andrew Geary's phone and see if you can find his car keys. And then, I think we'll let Tristan Daniels go.'

CHAPTER THIRTY-FIVE

PC MELLINGS WAS BACK on duty as the FLO at Journey's End.

'Hiya,' Rhys said brightly when she opened the door.

For once, the rain had stayed away and low sunshine lit up the courtyard, illuminating the FLO in the doorway. For a moment, Catrin looked a little flummoxed at Rhys's cheery response. But then she took in the PC's big smile and blonde hair and understood.

To her credit, Mellings remained completely professional despite being faced by the human equivalent of a dog with its tongue out scenting a bone. Just as she'd done with Warlow, she stepped out and briefed the two detectives in efficient, hushed tones.

'Ralph's just come back from the hospital. They've told him to go back in tonight. Celia needs some rest and they're arranging for a psych assessment. Fran's made everyone a cup of tea and they're all in the living room.'

'Great,' Catrin said. 'Did you tell them why we're here.'

'I did. I don't think Ralph really understood so you may need to go through things again.'

'Okay.' She turned to Rhys. He was still standing there with a toothless smile.

'Got the phone, Rhys?'

Momentary panic overtook DC Harries as he reached into his pocket. But he fished out Andrew Geary's phone, still inside its see-through evidence bag, and waved it at Catrin. Mellings suppressed a giggle before turning away and walking into the house before them.

'When you can, reel in your eyeballs and let's get this done,' Catrin said. 'And stop salivating, you're making a mess on your shirt.'

Rhys glanced down at his shirt front before twigging the joke.

'Like DC Mellings, do you?' Catrin asked with theatrical nonchalance.

'We were in school together. She was a couple of years above me.'

'Ah, the lure of the unattainable. That explains it.'

'Explains what?'

'Why I'm being doused in a testosterone fug.'

'Gina's a nice girl—'

But Catrin had already stepped across the threshold before Rhys could finish his explanation.

'Mr Geary.' The Sergeant greeted Ralph as soon as she was inside. 'I hope Mrs Geary is feeling better.'

Ralph stood up as was his custom, trying to keep a straight back but wincing as he did. The result of too many sleepless nights, no doubt. 'Better than when you saw her. Has the mother of all hangovers, but she's on a drip and she's stopped throwing up. They were checking her bloods again as I left. I'll take some fresh clothes in for her this evening. Thank you for asking.'

Catrin gave him a thin smile. 'Oh and please, don't let us disturb you. Mr Warlow needs something checking out. This won't take long.'

Rhys had donned gloves and took the phone out from the evidence bag. They'd already tested it with gloves. Rhys, wearing his nerd hat, explained to Catrin that there'd be no problem. Screens were capacitive and worked by detection of an electrical charge, not touch. The nitrile gloves were thin enough to function just like a finger.

'Is that Andy's phone?' Fran Dee asked.

'It is,' Catrin said.

Rhys pressed some buttons and the phone let out a regular three tone beep. He showed the screen to the DS. The directional red arrow pointed to the back of the house.

The officers exchanged satisfied glances.

'What is that?' Ralph asked.

'Andrew's car keys,' Catrin said. 'Do you mind if Rhys fetches them?'

'Carry on,' Ralph said. He seemed to have shrunk since Catrin had seen him in the early hours of the morning. Fallen in on himself.

Rhys took the stairs and, three minutes later came back down. 'On the dresser,' he explained.

'I could have brought those in.' Fran stood, both hands cupped around a mug, wearing a bemused expression.

'Of course you could. But we wanted to test out the app on Andrew's phone. He's tagged the key fob electronically with this little square.' She held the keys up and pointed to the tiny black oblong stuck on the fob. 'We wanted to see what sort of distances the app worked from in the real world.' She nodded to Rhys. 'Go on.'

He turned and walked out of the door. Catrin took out her phone and called him up once he was out of sight. 'Let me know when the indicator drops out.'

'Got you.'

Footsteps crunched and then disappeared as he

reached softer ground. Thirty seconds later, Rhys said, 'Gone.'

'Retrace your steps until it appears again.'

'Okay.'

'Right, now press the recall button.'

'Done… It's showing up now.'

A faint echo of the three beeps she'd heard first in the Incident Room when Rhys demonstrated the Reperire app reached her.

'On the way back,' Rhys's voice came through the speaker on Catrin's phone.

Thirty seconds later, he reappeared next to Catrin. 'Fifty, maybe sixty yards, I reckon,' he said.

'Good range then.'

'Sounds fascinating,' Rob said, looking bemused.

'Reperire,' Rhys said. 'Helps you find lost things. Like Andrew's water bottle and car keys, his wallet and BK, which DCI Warlow thinks might stand for Batknife, Andrew's very expensive camping knife. Things of importance, you know.'

'I've read about that. I had no idea Andy had one,' Rob said. 'Can I?' He stepped forward.

'Unfortunately, not,' Rhys said. 'The phone is still evidence for now.'

'Right.' Catrin smiled at the assembled crowd. 'Job done. Can I give the keys back to you, Fran?'

Fran got up from her seat and opened her palm. Catrin dropped the keys in.

'I hope Mrs Geary feels better, soon, Mr Geary,' the DS said, as they made for the door.

Once they were back in the car, Rhys sent Gil a text confirming that the app had a two-hundred-foot search radius and that there'd been no sign of the Batknife at Journey's End.

———

THEY RECONVENED at eleven in the interview room at Ammanford. This time Warlow sat with Jess opposite Daniels and Briggs. This morning, the solicitor had opted for an African-themed outfit. Huge wooden beads clacked on her chest when she moved and she wore a vibrant head-scarf that made Warlow wish he'd brought his sunglasses when he looked at it.

'Thought of anything more you'd like to say to us, Tristan?' Warlow asked after the usual preliminaries.

'No.' Daniels stared back at the DCI.

Warlow nodded and looked at Jess who had a couple of items on the desk in front of her. Both locked inside clear evidence bags. 'Detective Inspector Allanby has some things she'd like to show you, Tristan.'

'Ever seen this?' Jess held up Geary's drinks bottle.

Daniels shook his head.

'For the record, Mr Daniels has shaken his head.'

Briggs looked on disapprovingly. 'Is this relevant?'

'Simple questions,' Warlow said. 'Simple answers.'

Jess put the bottle on the table. 'We think Andrew Geary dropped this bottle and it was found by someone else. We got it back and it showed us something rather remarkable.'

Jess was already wearing gloves. She stood and placed the bottle in the far corner. Both Briggs and Daniels watched. Then Jess took Geary's phone out of the second bag, pressed some buttons, and everyone heard the phone give out three tones. She turned the screen so that Daniels could see the little directional arrow as she explained. 'It's an App designed to find misplaced things like lost drinks bottles, wallets, keys, and anything else you might consider precious or valuable.'

'Like a watch say… or a knife even,' Warlow added. 'If

you know anything about an item like that, now would be a good time to tell us, Tristan.'

Daniels watched the little demo without showing any emotion. 'Why would I know? What's this got to do with me?'

Jess sat back down. 'It's a useful tool though, you have to agree. One of many we'll be using to comb the forest on the lookout for anything that will help us. Unless you'd like to save us the trouble, Tristan.'

Daniels slouched back in his chair, arms folded. 'No comment.'

Warlow sat back. 'Okay, that's it. You're free to go for now.'

Jess ended the interview formally and turned off the recorder. Briggs frowned. Daniels sat up.

'We don't want you leaving the area,' Jess said. 'I'm sure we'll need to speak to you again soon.'

'I can go?' Daniels asked.

'Yes. Bit of paperwork, and you're off.' Warlow tidied the bundle of papers in front of him, lifting and tapping the lot on the table to straighten them. 'Unfortunately, your dirt bike and the push bike are still with the lab. But we could arrange a lift for you back to the caravan if you like?'

'No thank you,' said Briggs. 'I'll arrange transport.'

Daniels shook his head. 'No. They brought me in. They can take me home.' He stared directly at Warlow. Another show of defiance.

'We'll gladly sort that out,' said Warlow. The door opened and a uniformed sergeant appeared to escort Daniels and Briggs out to complete the paperwork.

When they were alone in the interview room, Jess spoke first.

'You think he's taken the bait?'

Warlow opened his arms wide to stretch his shoulders and back. 'Who knows. But we'd need a good reason to keep him much longer. Reasons we do not at present have. Hopley can't identify Daniels as the attacker. Forensics have come up short.'

Jess didn't need this explaining. But Warlow read doubt in her expression and felt obliged to reassure her again. 'And yes, I'm chancing my arm. You may think it's reckless. I think it's worth a shot.'

'For what it's worth, so do I.'

Warlow nodded. He was grateful for the vote of confidence.

'Is everything set up?' Jess asked.

'By the time we get Daniels back to his caravan they will be.' He glanced at his watch. 'You're with Catrin. Let's see what happens.'

CHAPTER THIRTY-SIX

FRAN DEE approached PC Mellings in the kitchen at Journey's End. The uniformed constable smiled at Andrew Geary's ex-fiancée, pleased that she looked a lot brighter than she had for the past few days.

'Would it be okay if I went out for a while?' Fran asked.

Mellings tilted her face. 'By out you mean what exactly. A walk?'

'A bike ride. I feel like I've been cooped up in here for days, which of course I have. And seeing Ralph looking so lost just gets me down.' Fran peered out of the window at the day. 'The weather's good so I thought I'd get out, blow away some cobwebs. Andy and Ralph have half a dozen bikes stored in the garage. I've never understood why you need more than one, but Andy...' She paused, brows bunching as if mentioning his name caused her physical pain. 'Anyway, I've convinced Rob to go with me.'

'What about his injuries?' Mellings asked.

'He's been out of the sling for a day now. Besides, I've convinced him that some fresh air will do him good, too. So long as I don't go too fast, he says he'll be fine.'

'Yeah, go for it. I don't see why not.' Mellings raised a pair of well-shaped eyebrows. 'You're not under house arrest.'

'No, but I thought I better check. I didn't know what rules your Chief Inspector had put in place.' Fran rolled her eyes.

'No rules that restrict your freedom,' Mellings replied. 'If you were off back to London, we'd need to know your location, obviously.'

Fran sighed. 'I'll need to go back soon I suppose, but I can't leave Ralph and Celia like this. Not until we know something. That's the worst thing, the not knowing.'

'Well, enjoy your ride. I'll have my phone if anyone needs me.'

'I can't believe it's actually stopped raining,' Fran said, stepping out into the courtyard with her face upturned.

Fran got bikes out of the garage and Rob joined her from around the side of the house, without sling, and gingerly checked the bikes over for size. He grimaced once as he mounted one but seemed to manage and cycled around the courtyard before getting off and changing the seat height. Both Fran and Rob adjusted helmets for fit before setting off.

Mellings watched them from the kitchen window. Their smiles were polite, the chat neutral. Normal behaviour damped down by the ever-present weight of circumstance.

Above, the sun burnt in a light-blue sky marred only by the ghosts of a few white clouds. It wasn't exactly warm but still a pleasant enough day with little wind. Mellings got back to making a sandwich for Ralph Geary. The least she could do for the poor man.

———

THE BETTER WEATHER HELPED, thought Warlow. It always amazed him how much difference a splash of sunshine made. A little after two in the afternoon and already he'd seen a dozen cyclists and a couple of walkers out and about making the most of it.

He sat behind the wheel of his Jeep Renegade in a lay-by about a hundred yards from where he'd parked previously for access to the crime scene, just to not make it look obvious. A crime scene clear of personnel this afternoon at his request. As plans went, it had taken little to set up. They'd borrowed a couple of Uniforms to man two of the hides; the one that partly overlooked the glade and the one farther out that gave a view of the trail that Daniels had supposedly taken in and out on his bike.

The third hide, after a quick inspection, gave no actual view of what needed to be surveilled, namely Ffrwd Y Dderwen. And so, he'd positioned Rhys in the woods under a quickly arranged bit of camouflage, forty yards in from Tristan Daniels' caravan. Gil manned the office, coordinating the operation. Jess and Catrin, meanwhile, were in Jess's car covering the road access to the old Daniels' place, on standby.

'Like the Sweeney,' Catrin had said when Warlow had outlined their roles.

'Sweeney?' Rhys had asked.

'Sweeney Todd. Flying squad,' Catrin had elaborated.

Rhys had given her one of his best open-mouthed smiles and nods. The kind that implied 'of course' but which meant that he had no clue what she was talking about. He'd perfected that look to a tee. Thinking about it now made Warlow shake his head and quash a half-smile. He'd even toyed with explaining to the detective constable how popular the seventies TV show of the same name had been. How it had brought that bit of cockney rhyming slang into common parlance. He suspected, as with many such series, you could probably find reruns on some channel somewhere at any given moment of the day.

But thankfully he'd seen sense before opening his mouth and risking one of those glances from Rhys that he'd seen so many times on his own sons' faces when he'd attempted to be the wise old sage, aka boring old git.

Warlow's phone buzzed. Everyone involved in the operation had their phones on silent. He hoped to God that Rhys had remembered that. Ironically, the message was from the DC himself.

Target released to caravan

K, Warlow texted back and got confirmatory texts from Jess and the two Uniforms in the hides. Now it was a matter of waiting to see what Tristan Daniels would do next.

Eyes on the target, Rhys? Warlow sent the message.

In caravan.

Warlow fiddled with the radio until he found something to lull his senses and settled for Classic FM, already regretting not calling in for a coffee and a sandwich on his way here. But he'd wanted to be in place. Thirsty and with his stomach doing an impression of a pride of lions, he settled back to wait and see if it had spooked Daniels enough to make sure the murder weapon he'd used was well enough hidden.

Assuming he'd used that weapon.

And assuming he'd tried to hide it.

And assuming said hiding place was within sight of one of the officers in the stakeouts. He didn't like the term much, but having outlined his plan, both Rhys and Catrin had rubbed their hands together, grinned, and said the word. There may have been a British acronym he could have applied, SSO, or special surveillance operation sprang to mind. But he'd let them have stakeout because he knew that was what they'd use when they talked about it later. In his report, he'd probably opt for mobile and static surveillance units. Terms that looked a lot better on paper.

Warlow didn't dwell on the flimsiness of his idea. It was simple, involved the minimum of sophistication and personnel outside of his team, and might give them the break they so needed. If it didn't work, then it meant he'd wasted a couple of hours sitting in a car in the Brechfa Forest and taken a few uniforms away from other duties. It's success or failure depended on how nervous Daniels might be. Because nervousness was a much under-used tool in the investigator's arsenal.

Make a man nervous and he twitched.

There were of course degrees of nervousness and by definition therefore degrees of twitchiness.

Not enough and you risked the head in the sand approach of say nothing and hope for the best.

Too much and you risked a suspect so anxious that they daren't risk getting further than two hundred yards from the nearest toilet for fear of not getting back there in time when the anxiety pangs hit the fan.

Or worse, there was cornered rat nervousness. So galvanised by fear that they abandoned all hope of escape or avoiding detection and lashed out.

Judging all that was a learned art. Warlow realised he was still on that learning curve because there were too many variables to apply any sort of science to it. Daniels didn't strike him as a head in the sand sort of guy. Or a cornered rat. The hope was he'd fall into the triggered anxiety bracket. Nervous enough to want to make sure, and canny enough to take the opportunity that a load of incompetent coppers had given him.

Twenty minutes later and with the Vienna Philharmonic well into the *Theme from Jurassic Park* on the radio, the phone buzzed again. Warlow's eyes flicked to the screen as he grabbed up the phone from where it rested on the seat and read the brief message from Rhys.

On the move

Where to? Warlow texted back.

On path. Towards Daniels' property.

Pulse thrumming, Warlow gunned the engine. He wanted to be ready if he had to move. As the crow flew, the Daniels' property was only a couple of miles to the west. A brisk half-hour walk if you knew the right paths to take. But on the road, it was a five-mile drive around narrow lanes to the point of access where Jess and Catrin were.

Stay out of sight. Eyes only, Warlow sent back.

By return he got an emoji of a pair of shifty eyes glancing to the left.

'Jesus Christ,' Warlow muttered, and fought, success-fully, the urge to fire off a suitably admonishing phrase. Instead, he put the phone down, took a deep breath, turned the music back up and waited.

CHAPTER THIRTY-SEVEN

FRAN LED THE WAY. Out along the lane to the road then winding up towards Keepers. A familiar route she'd travelled many times with Andy on her trips down to Wales. Fran peddled hard, enjoying the physicality after the long days of sitting around waiting for the police to come up with something.

She had not enjoyed her brief chats with DCI Warlow. He seemed to stare right through you and had the unnerving ability to make you feel guilty. It was the way he scanned your face when he talked to you, looking for little give-aways, his eyes sparking with energy.

She'd seen a TV programme once about an investigator who could supposedly predict when someone was lying by picking up on the tells: dilated pupils, microexpressions lasting less than a second, voice clues, body language, blah-de-blah.

She'd asked her sister, Alex, to quiz her psychologist partner if that stuff was true. He had come back with a typically vague answer. A highly inexact science had been his reply. The good liars always told a plausible story and were vague about details. The trick was to mix in a little bit of truth with the lies. That way made them harder to doubt.

So not an actual thing then, detecting lies. But Warlow seemed to be the nearest damn thing to a human lie detector she'd ever come across.

She was puffing up an incline when she risked a glance back. Rob was following, his damaged left arm a little lower on the handlebars than his right. Even so, he seemed to cope with the exertion.

'Okay?' she yelled over her shoulder.

'Fine,' Rob shouted in reply.

The way up to the forest car park was mainly uphill, with a couple of welcome flat stretches. Only four miles. Half a dozen cars and a few cyclists passed them but no one else. Fran enjoyed the rush of wind on her face and, when it appeared from behind the clouds, the feel of the sun on her back. Her legs burnt with lactic acid as she sucked in air and dropped the gears down to assault a tough stretch, one bend after another. By the time they reached the almost empty car park, she was a good three hundred yards ahead of Rob.

He arrived a few seconds later. 'You didn't… tell me… you were so fit,' he said, huffing.

'I'm not. At least not as fit as I used to be.' Fran straddled her bike and took a sip of water from her bottle.

Rob did the same. 'Did you come up here with Andy?'

'We did. All around here. Like you used to do.' A thought struck her, and the bottle paused an inch from her lips. 'How far from here? Where it happened, I mean.'

'The glade?' Rob asked. 'About three miles I'd say.'

'Can we go there? I'd like to see.'

Rob took his helmet off gingerly, wincing a little as he raised his left arm to fiddle with the chin strap. 'I don't know if that's even allowed. The police may still be all over it, blocking off the whole area.'

'I don't want to go to the actual spot; I just want to see where it is.'

Rob adopted a pained expression. 'What good would that do, Fran?'

She mulled over the question before answering. The idea caused her pulse to surge. She hadn't planned this, but now the idea had sprouted legs she wanted to run with it. 'I realise how morbid it sounds, but I think this might help ease my mind. Now all I have is this vague knowledge of Andy being attacked in the woods. My imagination does all the rest. I'm not Celia, Rob. I'm sure I could cope.'

Rob ran a hand through his sweat-matted hair. 'I don't know, Fran.'

'Please?'

He blew out his cheeks but dropped his shoulders in defeat. 'Okay. There's more than one path in. We can approach from the east. That way you'll get a reasonable view.' He slid his helmet back on. 'Follow me.'

Rob set off back down the road for half a mile and then pulled off through the woods. She couldn't remember ever riding through this part of the forest and the trees here were huge Douglas firs, the path wide and leaf strewn until Rob hitched a quick turn and took them through a narrow, winding trail past a section of older trees completely covered in moss. Something to do with their positioning, the microclimate, and the dampness colluded to make this a place from a fairy tale. As if some strange disease had claimed them and was gradually encasing them in green fur from the roots up. Fran had seen nothing quite like it before.

She realised then how a forest this big could be full of surprises. Harbouring secrets around almost every turn. People and animals used the path, but a few steps away into the trees and you were in unknown territory.

Then they were climbing again, and she dropped the

gears until they crested a rise and came out of the trees on the edge of a clear space.

'The glade,' Rob said, as she came to a halt next to him.

Spread before them was the killing ground, still with police tape fluttering in the breeze way off on the other side of the open space. In places, rocks jutted through the moss in jagged clumps and tussocks of grass here and there hinted at the thin nature of the soil beneath.

Neither of them spoke. Instead they stared solemnly across the expanse, broken here and there by a brave patch of gorse that had found enough purchase in the soil to establish some growth. And surrounding everything, always the silent trees. Row upon row, standing in funereal silence.

'It's bigger than I thought it would be,' Fran said. 'Do the police always keep their tape up?'

Rob shrugged. 'No idea. If they don't take it away, the wind and the rain will.'

They stayed quiet for half a minute. Until Fran spoke. 'I'm not going to ask you about it. The details I mean.'

'Just as well. It was dark. It's all a big blur.'

'How did you get out of here?'

Rob looked about, trying to orientate himself. 'Good question. After he went, the bloke on the motorbike, I went to Andy and... I found a torch. I dropped it before I got out on the road, but it helped a bit. I went to the line of trees just south of here and I found a trail and followed it. In fact, I think I can see the beginning of it a hundred yards down from here,' he pointed to a gap in the trees. 'There.'

'You walked out from there?'

'I must have. I don't even know how far it is. Shall we look?'

Fran shrugged.

'If we stay with the tree line, we should hit it.'

Rob set off. There was no path as such and they had to wind their way between old tree stumps. Sometimes riding, sometimes getting off to push the bikes. But they found the gap where the grass looked flatter. The police tape was much closer now, but though Fran peered closely, there was no sign on the ground of anything suggesting a fight had taken place here. All the evidence had been removed either by the crime scene investigators or by the rain that had teemed down over the last few days.

'This must be it,' said Rob. 'Looks very different in daylight.' His voice sounded strained.

'We don't have to,' Fran said.

'We're here now. Besides, it's probably the quickest way back to a half decent road. Now that I'm here, I realise it's a trail me and Andy sometimes used. Come on. Might as well get it over with.'

Fran turned to take one last look at where her fiancé was murdered before setting off in pursuit of the man who had survived the attack.

CHAPTER THIRTY-EIGHT

RHYS SAT on a tree stump behind the makeshift camouflage screen of branches, watching Tristan Daniels take the path between the caravan and Ffrwd Y Dderwen. He didn't want to move too early and risk making a noise, though the wind was up and with a bit of luck, any noise would be carried away. Even so, he waited until Daniels was a good forty yards along the path and about to turn out of sight before he took off on a diagonal route that would bring him up behind the man. If he'd got it right, that is. He moved quickly, eyes down to avoid the bigger branches that might snap and give the game away.

Daniels was almost at the bend where the path opened out. Rhys veered left to the edge of that same path and hid behind a large tree. He took out his phone and sent off a quick text.

In pursuit. Stealth mode

Stealth mode??? Warlow's text came back. Rhys smiled on reading it and the implied annoyance his using it must have induced. *Stay well back. Will contact JA and CR to approach from east.*

Rhys sent back an *Okay* before stepping out into the

path and hurrying after Daniels, slipping behind what cover he could find as he kept the man in front within view. But Daniels seemed like a man on a mission as he strode purposefully along a way that he must have travelled hundreds of times in the past, safe in the knowledge he would encounter no one in this isolated patch of the woods.

Safe and unsuspecting, so Rhys hoped.

When the path opened out onto the cleared area where Ffrwd Y Derwen stood, Rhys hung back. There was excellent cover here at the edge of the trees, and he could surveil Daniels as he remained in full view.

The suspect moved with purpose. At the side of the longhouse, he leant over and picked up a bucket that rattled when he lifted it. He reached in and took out the source of the rattling noise.

Rhys watched, heart thumping in his chest. Surely it wouldn't be as simple as that? No way would the Crime Scene Techs have missed a knife hidden in a bucket.

They had not.

What Tristan Daniels held in his hand was not a knife, but a trowel. The type with a small, curved end you might use for weeding.

Or digging something up that you'd buried.

Satisfied, Daniels turned abruptly and walked away from the house, down towards the edge of the little overgrown garden to a path that led towards the bottom of the valley.

Rhys had time to punch in the word, 'Following' before he moved. Quickly, silently, and making use of the house as cover, the detective constable set off in pursuit.

———

FRAN KEPT Rob in her sights as they negotiated the much narrower trail he was taking. This was nothing more than an animal path, though the multiple lines of tyre tracks told her that some people must have known of its existence. Two minutes after setting off, Rob slowed to a halt.

Fran pulled up behind him.

They were deep in the forest here, the trees tall and dark on either side. But in front, the way descended into a ravine with a tiny stream trickling through it. The tall firs disappeared to be replaced by a patch of deciduous woodland. Rob got off and wheeled his bike down towards the bubbling water. Fran followed.

'We called this the grotto,' Rob said. 'See that big oak tree? We reckon it's at least five hundred years old.'

Rob's pointing finger picked out a gnarled trunk with strangely curving lower branches. 'Look like hugging arms, don't they?'

'Wow,' Fran said.

'Andy and I used to come here a lot. We called it Treebeard.'

Fran let out a little laugh.

'I know,' Rob apologised. 'Tolkien has a lot to answer for.'

He put his bike against a nearby trunk and walked down the slope towards the tree. 'We used to climb this. Sit on the thick branches and pretend we were in Lothlórien.'

'More *Lord of the Rings*?' Fran asked, with a rictus grin. 'I won't pretend that I'm the biggest fan. Fantasy never did it for me.'

'It's okay. There's no accounting for taste. But we were into it. Andy was Frodo, I was Sam Gamgee. Look, you can even see where we left stupid messages.'

Fran parked her bike and joined Rob. Carved in letters that were now black scars in the bark were the words "Frodo and Sam were here."

Rob laughed. 'Mad. We even cut footholds in the bark as steps, here, see.' He pointed to more dark marks where the bark had rounded out in an attempt at healing. 'I wonder,' he said. With his right arm, he held on to a branch, and, with one foot in the foot hold, pulled himself up. 'Yes, see, they curve around behind in a spiral.' With that he disappeared around the enormous trunk until he appeared on the other side of it, but eight feet up off the ground now looking down at her.

'Mind your arm.' Fran sang out a warning.

Rob continued to climb as Fran took in her surroundings. 'What's that?' she asked, pointing to something hanging from a low branch in an adjacent tree. A dangling cross of tied together sticks with a fir cone at its centre.

'It's the sign of the beast,' Rob said.

'The what?' She shot him a wide-eyed glance.

'They're all over the woods. Just kids messing about, pretending that there's something weird in here.'

'Weird as in supernatural weird?'

'That's it. I'm not surprised they'd hang that here, though. I mean, this is a pretty special place.'

Fran took a moment to study her surroundings. Rob was right. Whether it was the silence, or the dappled light, or the odd shape of the trees, Fran was suddenly struck by the timeless beauty of the place.

'Makes you wonder if the Druids might have come here to do their thing,' Rob said.

'Druids? You mean sacrifices and things?'

'Who knows? I read Tolkien was heavily influenced by the Welsh and Celtic culture. This place looks as if it would fit right into the Hobbit. I even think—' Rob stopped, his eye caught by something he'd seen just next to where he was sitting a dozen feet off the ground. 'Looks like someone's been here before us,' he said. 'I remember being up here years ago. There's a hole where an old branch fell off.

A squirrel tried to nest in it once. But there's something…'
Rob reached in and pulled out a red and blue Tesco bag.
'Whoa. Treasure!' He grinned.

'What is it?' Fran asked.

'It's tied up. Hang on, I'll need both hands. I'm coming
back down.'

———

RHYS CREPT to the corner of the house from where he
could watch Tristan descending along a winding path
towards a stream.

He crouched again, reached for his phone, and texted.
Target has bucket and spade

Warlow's text came back with *What is this, an away day in
Tenby?*

Rhys frowned. And texted back. *Brechfa Forest, sir*

Warlow responded. *Irony, Rhys. Observe only. Wait for JA
and CR*

They'd given him a camera to use. A proper one with a
good lens. Rhys unhooked his backpack and took out the
SLR, held it up to his eye and focused in on his target.

The lens brought Daniels into focus. A grim,
purposeful expression on his face. But he was moving, and
a few steps took him into denser foliage and the view disappeared. Cursing, Rhys looked up to see where he could go
to get a better view. Nowhere other than the path that
Daniels had taken.

He looked up and around. No sign of Catrin or DI
Allenby yet.

'Observe it is then,' Rhys muttered and set off in
pursuit. He hurried across the little garden, camera in one
hand, phone in the other. He didn't notice the loose stone
until his big foot met with it and send it sliding from
beneath him.

His one thought as he lost his balance was to make sure he didn't damage the camera. With that in mind, he tucked his shoulder in and rolled into the fall. Gravity and the slope did all the rest. It wasn't so much a clatter as a thump and scrape. Loud enough to be heard by anyone within fifty yards. More than loud enough to alert the man lower down on the path. When he clattered to a stop, Rhys was much closer to Daniels that he'd ever meant to be and in full view.

For a moment, both men regarded one another. It was Daniels who spoke first as he clambered back up, pointed trowel in one hand.

'You need to watch your step, DC Harries. You could do yourself an injury.'

Rhys realised three things instantly as he pushed up from the ground. One, that he'd lost his bloody phone. Two, putting weight on his ankle was a terrible idea. And three, Warlow was going to kill him.

'They know I'm here,' Rhys said.

But all Tristan Daniels did was shape his mouth into a smile that got nowhere near his eyes, shake his head, and kept walking up the slope towards the injured and immobile officer.

CHAPTER THIRTY-NINE

CATRIN AND JESS were hurrying on their way to Ffrwd Y Dderwen in response to Warlow's text when Jess's phone buzzed for the fourth time in a minute. She stopped and stared at the screen.

Warlow again: *Heard from Rhys?*

Jess shook her head. Texting was too time consuming, and they were still half a mile from their destination. She decided to risk a call. She pressed the *dial* button. Warlow answered immediately.

'No, nothing for the last five minutes,' Jess said.

'Where the hell is he?'

'Maybe there's no signal.' A distinct possibility in these remote locations.

'He had signal until five minutes ago.' Warlow's voice was gruff with frustration.

'Should we phone him?'

'No,' Warlow said. 'We daren't risk giving him away. He may be in a delicate spot. But I said text every couple of minutes. I swear that boy will be the bloody death of me.'

'We're probably ten minutes away.' She looked up at

Catrin who nodded in response. Both women had not stopped walking.

'The last thing we bloody need is Rhys buggering this up. If Daniels has hidden that knife, I want it found.'

'That's if he had it in the first place,' Jess said.

'I know,' Warlow growled. 'Right, well I'm not sitting here. It's obvious he's not heading this way. No point me staying put. I'm on my way.'

He ended the call.

Catrin sent Jess an inquisitive glance.

'Our DCI is tetchy.'

'Rhys?' Catrin asked.

'Off the radar.' Jess put her phone back in her pocket and upped the pace. The next ten minutes were probably the longest of her life. They ended up in a half jog, hampered only by the uneven ground.

Finally they arrived at the edge of the clearing where both women stood, sucking in air. Jess had not been to Ffrwd Y Dderwen before, so the forlorn air of decay and emptiness that pervaded the place was new to her. Nothing moved. Quiet as the grave. Jess trod on the thought.

'So where do we go from—'

'Shh.' Catrin held up a finger.

Both women listened. Both heard the faint sounds of voices followed by a low groan of pain. Noises from somewhere in the house. Both officers withdrew their batons. Jess took out her PAVA spray. With a nod from Jess, they moved carefully towards the house and as they neared, the voices got louder.

'Don't move, mun.'

That's Daniels, mouthed Catrin to Jess.

The DI nodded and strode to the front door. It was open. All the invitation she needed. She nodded to Catrin who stayed behind her, and, with two quick steps, she stepped into the building and upon a sight she would never forget.

———

Rob stood in front of Fran with the Tesco bag in his hand. Slowly, he undid the knot and reached inside. What he took out was a black sheathed knife.

'Well, look at this,' he said.

'My God, is that… is that Andy's Batknife?'

'Looks like it could be. What do you think?' Rob held it up for her to see. But Fran didn't touch it. All she could do was glare at the thing as if it was alive.

'It looks very much like it. From what I can remember. But who… I mean what on Earth is it doing here?' She looked up into Rob's face.

'No idea. No one except Andy and me knew about this place.'

'What about Ralph? Could he have known?'

Rob was shaking his head. 'It's possible. I know they used to ride together when Andy went home sometimes. But Ralph? His own son?' Rob dropped the knife back into the bag. 'You'd better ring Mellings. Tell her what we've found.'

'Good idea,' Fran said. She slid off her backpack and reached for her phone.

———

Warlow was driving when he took the call.

'Evan, it's Jess.'

'And?'

'We're in Ffrwd Y Dderwen with Tristan Daniels and Rhys.'

'Is Rhys okay?'

'No, he's not. The poor sod has twisted his ankle. I'd estimate no rugby for a month at least.'

'Jess. What's going on?' Warlow could barely hold back his irritation.

'Rhys fell and hurt himself following Daniels downhill. Assuming Daniels was going to dig up the murder weapon, he says. But Daniels wasn't doing that. There's no knife there, Evan. There's a patch where he's scattered his dad's ashes. He planted a rose garden and a little cross and planned on doing some weeding. Rhys saw the trowel and added two and two together to get five.'

'You believe Daniels?'

After a beat Jess said, 'Yes, I do. I've seen it. I'm sending over a photograph of the spot for you. Looks genuine to me, but you can decide for yourself. We could get Povey out here with her metal detectors, but she wouldn't thank you for it. Daniels wouldn't have been so open if he had something to hide.'

'Damn,' Warlow cursed and slapped the steering wheel with his open palm. With commendable restraint under the circumstances. 'Does Rhys need to go to hospital?'

'No, he needs elevation and a bag of frozen peas strapped to his ankle. Oh, and he needs to find his phone. He's more worried about that than his leg. We're on that now. Right, sending you that photo.'

It had been a gamble right enough, letting it slip to Daniels they'd be using technology to find the knife. He wasn't to know that they had no idea if Geary had tagged the knife like the car keys and drinks bottle. Nor that they had no evidence of the knife – Geary's knife – being used at all. But it had been worth a go.

He wasn't that far from Keepers now. He pulled in to let his heart slow down and the photo download.

It came through after another twenty seconds. A valley bottom with a stream and a little wooden bridge across it.

Just above on a cleared terrace, Daniels had planted half a dozen roses. White, yellow, and red. The ground beneath the bushes was mulched but one or two little weeds were creeping back. Reason enough for a trowel.

In the middle of the roses were two simple stone crosses. He read the words of the first.

BOED TANGNEFEDD Y SER UWCHBEN

Deep peace of the stars above

And on the second:

ER COF ANNWYL MAM a DAD

In fond remembrance of Mam and Dad

Warlow saw it immediately for what it was. Whatever people thought of Daniels Senior, he'd probably made this little commemorative garden for his wife. The dedication a secular one, no non-conformist frills. And his son had placed his father with her. It struck him as a nice, honourable, and meaningful thing to do.

He liked the words and the setting. Warlow decided he'd keep this image.

Images, he thought. *So powerful because they didn't lie.*

Something twitched in his head at that. Something to do with images and lying.

Something just out of reach.

Come on, Evan. Wake up.

But it wouldn't come. Not immediately. There seemed no point rushing back to HQ yet. The Buccaneer wanted him to talk to the press, update them on how the investigation was progressing – not.

No point at all in him going to the Daniels' property either. Not with over half his team already there. Jess would figure out a way to get Rhys transported out.

So Warlow took five. Distraction free, he sat in the woods and thought.

CHAPTER FORTY

FRAN HAD her phone in her hands. She had Mellings' number in her contacts but there was no signal down in the hollow.

'Let's go back up to where the bikes are. Try there,' Rob said. He led the way, the Tesco bag dangling from his hand. Fran followed, one eye on the signal meter, hoping for one bar to light up.

They climbed in silence, past where they'd left the bikes, back up towards the path until Fran exclaimed. 'Yep. We're fine. I've got a sig—'

Without warning, Rob snatched the phone from her hands.

'Hey!' She looked up. The quick spurt of shocked anger quickly evaporating as her eyes focused on the point of a black blade inches from her face.

'Sit down on that stump, Fran,' Rob said.

'Rob? What are you doing?'

'Sit down on that stump.'

'No, I—'

Rob struck without warning. One swift thrust and the

knife entered her leg just below and to the outside of her left hip. One thrust, in and out. Fast and painful.

Fran screamed and clutched at her wound.

'Sit down. Otherwise I'll do it to the other leg and then your arm. In fact we can do this all day until you bleed to death.' His mouth quivered with an unnamed emotion, eyes blazing.

Whimpering, Fran staggered to the stump and sat, blood oozing between her fingers. Through tears of pain she watched Rob's fingers move over the phone's screen. He looked up only once to make sure she complied, then turned his face back to the screen to read what he'd written and used his thumb to send a message.

'Walk back down to the stream,' he ordered.

Fran was crying. She didn't respond.

'Walk back down!' Rob bellowed.

Fran jerked and let out a yelp of fright. She hobbled back down the slope, Rob behind her with the knife held out in front of him.

When she got to the bottom, she realised he was no longer following. Fran turned. Rob had stopped halfway up the slope where they'd parked the bikes. She watched him stick the knife into the front and back tyres of her bike and heard the high-pitched hiss as they deflated.

Rob still had her phone. He turned and launched it into the middle of the trees on the slopes of the ravine. And, as she stood below him, with the knife in his hand, he said in a voice heavy with regret, 'Sorry it has to end like this, Fran. But you know as well as I do why it does.'

———

WARLOW WAS STILL SITTING in his car when he took the call from a breathless Mellings.

'Sir, I've had a text from Fran Dee. She's in trouble. She's been attacked.'

'What?' Warlow sat up, mind clicking into gear.

'She sent me a location pin. She says her bike is trashed, and that someone is after them. She can't speak because whoever it is is close by. They're hiding—'

'They?'

'Fran and Rob went out for a bike ride and—'

He didn't hear the rest because his stomach started knotting up. His brain was desperately putting two and two together, calculating like a computer on heat.

First time I've seen that photograph.

A lie hidden in a truth.

'They went out together. But she's not answering her texts, sir. Her phone must be in and out of signal.' Mellings sounded desperate.

'Where are you now?'

'On the way, sir. But the pin is in the middle of the forest.'

Christ.

'Call DS Jones. Tell him to get the two Uniforms in the hides down to help you.'

Mellings' voice sounded shrill with anguish. 'I shouldn't have let them go. I shouldn't have—'

'Officer Mellings,' Warlow said, deliberately loud so that she'd jump. 'You are not their bloody keeper. How long ago was the text?'

'Ten minutes.'

'And where is Ralph Geary?'

'At home. About to have a shower and prepare to go back in and see Celia.'

Warlow gunned the engine and jammed the car into reverse, wheels spinning as he reversed and then forwards out onto the road, still with Mellings on the line.

'Stop the car and send that pin to DS Jones now. Tell

him to contact the Uniforms in the Hides. Your job is to find Fran Dee.'

'Yes, sir.' The noise of a slowing engine came through the speaker. 'What about you, sir? Should I send the pin to you?'

'No need. I don't know where Fran is, but I've got a pretty good idea where her attacker is going.'

Warlow killed the call and concentrated on driving.

He'd missed it. He'd missed the signs. The truth that hid a bigger lie. And now here he was driving like a madman towards the man that had fooled him and everyone else.

How appropriate, he thought, *to be heading down these bends and hills like a mad racing driver.*

Because he'd never felt more like a James Hunt in all his life.

No point being subtle about arriving. Warlow roared along the lane that led to Journey's End. He clocked the bike on its side, prayed that the back wheel was still spinning.

It wasn't.

Ralph's car sat in its usual place two feet in from a side wall, two feet from the garage door, neat and tidy and precise. He hadn't left for the hospital.

Damn.

Warlow screeched to a stop at a crazy angle inches from the tree in the centre of the courtyard. He threw open the driver's door and didn't bother to close it. He had a baton in the boot of his car. It took a precious few seconds for the boot to open on its damped hinge and he cursed safe, modern technology for being so bloody slow. With the boot half open he grabbed for the weapon and turned away.

Then he ran for the front door.

He didn't ring the bell. Didn't need to as the door stood open.

Warlow paused and inhaled, letting his pulse slow down, breathing easy and listening. It took fifteen seconds, but he heard it. A something. A noise. The scrape of some small piece of furniture above him followed by a rasp or a groan. Maybe both.

From upstairs in a house he was not familiar with.

He could call out. But everything about the initial silence had made his hackles rise. There was something wrong.

Quietly, swiftly, Warlow made his way through the living room to the door that Fran Dee had appeared through when he'd first interviewed the Gearys. She'd come from upstairs. Where he now wanted to be. And Mellings had told him that Ralph Geary had been about to take a shower.

Warlow pushed through the door and crept up the stairs. All doubt evaporated the moment he saw the discarded towel on the landing, and the wet footsteps on the carpet next to the others.

Muddy footsteps.

Celia would have had a fit. No shoes on upstairs. But someone wasn't bothered by the rules. Someone had bigger, darker, duplicitous fish to fry.

Another sound, a straining, half muffled groan again from a room at the end of the landing with its door ajar.

Warlow moved forward. Under the carpet, floorboards creaked. It didn't matter. The time for stealth had gone with the sight of those muddy footprints.

He pushed open the door.

The first thing he saw was the blood. A lot on the floor, on the bed, some streaked on the wall. Ralph Geary was naked, knees on the floor, hands tied behind him, a plastic

Tesco bag around his head being cinched tight by Rob Hopley.

He looked up when Warlow appeared but said nothing. That was when Warlow knew that what Rob Hopley had once been – the young engineer with his life ahead of him – no longer existed. Something else sat on the bed slowly killing Ralph Geary.

It had taken Warlow eight minutes to get to this bedroom, eight minutes during which Hopley could have finished the job. But he hadn't. A quick death clearly wasn't on his agenda. Blood oozed from the many stab wounds on Ralph Geary's thighs and abdomen and arms. Wounds inflicted by the knife Hopley held in his right hand.

Black, serrated, about six inches long.

The bloody Batknife.

It took a second for Hopley to allow Warlow's presence to intrude into whatever circle of hell he was in. When it did, surprise flickered. He eased the pressure on the bag and Geary coughed, sucked in air, and made a noise like a screeching child.

A noise which shut off the instant the black knife pressed into the skin of his neck over the big vessels.

'Rob, this is over,' Warlow said.

The knife trembled in Hopley's hands and for a moment, the dead, lost look in his eyes changed.

'I knew it would be you. If anyone worked it out, it would be you.'

'Any second this place is going to be crawling with police.' A lie, but Warlow needed to buy time. He took a small step into the room but stopped when Hopley shook his head.

'Don't.'

Warlow looked at Geary. He was slumping, only half conscious. Difficult to say how much blood he'd already lost. How much he had left to lose. 'Don't make this any worse, Rob.'

'It can't be any bloody worse.' Hopley's, mouth twisted in derision. 'How can it be any worse?'

'Let Ralph go.'

Hopley shook his head. 'You have no idea what this man is, do you? What he's done.'

'Whatever it is, we can—'

'Work it out?' Hopley laughed.

Warlow's skin crawled at the sound of that laugh. He sent his eyes left and right, keeping his face forwards. This was the master bedroom. To his right was a bureau full of Celia Geary's things. Jars of creams. A hairbrush. Hair dryer. A mirror. To his left, a floor to ceiling unit with all the doors shut. On the floor at the foot of the bed, Geary's folded clothes.

'Is Fran—'

'She isn't a part of this. I left her alone. But I did her a huge favour when I killed Andy fucking Geary. She doesn't know that yet, but she will.'

Warlow shifted a little to his right.

'Stay where you are,' Hopley hissed. 'This is a very sharp knife.'

Warlow had the baton, in his hand, but Hopley was a dozen feet away. One thrust of that knife would be the end of Ralph Geary.

'We've spoken to Tristan Daniels.' Warlow fixed Hopley in his gaze. 'He trashed your tents, didn't he?'

'You really want to know? What does it matter?'

'It matters to Daniels.' Warlow shifted his weight again, inched a little more to his right. 'Be good to get his side of things straight, for the record. You owe him that.'

For a fraction of a second, Hopley's eyes narrowed as if Warlow's words had hit a painful target.

Ralph Geary moaned and tried to move. Hopley

yanked the plastic bag tighter. The taut material moved in and out over Geary's mouth as he tried to heave in air. 'Don't move,' Hopley said through gritted teeth.

It might have been anger, but Warlow sensed that the yanking of that bag's opening had cost Hopley something in effort. He'd used his left hand. His weaker hand. Warlow's eyes drifted up to the man's left shoulder and saw a glistening damp smudge of darkness. He was bleeding from his sutured shoulder wound.

'Daniels isn't totally innocent,' Hopley said. 'If he hadn't trashed our tents and our bikes, then Andy wouldn't have lost his shit.' Hopley's gaze was fixed on Warlow, but his mind was seeing something else. 'We headed back from seeing the sun go down. We heard the motorbike, saw it smashing our tents, ruining the bikes. We sprinted down, but Daniels saw us and left. He stopped thirty yards away and took off his helmet. He shouted at us. "That's for Iona." Something like that.' Hopley shook his head. 'Andy went ballistic. Said he knew where Daniels lived. That we should go after him. Wait until dark and find him. Commando style, he said. It was like someone had thrown a switch in him. That was when he showed me the knife. That was when it all happened.'

'The knife in your hand?'

'He called it his fucking Batknife. Typical Andy. Like a big kid. I couldn't stop him talking. He called Daniels names. Said we should have killed him and his sister when we had a chance sixteen years ago. Buried them some-where no one would have found them. Andy could be full of himself, and full of crap. But there was something different about him that night. He asked me if I ever thought about what we'd done. About what we should have done. For the first time he told me what he'd said to Iona Daniels under that fallen tree. I thought he'd told her to stay hidden, like part of a game…'

Hopley lifted the knife away from Geary's neck and wiped his nose on his sleeve. He might even have been crying silent tears. But the light from the bedroom window glowed behind him throwing him into silhouette, darkening his features.

Hopley, though, hadn't finished. 'What he said to her, a six-year-old girl, was that if she moved, he'd come back with a very sharp stick and… oh shit. A six-year-old girl, Jesus. I couldn't believe it. I couldn't believe he was telling me this and that he now wanted to go after Daniels and "finish the job". His words. I knew Andy was full of *Call of Duty* crap, but he admitted that night what he thought about when we had Iona hidden all the time ago. That there were some remote villages in Cambodia where people would sell you a girl for the right money.' Hopley blew out air twice in succession. 'He was talking about reliving something… something I've spent every day trying to forget…' He swallowed loudly and made a face as if it was bile he was trying to push back down. 'I told him to shut up then. That he wasn't talking any sense. But I could see it in his eyes. The way they shone. He was getting off on all this stuff.'

A long beat followed as Hopley replayed it all in his head.

'Is that why you killed him?' Warlow asked.

Hopley blinked and shook his head, frowning in response to Warlow's question, zeroing in on the truth of the matter. 'No. I killed him because of where he bought the knife.'

CHAPTER FORTY-ONE

Warlow waited.

Ralph Geary's laboured breathing added a distressing gurgle, though the bag wasn't tight around his neck. Geary's oxygen capacity would have been severely compromised by the loss of blood. Being held upright was doing his brain no favours.

'Why the knife?' Warlow asked.

Hopley let out a wheezy laugh while his expression remained fixed. 'He didn't even know he'd said it. He was so pumped by what Daniels did he didn't think twice about telling me about buying a hunting knife in a Canadian hunting store where he'd taken his fucking girlfriend on their summer fucking holiday.'

Hopley looked at the knife in his hands and gripped it a little tighter. 'I thought he'd gone to Thailand last summer. No need for DBS checks to visit Thailand. He let me hold the knife like some big treasure. He gave it to me and spent five minutes telling me how wonderful it was and all the while I'm wondering about how to ask him the question. In the end, I just did. I asked him how he got a visa to visit Canada.'

Warlow took a further step to his right. This time, Hopley didn't notice. His eyes were on Ralph Geary's neck and the knife, but his mind had gone back to that night in the glade. 'That stopped him in his tracks,' Hopley went on. 'He knew he'd made a mistake. Knew he should not have mentioned Canada.' He looked up, searching Warlow's face, appealing for understanding. 'Three months ago I'd told him what had happened to me and Hannah and he'd listened on the phone and told me how tough that must have been. Sympathised with me.'

Hopley's eyes narrowed and his voice dropped to an incredulous whisper. '*Sympathised with me.* The bastard. Can you believe that? Said it was a bummer.' He tittered. 'A *bummer.* I'd been on my way to Vancouver to look at a job. Be with my girlfriend. I hadn't said anything on the visa application about what happened sixteen years ago because I thought the caution faded away. But it hadn't. It never would. I know that now, but I didn't know when I applied. It flashed up neon on their DBS check. When I phoned the Canadian embassy, the woman I spoke to said their policy was not to allow anyone who might be a danger to their citizens enter the country.'

Hopley squeezed his eyes shut. 'A danger. How do you think that made me feel? Imagine what it did to Hannah, my girlfriend, when I told her? It ended there, what had been between us. I saw it die in her eyes.' He looked up from the knife, blinking away tears. 'And she was the one, you know? A two-year relationship up in smoke because she said she couldn't trust me anymore.'

'Andy hadn't told you about him having the caution expunged?'

Hopley let out another thin laugh. 'Oh, he did in the end. In that glade in the dark. I made him tell me. How good old Ralph here asked him not to mention it to me to avoid complications. That's what this piece of shit sees me as. A complication.' The word came out through gritted teeth and Hopley yanked the bag tighter. 'If it hadn't been for Daniels and his bike I would never have known. Andy would have continued to bullshit me. You bought into Andy's fantasies if you wanted to be a part of his life. Most of them were macho crap. But I held the knife, so I knew that was true. I'd seen Daniels hurl abuse at us for what we'd done to him and his sister, so I knew that was true, too. And I'd listened to Andy tell me about his little trips to the Far East, and not all of that was fantasy either. I realised then he'd *enjoyed* inflicting terror on Iona. Enjoyed it and wanted to relive it all over again. That's what I understood in that one moment. That he didn't give a shit about our friendship. But more than anything I saw a regret. Not for what he had done. For what he had not done. To Iona that day.' Ralph's mouth became an ugly shape. 'And I saw his appetite for more. Maybe not here in the UK, but somewhere else; some remote place where no one gave a crap. Only this time he'd make sure he'd have a big knife with him as well as a sharp stick.'

A sick, harrowing smile spread over Hopley's mouth. 'No red mist for me. I had a full technicolour starburst. Anger, hate, revenge for my ruined life, the need to cut the head off a snake before it bit someone again. Take your pick. It all came out in one big unstoppable surge. It was all over in three minutes. He didn't stand a chance.'

Hopley tilted the knife back and forth in his grip, staring at it.

'And afterwards I sat in this house and listened to Ralph here placate Celia, who'd tagged Andy as a rotten fucking apple from the word go. And sixteen years ago, after it happened, I listened behind half open doors to him tell her that their boy would be fine. That he'd made mistakes but that they could be rectified. I didn't know what they'd meant then. I do now. Andy was flawed.

They knew he had something wrong with him. But Ralph is the enabler here. He's the one that introduced Andy to the Far East and let him do God knows what there. He's used his money and influence to protect Andy for years.

'Killing Ralph won't solve anything, Rob.' Warlow spoke softly.

Hopley looked at the DCI as if seeing him for the first time. 'The Gearys took everything from me. Self-respect, the woman I was going to make a new life with, everything. No more.' The last two words came out as a distorted snarl.

Warlow sensed that there would be no more talk. Hopley was a man beyond redemption for his crimes. The cornered animal with nothing to lose.

But perhaps he could be stopped from making it a whole lot worse.

Warlow snaked his arm out, grabbed the nearest jar from the bureau and threw it. Hopley's head was above Geary's, but Warlow hadn't aimed directly. The half-full jar felt heavy as it sailed past and hit the wall behind Hopley, smashing into a hundred pieces, showering glass and cream over the man's head and neck.

Not a direct hit, but that didn't matter. All he wanted was to make Hopley duck away.

Warlow hadn't played cricket in years, but he threw a ball for Cadi regularly. The second throw with the second jar came within three seconds of the first, and this time Hopley's reflex response was to duck before it hit the wall.

Warlow crossed the gap in three strides, baton extended and aimed point first towards Hopley's damaged left shoulder. Metal met flesh and bone. Hopley yowled and jerked away, his head thudding against the wall behind him. Warlow grabbed the wrist holding the knife, bending it forward sharply. The knife clattered to the floor and

Hopley let go of the plastic bag around Ralph's neck as he writhed away from the DCI.

Ralph Geary fell forwards onto his face. Warlow yanked off the bag.

Ralph didn't move.

Neither did Hopley.

He'd fallen back onto the bed, white with shock and pain. All the fight had gone out of him and his expression went slack as realisation finally seeped in.

Warlow kicked the knife away as the noise of sirens drifted in through the open window. He reached into his pocket for some handcuffs, looked down at the man on the bed and said, 'Robert Hopley, I'm arresting you for the murder of Andrew Geary.'

CHAPTER FORTY-TWO

WARLOW AND JESS sat in the Jeep watching a small army of police, ambulance, and crime scene investigators swarm all over Journey's End. The press were already encamped at the entrance to the property, but since that was about fifty yards away, Warlow found a spot under a tree out of the way of all the other vehicles and hoped the press's telephoto lenses couldn't get through the foliage.

Jess had just brought him a fresh cup of tea in a paper cup and Warlow was sipping it, wondering why some shredded leaves in a bag suffused with boiling water made for such a wonderful cure for feeling like *cachu*.

He said as much to Jess. She didn't need to ask for a translation of *cachu*.

Mellings and the Uniforms had found Fran Dee shaken and injured but alive half a mile from the glade and walking into the forest rather than out of it.

They'd need to take her statement.

But not now.

Not yet.

'Rhys?' Warlow asked.

'At home being mothered. He probably has his foot up

on the sofa, *Taskmaster* on the TV, and an ice pack on his ankle. Nothing broken, apart from his pride. Just a bad sprain.'

'Good.'

A crime scene tech crossed the courtyard with a box full of what looked like IT equipment on the way to one of their vans. 'Do you think your little demonstration of Andrew Geary's Reperire phone app triggered Hopley?'

Warlow pushed his head back into the car's headrest. He'd asked himself the same question. One of dozens that came at the end of an investigation. That began with "what if?" morphed into "why didn't we?" and ended with the feeling that there were half a dozen eggs ready to be scraped off his face. 'It was meant to scare Daniels. Perhaps it did get Hopley worried about where he'd hidden the knife. But I think Celia Geary's attempted suicide played a bigger part. The ultimate confirmation that the Gearys knew what sort of monster their son truly was.'

'Are we going to charge Daniels for locking Rhys and Catrin in the generator shed?'

'No,' Warlow said. 'Though it would make a great opening scene for a sitcom.'

Jess chuckled.

He looked over at her. 'Nor should we charge him for owning a bike with no insurance or a licence. In fact, I thought we might have a whip round and see if we can get him some lessons.'

Jess had her cup to her lips, but it froze there as she swivelled her large eyes towards Warlow. 'Bloody hell, you're nothing but a big softie, Evan Warlow.'

Warlow gave her a stony look. 'Many people have made that mistake and lived to regret it. Please don't be one of them.'

Jess shook her head. 'You did good, Evan. Another ten

minutes and I reckon Ralph Geary would not have survived.'

He didn't respond immediately. He'd had the same thought himself. Not the doing good bit. Just the sapping worry that he might have arrived too late. As it was, Ralph Geary was in intensive care with a punctured lung, a hundred sutures, and on his second transfusion. But he was alive. He'd recover well enough to regret all his actions.

Warlow had his own set of demons who'd drop by in the dark watches of the night to taunt him. But he did not fancy meeting any of the ones lining up to appear at the end of Ralph Geary's bed with all the lights out. The man had that to look forward to once his physical wounds had healed.

'Ralph Geary may not be dead, but we should have done better,' he said. 'I should have sussed out Hopley's game.' Warlow recalled his visit to Fran Dee, showing her and Hopley a photograph of the knife. Hopley's reply had been odd. The way he'd chosen to answer by saying he'd never seen the photograph before. Misdirection right there and right under his nose. Warlow knew he should have picked up on that. The dark lie underneath a moment of truth and Warlow had missed it. A miss that could well have cost Ralph Geary his life.

Both officers sat in contemplative silence, sipping their tea. Above the trees, the sky hinted at a new weather front coming in from the west and a line of dark inched ever closer.

'More foul weather on the way,' Warlow said.

'When isn't there,' Jess replied. She stayed silent for a couple of beats as the clouds encroached. But Hopley would not go away. 'Do you think he'll offer some kind of plea?'

Warlow had pondered that same thought a dozen times. 'I don't think he was in his right mind when he killed

Andrew Geary, but it'll be up to the trick cyclists to prove that. If you're asking me if I think maybe Hopley did the world a favour, then the answer is yes. And I know how that sounds coming from a copper, but eventually, Andrew Geary was going to do something worse than simply frighten a little girl.'

'Agreed,' Jess said.

'Hopley may have lost it in the glade, but everything else he did with calculation. Self-induced defence wounds, the works. Luckily, he did too good a job on his left shoulder. That was his weak spot in the end. Bastard fooled all of us.'

'Almost all of us. You got to him before he killed Ralph, though.' Jess murmured, staring into her cup before gazing out over the expanse of the forest. 'I can't help feeling half an ounce of sympathy for him. His bad luck to have bumped into Andrew Geary that first day of school. Could have been any of us.'

You weren't supposed to think like that, of course, but police officers were only human, the majority at least. And now and again it struck Warlow that crimes of passion – not the jilted lover kind, the type where emotion took over and steam-rolled sense and sensibility into a pancake, allowing violence its head – were more crimes of balance. Where seeing the remains of a dead woman, or a mutilated child, or the demon within demanded redress. The law put itself up as a barrier to that sort of rough justice. And that made Warlow's job easier and at the same time harder. His brief stopped at the arrest, thank God. Let the buggers in wigs sort out the punishment. Harder, sometimes, was keeping an urge to mete out punishment yourself at bay. Hopley killed Andrew Geary. For that, he would pay his dues.

But perhaps, as human beings, Warlow and Jess could allow themselves the tiniest smidgen of relief.

Time to move on. Warlow shook himself free of his morbid thoughts. 'Have you had a word with Mellings?'

Jess nodded. 'She's beating herself up about it, but I've told her not to.'

Warlow turned his head to look at the forest proper. The dark line of firs started about twenty yards from where they were parked. 'Wonder if we could convince the forestry people to move one of their hides here.'

'Why?' Jess asked. 'Monitor the property? Bit late for that.'

'No. I fancy sitting up there with an airgun waiting for one of the hyenas to send up a drone.'

Jess grimaced. 'They wouldn't dare. I think you frightened them off the last time.'

'Oh no, they'll be back. They're like herpes. You pick off one lot of scabs only to find the bastards hiding in the good flesh underneath. You can never be rid of the sods.'

Jess shook her head and laughed silently. 'What a charming image it is you conjure, Chief Inspector.'

'It's a gift.' Tea finished, Warlow squared his shoulders and jabbed the Jeep's starter button. 'Once we finish this, I'll get back to HQ. Start on the paperwork.' The engine coughed once and then spluttered into an idle. The thing needed a service.

'Catrin's already made a start. You know how she is.'

'Frighteningly efficient.' Warlow nodded. 'No need for her to know that, of course.'

Next to him, Jess smiled and blew on her tea.

Grumpy, relentless, clever old bastard, she thought. *Thy name is Warlow.*

———

WARLOW BRUSHED leaves into a trug and carried them to a growing pile in the corner of his small garden. He heard a vehicle pull in and walked the length of his lawn to the point at the side of the cottage where he could see his front yard. A postman in shorts got out of the red PO van with a small bundle of letters and shoved them through his door.

Warlow raised his hand, but the postman was in too much of a hurry to respond.

A cool, dry day. Ideal for leaf blowing, or sucking, or collecting. He'd done all three, but still a few dried brown strays skittered over the grass like blind mice.

Bugger it.

He put away the brush, upended the trug, and washed his hands in the sink before retrieving the mail. He filed away the bills on a side table and the circulars into the bin and was left with a brown envelope.

He recognised the handwriting immediately.

Another one. Must be his lucky day. Again.

Worryingly, the envelope was a little thicker than usual. But he was more surprised because he'd received one only a few days ago. Karen Geoghan usually sent one of her poison pen letters when there was an occasion. Birthdays, Easter, Christmas. But, as far as Warlow could recall, today was not one of those.

He fetched some gloves and slid them on before using an old paring knife to slit the envelope open. The grey transparent edge of some thin bubble wrap presented itself. Warlow slid it out and placed it in the sink. Inside the wrap was a desiccated bone with four elongated toes.

A bird's foot.

A few inches of red wool tied to the leg joined a piece of paper marked with a single symbol in Runish. He'd learnt to recognise the symbols, but had no idea what they meant.

Tied to the other foot was a piece of paper folded into a half-inch block loosely attached to a folded-over news-paper cutting. Warlow put on his readers.

. . .

Ex Carer wins lottery.

Karen Geoghan, a retired nursing home worker from Townhill, Swansea, is celebrating her success having won a quarter of a million pounds on the National Lottery.

"Karen is a regular. Comes in three times a week for her ciggies and magazines. We couldn't believe it when she came in the next day as usual and told us she'd hit the jackpot," store manager, Mick Lenden, told the Mail.

"She doesn't always buy scratch-cards – but decided, this time, to have a dabble. It's been a good experience all round. Her win has brought more people to the shop in the hope some of her luck is rubbing off.

Mrs Geoghan was unavailable for comment, but a friend told the Mail that she will use some funds to help her husband fight his jail sentence."

Warlow read the article twice. 'The devil looks after his own alright,' he muttered. Only then did he unfold the second piece of paper.

Now we have money. Bad things are coming your way. I hope you have an accident soon and a bird shits on the open wound.

Warlow sighed. Was it surprising he didn't like people much?

He looked at the clock. Just after ten in the morning. Half an hour until he had to leave to pick up Cadi. Just time for a quick shower and to change out of his leaf-collecting clothes. Which were the same as his dog-walking, roof-repairing, and re-pointing-the-wall-at-the-rear-of-the-garden clothes.

Molly Allanby was cooking lunch. Which meant Jess

was cooking lunch and Molly was laying the table. Having tasted Jess's cooking a few times, and Molly's just the once, that was fine by Warlow. He'd take a good bottle of wine but couldn't help thinking that this was all slightly back to front. It was him that should thank the Allanbys. Molly had been dog sitting Cadi for almost a week because of the extra paperwork and meetings and interviews Warlow needed to attend to following Hopley's arrest.

But he was free of all that now and he wanted his dog back. Needed his dog back.

On the table near the front door, next to his keys, was a nicely wrapped copy of *Something Wicked This Way Comes*, the Ray Bradbury classic.

He really hoped Molly liked it.

Tomorrow was a Sunday, and he had a big walk planned. Just him and Cadi and the elements. But the weather didn't look too hot. Gales and rain were forecast. But he'd believe it when he saw it. The met office sometimes looked like they'd mixed Pembrokeshire up with somewhere of the same name but on a different planet. He'd toyed with the idea of the coastal path, but if it turned out to be squally, he'd need a back-up plan.

There were always the woods.

On second thoughts, maybe he'd give the woods a miss for a week or two.

Beach it is, then.

Warlow glanced once more down at the Geoghan envelope before stuffing the contents back inside, scrunching the lot up, and tossing it in the trash.

He gazed out of the window to the Ash at the bottom of the garden and the totem made up of a cross of sticks with a fir cone at its centre. The mark of the beast. A totem he'd recovered from the Brechfa Forest. He thought it might look good in the garden. An antidote to the witch-craft tosh that Karen Geoghan kept sending his way.

It was all balls, really. But somehow having the sign of the beast in his garden made him feel better. Especially since the Geoghans were spoiling for a fight.

Ah well, thought Warlow. *Two could play at that game.*

THE END

malevolence at work? One with its sights on bigger, two legged prey.

Only one thing is for certain; Warlow will not rest until he finds out.

———

By joining the club, you will also be the first to hear about new releases via the few but fun emails I'll send you. This includes a no spam promise from me, and you can unsubscribe at any time.

ACKNOWLEDGMENTS

As with all writing endeavours, the existence of this novel depends upon me, the author, and a small army of 'others' who turn an idea into a reality. My wife, Eleri, who gives me the space to indulge my imagination and picks out my stupid mistakes. Sian Phillips, Tim Barber and of course, Martin Davies. Thank you all for your help. Special mention goes to Ela the dog who drags me away from the writing cave and the computer for walks, rain or shine. Actually, she's a bit of a princess so the rain is a no-no. Good dog!

But my biggest thanks goes to you, lovely reader, for being there and actually reading this. It's great to have you along and I do appreciate you spending your time in joining me on this roller-caster ride with Evan and the rest of the team.

CAN YOU HELP?

With that in mind, and if you enjoyed it, I do have a favour to ask. Could you spare a moment to leave a review? A few words will do, but it's really the only way to help others like you discover the books. Probably the best way to help authors you like. Just visit my page on Amazon and leave a few words.

AUTHOR'S NOTE

Caution Death at Work has its roots in the many and varied walks we have done with Ela and her predecessors. It really can feel wild and wonderful in the vast woodland tracts dotted around Carmarthenshire. Brechfa and its forest is real and a world class mountain bike venue. And sometimes phone reception up there can be a bit iffy. You could get up to all sorts and no one would be any the wiser…

Why the Black Beacons?

Spread over 500 square miles, the Brecon Beacons mountain range sits like a giant doorstop at the heads of the South Wales Valleys. To the north and west, they nestle in the crook of the ancient kingdoms of Powys and Dyfed, stretching from the eastern borderlands to the wild western coast. Many of the mountain peaks in the range have names. Others are simply referred to as *black*. It's in this timeless landscape that the books are set.

I am lucky enough to live in this neck of the woods having moved here in the 1980s. It's an amazing part of the world, full of warm and wonderful people, wild coastlines, golden and craggy mountains. But like everywhere, even this little haven is not immune from the woes of the world. Those of you who've read *The Wolf Hunts Alone* will know exactly what I mean. And who knows what and who Warlow is going to come up against next! So once again, thank you for sparing your precious time on this new endeavour. I hope I'll get the chance to show you more of this part of the world and that it'll give you the urge to visit.

Not everyone here is a murderer. Not everyone... Cue tense music!

All the best, and see you all soon, Rhys.

READY FOR MORE?

DCI Evan Warlow and the team are back in...

ICE COLD MALICE.
DCI EVAN WARLOW CRIME THRILLER BOOK 2

Revenge is a dish best served... icy cold.

While beach combing on MOD property, two young boys stumble across a reeking mound of tangled kelp. But it isn't the seaweed that stinks. It's the decomposing corpse beneath it.

Called in to investigate, DCI Evan Warlow's team is faced with the mystery of how and why the body of a struck-off doctor ended up on a lonely Carmarthenshire beach within sight of Laugharne's famous Boathouse.

But this is no innocent victim. This is a man with more enemies than friends. A fact that muddies the waters no end as Warlow unearths more and more of the dead man's sordid history. Not to mention a long line of suspects.

With a killer in their midst hell bent on achieving a deadly goal and determined to let nothing and no one stand in their way, the team need to be on their guard.

Unless they want to end up as victims, too.

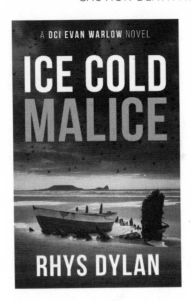

ICE COLD MALICE

Alex Maitland ran his bike down the concrete slipway onto the beach with glee. He turned and beckoned to his younger brother, James.

'Come on, Jam.'

James, ten, younger by a year and a half, looked red in the face from the two-mile ride through the marshland to the shore. He stood astride his bike, gulping down water from a plastic bottle.

'Wait for me, Al.' He screwed the cap back on and fought against the buffeting wind as he dismounted.

But Alex was in no mood to linger. They'd made it to the beach. He'd checked yesterday on the *QuinetiQ* website to make sure the firing range was shut and the beach was open. When he'd woken up that morning and found the sun gleaming in a cloudless sky, he knew there'd be no excuses. He'd told their parents they were following the track next to the stream known as Railsgate Pill, towards one of the estuary inlets. A muddy path on a wet day, a glorious bike ride in the dry. One they'd done many times with their dad. But this time, like the big boys they were, they had the entire afternoon to do it alone.

Supposedly.

Alex, however, had other plans.

Once out of the caravan park, instead of taking a left over the cattle grid, they'd kept going, straight down the wetlands and through the gate onto Ministry of Defence land.

Ginst Point drew Alex like a moth to a flame. Remote and wild, accessible only when they weren't testing munitions. Mr and Mrs Maitland had taken them on a blustery *let's-go-for-a-drive* day the year before. James and his mum had been happy to stay in the car rather than get blown away. Only Alex and his dad had braved the August squalls and walked the few yards to the public beach.

It had been deserted, and they hadn't lingered. A five-minute stroll to stretch the legs, his dad had promised. But then Alex saw the signs. Read them in awe. This wasn't just any beach. This beach had secrets. Alex, smitten, dreamt about going back there ever since.

Today was the day.

'Hurry up, Jam,' he urged his brother once again. James arrived, and they put their bikes flat against the pebbles. Alex turned to survey the vast expanse of sand that stretched away in front of them. The tide was halfway in, but still waves lapped a hundred yards away from where they stood.

'There it is,' Alex said, and sprinted towards a yellow sign on a metal board. James joined him a minute later, and the boys stood in wonder beneath it. The sun on their backs, wind whipping their hair while Alex read aloud the information that had thrilled and inspired him the first time he'd read it.

MINISTRY OF DEFENCE

When the beach beyond this point is open to the public, you must proceed with caution.

Observe the speed limit and comply with the Road Traffic Act. Do not pick up any object. It may kill. Report the presence of any bomb or missile to the QuinetiQ Security Service.

The use of metal detectors on the MOD beach is prohibited.

'Wow,' James said. 'Are there really bombs and bullets and stuff on this beach?'

'There's tons,' Alex replied, his eyes alight. 'They fire missiles all the time. They'll get duff ones that land unexploded. Must do.'

James stared at his brother. 'A whole one?'

'Yeah. Course.'

'But we don't want a whole one, Al, do we?' James asked, anxiety angling down the edges of his eyebrows.

'No, just a bit of one. A bit of shell casing or a detonator. We could sell that for shitloads on *eBay*.'

The boys hailed from the outskirts of Bristol, and Narrowmoor Farm Caravan Park was their regular Easter and summer holiday destination. With Carmarthen Bay on their doorstep and the Southern Pembrokeshire coast next door, so long as the weather was good, there was enough to do. But Ginst Point remained the jewel in the West Wales crown for Alex.

'Keep your eyes peeled, Jam. If you see anything don't touch it,' Alex ordered, designating himself a munitions expert. 'Let me see it first. But grab some ammo to throw at anything we find. That way, we'll see if it's safe. If it blows up, we run for it.'

The boys ran to the pebbles that spanned an area in

front of the dunes and stuffed their pockets with small, smooth stones.

'Let's go down to the water and work our way back.' Alex started off, pockets bulging.

James didn't move. He'd turned his eyes west to where Laugharne Sands became Pendine Sands for some seven miles.

'It's massive,' James muttered, awestruck.

'That's where they do the land speed thing. Rocket cars and that.'

'Wow.'

'But we're not going over that way. We'll stay this side. Come on.'

The boys started walking with the wind at their backs. The beach was deserted except for some fishermen far off to their right with rods set up vertically in the sand, tips bent with lines deep in the surf. But they were a long way off. Stick men on the far horizon.

'What's that?' James asked, pointing towards a spot at the water's edge where seagulls congregated above a dark unmoving shape.

'Dunno.' Alex put a hand over his eyes to shield them.

The birds kept up a constant racket, wheeling above and landing on the shapeless blob.

'Could be a whale, or a dolphin.' Alex's voice rose at this suggestion. 'Sometimes they get beached.'

'Is it dead then?'

'Duh. If it's not in the water then yeah, it's dead. Let's have a look.'

Alex started running. James called after him, 'No, Al. I don't want to see a dead dolphin.'

Alex stopped and turned. 'That's mad. It can't do nothing to you.'

'But it'll probably stink.'

'So? Hold your nose you mong.' Alex pinched his nose in demonstration.

'Let's stick to missiles,' James argued, knowing this battle was already lost.

'Come on. Maybe there'll be a harpoon.' Alex started jogging backwards, his face animated. 'We can stick that on *eBay*, too.'

James kicked at the sand and reluctantly followed.

The shapeless mass remained formless but got bigger the nearer they got. Shells crunched underfoot and patches of sand were firmer than others. Where it was damp, the boys' footsteps appeared and then faded to nothing as they ran, ghostly and untraceable. James struggled to keep up with his older brother. And all the while the gulls kept up their noisy performance until the boys were within thirty yards. Then the birds finally took flight, squealing out their objections.

James pulled up, hands on his knees, heaving in breaths, but his eyes glued to the object of their quest. 'What's that brown stuff?'

'It's seaweed,' Alex explained.

Tendrils of brown-stalked kelp reached out like the arms of some sea monster from the main mass.

'I expect it got wrapped around the dolphin when the sea brought it in,' Alex added.

He delivered this with a surprising confidence. He found it best to provide explanations when he was with James. His younger brother got nervous, let his imagination run away with him.

'What if that thing moves, though?' James said. 'What if there's something alive in there?'

'Seagulls wouldn't be landing on something alive. No way.'

James wrinkled his nose. 'It stinks, though.'

'It's the rotten seaweed. I told you.'

'Let's leave it, Al. Let's search for bombs instead.'

'We're here now,' Alex insisted. 'We'll take one look and then go back up the beach. Do a sweep. Look' – he pointed – 'there's a big piece of driftwood we can use to poke a bit of seaweed off.'

James retrieved the bleached curved branch and handed it to his brother.

They inched onward towards the clump of seaweed. It was dense and thick, with no sign of anything obvious underneath. James clamped a hand over his nose when they were within poking distance.

'Wow, that's so manky,' he said.

Alex held the stick in both hands and began peeling away the seaweed with clumsy strokes. 'Na, nothing...' He replaced the sweeps with a poke. As the stick hit the centre of the mass, the whole mess moved in response. Alex grinned. 'See that? There's something solid in there.'

'I don't like it,' James said in a voice that made him sound two years younger than he was.

'Here, you take pictures on my phone.' Alex held out the iPhone.

'I don't want to.'

'Come on, Jam. This is part of it. This is our adventure. You said you wanted to come.'

'I wanted to look for missiles.' James dropped his head, his voice petulant.

Alex gritted his teeth. He hated that whining voice his brother used when he couldn't get his own way. 'We will. Honest. But let's get a snap of this dolphin first. We could stick it on *Insta*. We'll get a million likes.'

James sighed but took the phone from his brother.

With exaggerated sweeps, like waving a cricket bat, Alex slashed at the kelp. After half a dozen strokes, strands of the rotting brown stuff flailed away. He kept at it, providing a constant stream of encouraging words to keep his brother happy.

'Yay, slash the dolphin. Slash the dolphin.'

Despite his misgivings, James laughed and joined in. 'Slash the dolphin. Slash the dolphin. Slash the dolph—'

When his brother stopped talking, Alex was laughing out loud mid slash. He turned to stare at James.

'What?' he asked, expecting him to come back with something rude. But he wasn't saying anything. He was staring, mouth slack, his face as white as the shells beneath their feet.

'Wha-at?' Alex demanded, expecting a silly reply.

'It's not a dolphin,' whispered James. There was something in his voice that made Alex frown. Though he kept a smile on his face, the laughter drained away. James was shaking. He'd dropped the phone but kept his eyes on the point where Alex had last slashed the seaweed. 'Don't look, Al. Don't look,' he whispered.

But Alex, still thinking his brother had suddenly found great acting skills, turned to stare at what James's eyes were glued on.

Through a tangled net of brown leaves, something pale and round was now visible. A moon shaped ball against the streaky brown. Alex leant in to stare, but then froze as his stomach lurched. Not a football, as he'd first thought. Because footballs didn't have mouths with grey lips, or noses with black choked nostrils, or eyes. Or at least something that once might have been eyes.

Memory of the seagulls swooping and pecking with their big sharp beaks, calling to others to join the feast, flooded his mind. But only for a moment before horror gripped him and he reared up and back, legs wheeling until he fell bum-first onto the sand with a thud, unable to drag his eyes away from what he'd seen.

Above, the gulls bugled their objections. The water

lapped as it crept in. It was only a few seconds, but later Alex would admit how it seemed like he sat forever staring as the thing in the kelp looked back with unseeing eyes. He scrambled to his feet, words tumbling from his mouth in a panicked rush. 'Come on, James. We can't stay here.'

He got no reply because James was already tearing up the beach to the bikes, not daring to look back even when Alex called his name.

A slight movement drew Alex's focus back to the thing in the seaweed. A crab scuttled out from under a broad brown frond over the face's forehead, above the point where it stared out with those ruined eyes.

Alex felt the wind gust, pushing him with one faltering step towards the tangled mess. He regained his balance, let out a low shuddering moan, turned and ran into the breeze after his brother.

Made in the USA
Columbia, SC
07 July 2023

20169416R00195